D0975823

19
YELLOW
MOON
ROAD

Books by Fern Michaels

Hidden
No Way Out
The Brightest Star
Fearless
Spirit of the Season
Deep Harbor
Fate & Fortune
Sweet Vengeance
Holly and Ivy
Fancy Dancer
No Safe Secret
Wishes for Christmas
About Face
Perfect Match
A Family Affair
Forget Me Not
The Blossom Sisters
Balancing Act
Tuesday's Child
Betrayal
Southern Comfort
To Taste the Wine
Sins of the Flesh
Sins of Omission
Return to Sender
Mr. and Miss Anonymous
Up Close and Personal
Fool Me Once
Picture Perfect
The Future Scrolls
Kentucky Sunrise
Kentucky Heat
Kentucky Rich
Plain Jane
Charming Lily
What You Wish For
The Guest List

Listen to Your Heart
Celebration
Yesterday
Finders Keepers
Annie's Rainbow
Sara's Song
Vegas Sunrise
Vegas Heat
Vegas Rich
Whitefire
Wish List
Dear Emily
Christmas at Timberwoods

The Sisterhood Novels:

Bitter Pill
Truth and Justice
Cut and Run
Safe and Sound
Need to Know
Crash and Burn
Point Blank
In Plain Sight
Eyes Only
Kiss and Tell
Blindsided
Gotcha!
Home Free
Déjà Vu
Cross Roads
Game Over
Deadly Deals
Vanishing Act
Razor Sharp
Under the Radar
Final Justice

Books by Fern Michaels (Continued)

Collateral Damage
Fast Track
Hokus Pokus
Hide and Seek
Free Fall
Lethal Justice
Sweet Revenge
The Jury
Vendetta
Payback
Weekend Warriors

Captive Innocence
Captive Embraces
Captive Passions
Captive Secrets
Captive Splendors
Cinders to Satin
For All Their Lives
Texas Heat
Texas Rich
Texas Fury
Texas Sunrise

The Men of the Sisterhood Novels:

Hot Shot
Truth or Dare
High Stakes
Fast and Loose
Double Down

The Godmothers Series:

Far and Away
Classified
Breaking News
Deadline
Late Edition
Exclusive
The Scoop

E-Book Exclusives:

Desperate Measures
Seasons of Her Life
To Have and To Hold
Serendipity

Anthologies:

Home Sweet Home
A Snowy Little Christmas
Coming Home for
Christmas
A Season to Celebrate
Mistletoe Magic
Winter Wishes
The Most Wonderful Time
When the Snow Falls
Secret Santa
A Winter Wonderland
I'll Be Home for Christmas
Making Spirits Bright
Holiday Magic
Snow Angels
Silver Bells
Comfort and Joy
Sugar and Spice
Let it Snow
A Gift of Joy
Five Golden Rings
Deck the Halls
Jingle All the Way

FERN MICHAELS

19 YELLOW MOON ROAD

KENSINGTON
PUBLISHING CORP.

www.kensingtonbooks.com

KENSINGTON BOOKS are published by

Kensington Publishing Corp.
119 West 40th Street
New York, NY 10018

All Kensington titles, imprints and distributed lines are available at special quantity discounts for bulk purchases for sales promotion, premiums, fund-raising, educational or institutional use.

Special book excerpts or customized printings can also be created to fit specific needs. For details, write or phone the office of the Kensington Special Sales Manager: Kensington Publishing Corp., 119 West 40th Street, New York, NY, 10018. Attn. Special Sales Department. Phone: 1-800-221-2647.

Library of Congress Control Number: 2021935303

ISBN: 978-1-4967-3117-3
First Kensington Hardcover Edition: September 2021

10 9 8 7 6 5 4 3 2 1

Printed in the United States of America

19
YELLOW
MOON
ROAD

Prologue

Present Day
Dade County, Florida

Gabby knew that if she kept looking back over her shoulder, it would slow her down. Why were The Haven's Guardians following her? The Guardians, known as "the Gs," were members of the organization—the organization where one resided in search of a higher meaning and a more spiritual life. They were an elite group of individuals assigned to accompany the Pledges when they went outside The Haven's compound, unless the Pledges had obtained special permission to do so, which did not happen very often. Their purpose, the Pledges had been told, was to protect members from harassment, but some thought it was a method of intimidation.

Gabby was supposed to be boarding a flight to Minneapolis to visit her mother in the hospital. But when she arrived at the security checkpoint at Miami International Airport, she discovered that her ticket and passport were missing from her backpack. She *knew* she had put them in there. She had checked several times. Her wallet was also missing. The only thing she had was the fifty-dollar prepaid debit card she had tucked in the pocket of her jeans.

Liam, the supreme guru of the organization, and his brother Noah, the general manager, had given her permission to travel, something not normally granted to a Pledge. One had to have been a member for at least a year and pass a series of tests before one could leave The Haven unaccompanied. But Liam had taken a special liking to Gabby and wanted her to be happy and content—and Noah wanted her content long enough for The Haven to gain access to the principal of the trust fund she would come into when she turned thirty-five. There were only a few months to go.

Trying to dodge the Gs, Gabby frantically weaved in and out of hustling, oncoming passengers. She could feel the heat on the back of her neck. *Why am I panicking?* She couldn't quite put her finger on it, but her inner voice was telling her to run.

Present Day
Washington, D.C.
Office of the Post

Maggie Spritzer stared at the phone sitting on her desk. The call had come in through the newspaper's toll-free line and went to Maggie's voice mail while she was conducting an interview on the latest political scandal. The message was from her former college friend, Gabriella (Gabby) Richardson. They were journalism students together and met when Maggie was a junior and Gabby a freshman. They say opposites attract. Maggie was outspoken, witty, and had an enormous appetite for food. Gabby was demure and often shy, and tried to maintain a vegetarian diet. Gabby's father had been in the diplomatic service, which had caused the family to uproot often, even as her mother tried to maintain her position as a college professor. The frustration her mother experienced moving from one country to the next, forcing her to leave one prestigious learning institution after another, became too much. She had finally filed for divorce when Gabby was a teen. When Gabby entered college, she was feeling displaced once again and was drawn in by Maggie's vivacious personality. Maggie hit the REPLAY button on her phone again:

> *Maggie, it's Gabby. I'm at a flower shop in Miami. I was trying to get on a plane to see my mom, but something happened to my ticket and my passport. I think some people are following me. I didn't know who else to call. Please call back on this number: 305-555-7416.*

The last Maggie heard was that Gabby had been on a soul-searching mission and joined an organization that sounded like an ashram or spiritual retreat. Maggie couldn't remember the exact name of the place. As she was drumming her fingers on her desk she thought, *Spiritual retreat, okay, fine. I get it. But who would be following her? And why?*

Chapter One

2004

Liam and Noah had been raised in a house on Sheridan Road, the upscale area of Wilmette, a suburb of Chicago. Their father, Sidney Westlake, had a seat on the Chicago Board of Trade, and had parlayed a modest stake into a large fortune. Their mother, Eleanor Adams Westlake, was aloof. A debutante when she was in her teens, she had picked her friends according to their socioeconomic status and continued to do so throughout her marriage. Only the wealthiest people in town were invited to the opulent parties hosted by "the Ice Queen," the name Liam and Noah would mutter when she dismissed her sons from a room. Any room. To describe her as cold would be like describing Warren Buffett as well-off. Even the sting of dry ice would be warmer than her personality. She could be most charming, but only bothered when being scrutinized by her peers. She was a perfectionist at maintaining a façade of grace and hospitality.

The brothers had attended boarding school from the time they were eligible. Prior to that, they were constantly under the tutelage and care of not one but two nannies. They rarely saw their mother, even when they were home.

Truth be told, Eleanor hated children. If it hadn't been for the pressure from her family, she would have skipped the revolting process by which they came into the world, but someone had to inherit her share of her father's estate. Her father had been a bit of a prig. He wanted an heir. An heir as in a male. As far as he was concerned, neither Eleanor nor her sister, Dorothy, qualified. They were women. He was adamant that the legacy would be handed down to Eleanor's and Dorothy's male children. Dorothy was still single, so it was up to Eleanor to do the heavy lifting, something Eleanor abhorred.

A few short months after they were married, Eleanor was with child. Not one but two. Twins. She despised being pregnant and refused to breastfeed the infants once they were born. Her disdain went beyond breastfeeding. She barely held them. She was thrilled that she had gotten all the dirty work out of the way in one fell swoop. The only time she exhibited any sort of emotion was when she discovered she was having twin boys. She would produce two heirs to the family fortune. Besides, she dreaded the thought of having a girl. Not only would a girl not be an heir, so she would have to go through the disgusting process all over again, but a girl would expect some kind of female bonding. Not Eleanor.

She couldn't bond with anyone even if she used Gorilla Glue. Eleanor was people-proof. The only reason she had a long list of social acquaintances was for everyone else's opportunity to mingle and network with other socialites. She knew it, but she didn't care. She only cared about all the accolades she would get in the lifestyle section of the newspapers—print and online. When it came to human feelings, Eleanor had only one: self-absorption. She was the ultimate narcissist.

On the surface, her marriage to Sidney appeared normal, with the exception of Eleanor's conspicuous consumption of goods, parties, and extravagant trips. Perhaps it was her way of dealing with the numerous extramarital relationships Sidney had had over the years. His dalliances were common knowledge, and most people secretly felt it was more her frigid personality than anything else that caused him to stray. But everyone looked the other way, since they reaped the benefits of association with the wealthy and entitled. It was a price everyone in her circle was prepared to pay.

Even with his money and influence, Sidney could never divorce Eleanor. He was always discreet as well as generous to the women with whom he had his dalliances. Also, many of the women were married, which meant that discretion was even more important. The affairs were casual, and he would show his gratitude with gifts. But he never took it to the point that could warrant his being accused of having "a kept woman." No, Sidney was careful. He couldn't afford a scandal, much less a divorce. Eleanor would take him to the cleaners and stick a hanger up his butt.

Eleanor knew about each and every one of Sidney's peccadilloes. She didn't care as long as he showed up at her side at the many social events they attended or hosted. She'd rather have access to all of Sidney's money than half of it. And everyone knows that the ex-wife becomes the social persona non grata, as she has to take a back seat to the trophy wife who replaces her. No, Eleanor was shrewd. Besides, she found Sidney's lovemaking revolting. She was happy to let someone else handle that repulsive bit of business. Eleanor provided the perfect partner for Sidney. They were locked into their soulless, loveless, controlled lives.

The sons of Sidney and Eleanor Westlake were privileged but not spoiled in the usual way. They didn't have the entitled attitude that so many of their peers exhibited. That was probably due, in large part, to Eleanor's lack of participation and interest. The nannies, the tutors, and their proctors taught them respect and kindness.

Liam was the more introspective of the two. He spent a great deal of time thinking, while Noah spent time playing. In boarding school, Noah would tease Liam when they had an opportunity to watch a rugby match. Liam preferred to sit among the books at the school's well-endowed library. He enjoyed getting lost in thought as he buried himself in the works of ancient philosophers. Noah would sneak up behind him and give him a flick on the back of the ear, causing Liam to holler and shrink in embarrassment while the librarian would give him a big "ssshhhh!" Liam was interested in psychology. He secretly hoped he could reconcile his feelings of abandonment. Intellectually, he knew that Eleanor would never win Mother of the Year, but emotionally, he felt a tremendous void in his heart.

Noah seemed immune to their mother's indifference. His way of dealing with it was simply to make the most of the situation, even if that meant making mischief at times. He never did anything horrid or dangerous. Mostly practical jokes, like short sheeting someone's bed, setting the table with a dribble glass, or leaving rubber spiders in the toilet. They were fraternal twins, so switching identities was not an option. But even as he was nearing his eighteenth birthday, Noah would be the one setting a bag of doggie doo-doo on fire and ringing the doorbell, in the hopes that the person would instinctively stomp out the fire, getting poop all over their shoes. That was probably the most horrendous joke he had pulled.

At least as far as anyone knew.

Regardless of their different personalities, the brothers had a very strong bond. As children, they soon realized that Mother didn't care much and Dad was never home unless Mother was entertaining. Their nannies were the only people who showed them any affection. Eleanor grudgingly gave them a hug when the boys went off to boarding school, but neither could recall any other displays of motherly love. When they were sick, it was the nannies who cared for them, administering cold medications, serving them soup and crackers, and reading stories. Stories. Their mother had never told them a story. Not a single time. Looking back, Liam couldn't remember if their mother had ever entered their bedroom when they were home from school. He had asked Noah if he recalled her coming to them, and Noah couldn't think of a time that it had happened.

Despite the frigid environment in which they were raised, Liam and Noah were well-adjusted. There is something to be said for "the best money can buy" when it came to their nannies and their schooling.

But, in a very short time, they would be emancipated and choosing which college to attend. Liam had contemplated joining the Jesuits but was quickly talked out of it by Noah. Noah had arranged for them to visit the University of Miami campus. The clear blue skies, swaying palms, vibrant blooms of the bougainvillea, and lovely, scantily clad young women sauntering across the great lawn would certainly change Liam's mind.

College life was going to be a totally different experience. They would essentially be on their own without the oversight and supervision of the boarding-school staff. True, there were resident assistants to monitor the dormitories and supervise adherence to the rules. But they had no control over what students did on campus or in the city. There were only eighteen campus police patrolling almost three hundred acres of land and seventeen thousand students, and not all of them were on duty at the same time. It was a very safe campus nonetheless, but it gave students a lot of autonomy and self-reliance.

Mother was not happy with the college they chose. She

had anticipated that they would attend Brown or Dartmouth, Ivy League schools that the children of her wealthy friends attended, and put up a bit of a stink. It was one of the very few times she had shown any reaction at all to her children's choices. And this despite the fact that anger and disapproval were her go-to emotional responses to most everything else. Rarely did a smile or word of encouragement surface in response to something her children had done or said. Without saying or explaining what she expected of them, she made it clear what her expectations were, expectations that always had to do with furthering her own social standing. And when those expectations weren't met, she would leave the room in a huff, slamming the door behind her. That's when she would go to Sidney and complain that he needed to "do something about those boys."

And Sidney, who couldn't care less, would shrug, explain to his sons how disappointed Mother was, adjust his tie, and leave the room.

Noah and Liam would roll their eyes and resume whatever they were doing at the time. Reading was Liam's passion. Video games were Noah's.

The day they were leaving for Miami, their mother refused to see them off, feigning one of her "headaches." Liam and Noah were used to her disinterest but got hugs and kisses from the staff—the people who actually cared for them. Even Sidney merely gave them a handshake and a thousand dollars each. "This is your allowance for the semester. Don't ask for any more." After which, he picked up his attaché case and left the grand foyer of their mansion in Wilmette, one of the most luxurious suburbs of Chicago.

Chapter Two

Christmas 2007
Chicago

Liam and Noah were in their final year at the University of Miami, and neither of them was certain if he was going to continue his education, take some time off, or look for work. They had managed to get through three and a half years of undergraduate school with good grades and good behavior. They were involved in sports and dated a number of girls, but neither was interested in having a committed relationship. Though Liam was the quieter and more moderate of the two, even he enjoyed his freedom. And if their parents' relationship was any indication of what married life was like, neither one of them was interested in entering into any long-term involvement. Casual dating and being "friends with benefits" was the norm for most students their age. And they saw no reason to deviate from that norm.

During school breaks, they would often go on "family" ski trips to Aspen or Vail. In the summer months, Liam, Noah, and a small staff would stay at the family vacation home in Shelby, Michigan. "A modest castle on the lake," is how

Eleanor would darkly refer to her husband's purchase. "Sidney wanted a place where he and the boys could spend time fishing." Part of that was true, but everyone knew that Sidney used the villa during the off-season for his frequent liaisons.

Regardless of where they were during school breaks, the family was surrounded by acquaintances, guests, and a variety of social friends. Heaven forbid they interacted with one another as members of a family. There were always other people around to keep the conversations banal. Liam and Noah referred to the multitude of people as "insurance." Insurance that nothing personal would be discussed. Occasionally, someone would ask, "So, Liam, how is school treating you?" Liam would think to himself, *Schools can't treat a person. The question should be, How are you treating school?* Liam was always the more perceptive of the two, but before he could get a chance to discuss his studies and interests, Mother would quickly change the subject. She never got over the fact that not only did they go to a school that was known as "Sun-Tan-U," but they actually were going to graduate from "that dreadful, crass place."

It was now their final Christmas holiday while in college, and, as per usual, some distant cousin and her brood were staying at the house. Eleanor hired professionals to handle the holiday decorating, the results of which always generated many disapproving looks. Nothing ever seemed to satisfy her.

It was late in the evening, and Liam had a craving for ice cream. He didn't want to bother the staff. They deserved some peace, especially since Eleanor was on her customary pre-party rampage. As Liam made his way down the long corridor, he overheard his mother hissing at his father. But the heavy oak door that separated the master bedroom suite from the hallway made it difficult to hear his father's reply. Sidney never raised his voice, something that invariably infuriated Eleanor. But rather than add fuel to her own fire, Eleanor would stop talking and leave the room, banging the door in her usual manner of expressing her discontent. She barely noticed Liam standing in the hallway and breezed right past him. Not a look. Not a word. She cruised her way to the guest bedroom suite, which was usually occupied by Sidney. But that night, she was hell-bent on making a dramatic grand exit, and that was the only other available bedroom.

The next morning, she was absent from the breakfast table. Nothing new there. She usually took her morning coffee with her dry wheat toast in her bedroom. Most of the time she never ate or drank either of them. She simply liked the idea that she had someone who could fix it and bring it to her. Margaret Drew, the family cook and head housekeeper, would scrape the uneaten toast into a small bowl. She would then break it into pieces and leave it outside the windowsill for the birds. Once Noah had spotted her recycling his mother's discarded breakfast and was happy to see it hadn't gone to waste. He gave her a nod of approval, which made Margaret smile.

With their college graduation a few months away, the pressure was on for the twins to decide what their next moves would be. Sidney had arranged for the family financial planner to meet with them before they returned to school.

Lately, when it came to money, Sidney's hands would tremble, and any discussion was immediately terminated. It wasn't as if the boys asked for cash on a regular basis, but conversations with their father tended to center on their making plans for gainful employment. And it was their impression that Father seemed to feel some urgency about their entering the workforce.

Edward Coulson had been the family's financial planner

for decades. Even though Sidney earned well over seven figures managing other people's money, it was important for them, he said, to have someone impartial advising them.

Eleanor came from old money, and with her came a sizeable dowry that had helped Sidney buy his seat on the Chicago Board of Trade and launch his career as a money manager. In the years that followed, Sidney's income was used to pay the family's living expenses, including the various homes, the boys' education, and Eleanor's sumptuous lifestyle. He felt that he had paid his dues but knew Eleanor would never view it the same way. She believed she owned half of everything, and, legally, she did. But things were getting dicey with the market, he said, and he was becoming increasingly agitated. He tried to get Eleanor to cancel her annual New Year's extravaganza, but she threatened to leave him. She didn't have to spell out the grounds for divorce and the high price he would pay. They finally agreed on what Eleanor considered a reasonable budget for her party—one hundred thousand dollars. She was determined to get Yo-Yo Ma to play for her guests, but he came with a price tag of forty-five thousand dollars an hour. Still, she couldn't resist hiring the world-famous cellist. It would be the talk of the town. She would figure out the rest of the budget later, including buying just enough Dom Pérignon for the first round of champagne. Then she would have the staff pour cheaper champagne into the empty Dom bottles. No one would know the difference. Tipping the staff more than usual would keep it her little secret. Eleanor had no shame when it came to pretenses. Neither did anyone else in her circle, for that matter.

Liam and Noah dreaded those social events. They were much more down-to-earth. Some people think that attending a boarding school causes people to be emotionally distant. In their case, "emotionally distant" described their home life.

Only *away* from their home did they receive any positive attention. At home, callous disregard on the part of their parents was the norm.

Christmas was a flurry of visitors coming and going. It was controlled pandemonium. Why people went through the exercise of buying gifts no one needed or even wanted had always puzzled them. The only explanation was to see who could outdo everyone else. It was over the top.

When it came to Eleanor's gift from the boys, she would pause very briefly and give the obligatory "Thank you. It was very thoughtful," knowing full well it was something she had ordered for herself. The only participation from Liam and Noah was to pick it up from either Nordstrom or Bloomingdale's, or one of the 900 North Michigan Shops.

The holidays were nothing more than another opportunity to show off. Liam and Noah were counting down the days when they could return to palm trees, autonomy, and not having to hold their breath while navigating Eleanor's stringent schedule. One more night of feigning enjoyment was up next: the big New Year's Eve gala, hosted by the social elitist Eleanor Adams Westlake.

Fortunately, most of the guests would be Sidney's and Eleanor's age, and the boys could weave their way through the crowd of more than a hundred without too much interaction. Saying "Hello," "Nice to see you," and "Happy Holidays" a few times would suffice. They referred to it as their "cameo appearance."

As soon as the musical entertainment was over, the boys disappeared into the kitchen, where they knew they could find the real champagne. A wink was all it took for Margaret to pull out one of the few remaining bottles of "the good stuff."

Liam gave Margaret a peck on the cheek. "You're the best." And to Liam, she was. Margaret had been with the family since the boys were infants. She had started out as one of the nannies and become head housekeeper once the boys went off to boarding school. She was reserved and efficient, qualities that Eleanor appreciated. And Eleanor appreciated very little. It was in Eleanor's best interest to keep Margaret rather than have to train someone in the family protocol. Eleanor had a way of losing staff in the same way Sidney was losing his hair. Fortunately for Margaret, she didn't have to be concerned with finding another job. She knew how to navigate the personalities, was very fond of the boys, and treated them royally when they were home. Margaret had never married or had children, and she nurtured the twins as if they were her own.

Noah grabbed the bottle from Margaret's hand. He didn't bother to pour it in a glass and took a big swig from the hundred-and-fifty-dollar bottle of bubbly. Margaret gave him a look of disapproval and motioned for the boys to scram before they got caught.

Liam and Noah headed out the back entrance and made their way to the pool house, which also served as their hangout when the house was jammed with people.

The fifteen-hundred-square-foot pool house was decked out with all the amenities. It had a vaulted ceiling, and a free-standing fireplace divided the living room and kitchen area from the king-sized-bed sleeping alcove. The bathroom suite contained a sauna and a steam room. It was big enough for a small family but also served as a guesthouse if the five other additional bedrooms were occupied.

Noah flopped into one of the chaise lounges. "So what do you think old man Coulson has to say?" He took another pull from the bottle, then handed it to Liam.

Liam paused. "Dunno. But don't you think Dad's been acting a little uptight lately? More than usual, I mean."

Noah grunted. "Maybe he's not getting laid enough. It is

the holidays, after all. People go on vacation, visit their families. I'm sure the trollops do the same."

Liam shook his head. Even though Sidney had been involved in many extramarital affairs, Liam chose to relegate it to the back of his mind. Way back. Noah looked at him. "Oh, come on, little brother." Noah liked to remind Liam that he was born twelve minutes earlier. "He's been doing it for years. I doubt he stopped just because we left for college and he wants to keep Mother company."

Liam took a swig and handed the bottle back to Noah. "Like that might happen. But Dad definitely does seem a little off."

They both sat in silence for several minutes. Liam got up and turned on the gas fireplace. Staring at the flames, he said, "Do you have any idea what you want to be doing next year? I mean, you changed your major, what, three times?"

Noah shrugged. "I really don't want to keep going to school, that's for sure, but college life has been the bomb."

"Yes, but even if you continued your education, you'd have to be gainfully employed at some point, no?" Liam was being circumspect with his brother.

"No!" Noah roared with laughter. "Not if I don't have to be!" He finished off the champagne with a guzzle.

Looking at his watch, Liam said, "We should be getting back to Mother's celebration before the ball drops."

"God forbid we miss all the phony air kisses!" Noah slapped his brother on the back, making loud kissing sounds.

When they got back to the main house the music from the ten-piece band was blaring. Eleanor had gotten them to play for free with the promise they would get exposure to some of the most influential people in Chicago. A master manipulator, Eleanor knew no one would give a hoot about the band, especially after listening to the world's greatest cellist.

Liam and Noah positioned themselves on each side of their mother and father. The mandatory stance. Liam thought to himself, *Fake news? How about fake family. Fake fun.*

People were shouting the countdown. "Three, two, one! Happy New Year!" Then came the fake kisses.

Sidney motioned for the boys. He wanted to introduce them to one of his colleagues. Daniel Josephson Ruffing, "DJ" to his friends and associates, Ruffing was a billionaire. He was hovering around the age of fifty but took every precaution to slow down Father Time. His salt-and-pepper hair was neatly trimmed around his Botoxed forehead, and he was in good physical condition. You wouldn't necessarily call him handsome, but his wealth made up for his lack of physical attractiveness.

He had an enormous estate on the coast of Cuba, rumored to be a "playground for the rich." Rich men, that is.

"Daniel, you remember my sons, Liam and Noah?"

"Of course. How are you gents doing these days? Staying out of trouble?" Daniel extended his hand to Liam, then to Noah.

Liam shook the well-tanned, manicured hand of the billionaire and thought to himself, *Why does everyone ask that same stupid question? No. I'm on parole. Duh.* "We do our best." He smiled.

Noah reached out next, much more amicably than his brother. He shook Ruffing's hand vigorously.

"That's some handshake you've got there, son!"

Ruffing beamed his dazzling, expensive white teeth at them. They were almost blinding. "I hear you boys will be graduating in the spring. I have a marina in Miami. Golden Shores. We sell yachts and also provide docking services. If you're in the market for a boat, I have some very fine high-performance cigarettes. Maybe your dad will buy you one for graduation." He elbowed Sidney, who almost went pale at the thought. Even a used one could cost upwards of three hundred thousand dollars.

"Hey, Dad. That sounds like a grand idea!" Noah eagerly jumped in.

Sidney took in a deep breath, trying not to reveal his discomfort. "We'll see."

Liam was getting a strange vibe from both his father and the billionaire. He couldn't put his finger on it, but he couldn't help noticing that his father was nervously tapping his foot. Sidney interjected, "Perhaps Daniel can give you boys a job." That's when his leg stopped shaking.

Noah almost balked at the word *job*. Instead, he answered with, "I'm thinking about continuing with my studies. Maybe get my MBA."

"That's a good plan, too." The billionaire's teeth gleamed as if they were about to take a big bite out of someone's hide.

"Yes, we've been discussing postgraduation plans with them," Sidney continued. "They have a meeting scheduled with Edward Coulson, my financial advisor, in a few days."

Liam remained silent during this exchange.

"Your financial advisor?" Ruffing asked curiously.

"Yes. It's time they took a bit of financial responsibility. They're going to be twenty-two by the end of the year. I was starting my own consulting firm by that age." Sidney stiffened.

Yeah, with Mother's money, Noah thought to himself.
And what about the trust fund?

"I suppose you're right. No time like the present to learn how to manage your finances, hey boys?" Ruffing patted Noah on the shoulder. "But if you ever want to go for a ride, let me know. We sponsor races all the time." He handed his business card to Noah.

"Thank you! We'll be sure to take you up on that offer, right, Liam?" Noah's enthusiasm was obvious. Sidney's was not. He didn't want his sons to get any ideas about buying a boat that cost at least three hundred thousand dollars.

Liam was about to remove himself from the cluster when his mother glided toward the four men. "Daniel, so what do you think of my boys all grown up now?" She could certainly be charming when she wanted. She threaded her arm through his.

"Yes, we were just discussing how Sidney should consider buying a boat as a graduation gift." Daniel's raising the subject again caused Sidney's blood pressure to rise and perspiration to form on his forehead.

"But what will you get for Liam?" Noah joked.

"Oh, I'm sure your father will come up with something marvelous for him as well." Eleanor squeezed Ruffing's arm. "Perhaps we can get matching boats. They are twins, after all." She batted her eyes at the billionaire.

Everyone but Sidney chuckled. "Will you excuse me? I have to speak to one of the staff. We'll catch up later, DJ." Sidney could barely catch his breath as he made his way through the thinning crowd.

Liam's eyes followed his father. Something was definitely amiss. Sidney never addressed the staff. That was Eleanor's territory.

As the last guests were departing, Sidney was conspicuously absent. He didn't care about Eleanor's wrath over his disappearance. He had retreated to his den, where he placed a phone call.

As directed, two days later, Liam and Noah went downtown to meet with Edward Coulson. They sat in the opulent waiting room and wondered why this meeting was taking place. "Something doesn't feel right," Liam said to Noah.

"Oh, aren't you the sensitive one?" Noah chided him. "Are you getting one of your 'woo-woo' visions?" Liam was much more connected to spiritual things than Noah.

"It's not 'woo-woo,' Noah. Don't you ever get a vibe about anything?" Liam was always defending his interest in the subject of metaphysics. "A gut reaction?"

"Well, sure, but that's not the same thing."

Liam cocked his head and smiled. "Are you sure?"

Noah gave him an affectionate punch in the arm. "Ouch!" Liam yelled, pretending to be hurt while the other people in the room looked on with displeasure. Liam laughed, recalling the times when Noah would try to embarrass him in the library.

The phone at the receptionist's desk buzzed. "Yes, I'll send them in." She nodded at Liam and Noah. They smiled, thanked her, and made their way down the hall to Edward Coulson's office.

Liam put his hand on Noah's arm and held him back. He whispered, "Doesn't this seem a bit odd? We've never had to meet with Edward privately."

"Oh, stop fretting." Noah patted Liam on the cheek. "It probably has to do with the trust fund."

Coulson stood from behind his desk as the boys entered the room. He looked pale. Paler than usual. "Sit down, please."

His tone was cold and even.

"As you know, your mother's father, Jerome Adams, set up a college trust fund for you."

"Yep!" Noah smiled and sat back in his chair while Liam continued to sit on the edge of his.

"Income from that trust terminates upon your graduation," Coulson continued. "So, should you wish to enroll in a graduate program, you would have to pay for your own housing and amenities."

"Wait. What are you saying?" Noah sat upright and forward.

"The trust only covers the tuition for advanced studies." Coulson waited for the information to sink in.

"You mean we would have to pay for housing? Food? Gas?" Noah was incredulous.

"I'm afraid so," Coulson said evenly.

"Hold on," Noah said sternly. "Pops had lots of money. I thought we were the heirs to his estate."

"Well, only part of it," Coulson explained. "Your grandfather set aside money for your studies, not your pleasure."

"Pleasure?" Noah was becoming agitated. "How are we supposed to continue our education if we have to get jobs?"

Coulson cleared his throat, and continued, "Your grandfather was a very traditional man. He believed everyone should earn their way. He gave you both head starts by setting money aside for your education. Keep in mind that he also paid for your boarding school."

Noah looked deflated, while Liam listened intently. Coulson continued, "You are both going to have to let me know your intentions before you graduate so I can release the funds if you choose to continue your education."

"But . . . what about our parents? Don't they have the money to help pay for overhead?" Noah was a few octaves shy of whining.

"You will have to take that up with your father. I am only here to inform you about the educational trust."

"So that's it?" Noah blinked several times, trying to absorb this new information. While the young men never behaved as if they were entitled, they assumed money would never be an issue, let alone having to get a job.

"Yes. Do you have any other questions?" Coulson stood.

"I guess not." Noah shrugged.

"Thank you for your time." Liam held out his hand politely.

"Remember, I need to know your decisions by the first of May. Good luck." Coulson moved from behind the desk and ushered them out.

As they headed toward the elevator, Noah hissed, "I can't believe this! Why couldn't Dad tell us this himself?"

"Probably because it wasn't his decision. It was Grandpa Adams who set up the trust." Liam took in a big sigh. "I was going to study for my master's in psychology, but I also wanted to travel a bit before I had to hit the books again." Liam was much more resigned to the situation than Noah.

"Well, this sucks. I'm going to have a talk with Mother about it," Noah huffed, as they made their way back to the waiting area and elevator bank.

Liam chuckled. "Yeah, good luck with that."

When they got home, Noah went in search of his mother. "Margaret? Where is my mother?"

"Oh, Noah. She left for London this morning. She is going to spend some time with her sister Dorothy. Didn't she tell you?" Margaret looked a tad confused.

"No." Noah was infuriated. "She threw us to the wolves!"

Margaret didn't dare respond. She wasn't used to either of the boys having a temper tantrum, and she feared she was about to witness one.

"Where's my father?" Noah demanded. Margaret gave him a blank stare.

"Liam! Liam!" Noah went yelling through the house. "Where the hell are you?"

Liam leaned over the second-floor balcony. "Up here. What seems to be the problem?"

"The problem?" Noah was about to explode. "Did you know Dear Mother has taken flight to London?"

Liam looked confused. "What do you mean, London?"

"London, as in England. Don't be a schmuck. She flew the coop."

Liam kept looking at his brother, waiting for more steam to come off, which it did.

"I can't believe this is happening! We're screwed, and there's no one here to explain why." By this time, Noah was climbing the stairs two at a time.

"Take it easy. We're not exactly screwed." Not only was Liam the more circumspect of the two, he was also the more levelheaded. "We just need to figure out a plan. Where's Dad?"

"Hell if I know. Probably in Michigan with one of his whores."

Chapter Three

Present Day
Washington, D.C.

Maggie punched the REPLAY button one more time before she dialed the number. "Hello, Flowers Exotica," a friendly voice answered.

"Hi, my name is Maggie Spritzer. A friend of mine left me a message asking that I call her back at this number." Maggie sounded her usual journalistic self. Pragmatic and polite, but her hands were shaking. Something wasn't quite right.

"Oh yes. A young lady was here about an hour ago and asked to use the phone. But she left with two men in a black SUV."

Maggie stared at the phone. "Did she seem all right to you?"

She was now taking notes.

"Well, it's hard to say. She seemed a little confused and nervous. I gave her a cup of tea while she waited for you to call her back."

"Did the men say anything to her? Did they come into the shop? Did she go willingly?" Maggie was rattling off questions like a machine gun.

"She saw the SUV and left the store as soon as one of the men got out. They had a very brief exchange, and she got in."

"Could you hear anything they said?" Maggie was tapping her pen on the desk like a drum.

"No."

"Did it look like some sort of altercation?" Maggie prodded.

"I don't think so. She seemed to know them."

"Did she smile at them?"

"I couldn't see her face."

"Did they touch her in any way? Grab her? Shove her?" The hair on the back of Maggie's neck was standing at attention now.

"No. Just a few words, and she got in willingly. I'm sorry I don't have any other information for you." The flower lady was trying to be as helpful as possible. "But there was one thing that struck me as odd."

"What was that?" Maggie listened intently.

The flower lady continued, "The men were dressed in exactly the same clothing."

"Like suits?" Maggie prodded.

"No. They were wearing big shirts. The kind men wear for yoga or meditation, but they were black. Like a tunic but with toggle-like frogs. You know, instead of buttons. The pants were white. They looked a little out of place for this part of town."

"Can you describe the men?"

"Just average Caucasian, with very short light brown hair," the woman said.

"Anything else you can think of?" Maggie pushed harder. "Did the shirts say anything? Did they have a logo?"

"Now that you mention it, there was some kind of symbol on the left."

"Did you recognize it?" Maggie was writing feverishly.

"Sorry, no. They moved too fast for me to see. Oh, and they looked pretty buff. Like they work out a lot," the flower lady added.

"You didn't happen to get the license plate of the SUV?"

"No. Most cars in Florida don't have state plates on the front, and I didn't think to look when they turned around."

Maggie was about to start biting her nails, a habit she had tried to break for years. At one point, she had regular manicures to cure her from the nibbling, but it had been weeks since her last visit to the salon. Her cuticles were ripe for the chewing. "Okay. Thank you very much. This has been very helpful. Can you please take down my number in case you remember anything else?"

"Of course, dear."

Maggie rattled off the toll-free number and her cell to the woman. As soon she got off the phone, she buzzed her boss, Anna (Annie) Ryland de Silva. Countess de Silva, one of the richest women in the world, who also happened to own the newspaper where Maggie worked. Annie was also part of a select group of women, known to many as the Sisterhood, founded by Myra Rutledge. Annie's life partner, Fergus, formerly of Scotland Yard, was an adjunct member of the group and a friend of Charles Martin, Myra's husband.

The Sisterhood began when Myra's daughter Barbara was struck down and killed several years before. The driver was never prosecuted owing to his diplomatic immunity. To make the situation more horrendous, Barbara was pregnant at the time.

That horrible situation threw Myra into a state of ultimate despair. The man who was now her husband was a former MI6 agent who had unceremoniously left the UK, leading him to look for work in the States. He interviewed for a position as head of security at Myra's candy company, where they began a lifetime, loving relationship.

In spite of all of his doting, Myra remained in a fog of hopelessness until one day she saw a news clip about a woman whom the legal system had failed. Staring at the TV, Myra had an epiphany. *No one else would be a victim of an injustice even if it meant taking matters into her own hands.* In a very short time, the group grew, with each woman bringing her own special talents to their cause.

Lizzie Fox Cricket was a crackerjack lawyer, considered one of the sharpest in the world. Nikki Quinn, Myra's adopted daughter, was also a lawyer. Kathryn Lucas, a graduate of MIT with a degree in nuclear engineering, had been brutally raped, while her husband, suffering from MS, was forced to watch. When her husband died, Kathryn took on his vocation as a big-rig, long-distance truck driver. She preferred the freedom of the open road over a desk job or a position in a laboratory.

Alexis Thorn, a beautiful African American woman, was wrongly imprisoned while the real criminals spent the profits from their stock scam. After her release, she went to law school and became a member of Nikki's law firm. She also happened to be a master of disguise. Yoko Akia owned and ran a plant nursery when she wasn't honing her exceptional martial-arts skills; and Isabelle Flanders owned her own architectural firm and was becoming a master computer hacker under the tutelage of her husband, Abner Tookus.

Maggie's first thought was to bring in the sisters, but not before she did a little research on her own. In the meantime, she would talk to Annie and get her advice.

Chapter Four

2008
South Florida

When their final semester was ending, Noah and Liam received a disturbing phone call from their family attorney. Their father had been arrested for running a Ponzi scheme that rivaled the one for which Bernie Madoff would eventually be arrested. Sidney's behavior during the holidays was beginning to make sense. He must have sensed that the FBI was onto him, but before he could make a move, they seized all his assets, indicted him, and stuck him in jail without bail until he could be tried. They were not taking any chances of his making bail and skipping the country.

It also answered the mystery of Mother's earlier departure for England. She had to have known something. Whether she had full knowledge of Sidney's financial shenanigans, and if so for how long, was her little secret, a secret she wasn't about to share. She had transferred a goodly sum of money into an offshore account prior to her departure, then transferred it to London upon her arrival in the UK. Her New Year's Eve gala was intended to create the illusion of normalcy.

Liam and Noah had been thrown to the wolves.

Noah was in a state of panic and rage. But Liam began to think about a plan. If he could make enough money to share an apartment with Noah, he could work on his master's degree in psychology. Liam decided to apply for a position as a graduate assistant and to get several side jobs tutoring. It wouldn't be a lot, and he would be living month-to-month, but he would be able to share the bills with Noah. At least the overhead. Noah was interested in leading a much ritzier lifestyle and thought he could afford it, for a while.

When Noah heard the news about the loss of his family's wealth, he was too furious to think about continuing his education. *What for?* No. He would figure out a way to make money. Lots of money. He dug through his contacts list and found Daniel Ruffing's number. Connecting with the billionaire would certainly be a good move. Even if it meant working for him. *How bad could selling yachts be?* Noah dialed his private cell number.

"DJ here." Daniel Ruffing's voice came through loud and clear.

"Hey, it's Noah. Noah Westlake. How are you, sir?" Noah's voice was a little shaky. He had never had to grovel before. Ever.

"Noah. Good to hear from you, but please drop the 'sir.' Makes me sound old," Ruffing said with a guffaw. "Call me DJ."

Noah was even more nervous. He hadn't expected the conversation to be so casual. What he was expecting were questions about his father, or that Ruffing would simply hang up on him *because* of his father. Noah had no idea as to the real relationship the two men had. But based on the tone of his voice, Ruffing was quite blasé. "What can I do for you, Noah?"

"Well, actually, I, uh . . ." Noah was stammering.

"Hey, I know about the situation with your old man. Tough break." That was even more casual.

"Yes, which is one of the reasons I called." Noah quickly added, "Not for money, but maybe discussing a job?" He cringed as he waited for a response.

There was a moment of silence. Noah thought perhaps they had been disconnected. Finally, Ruffing cleared his throat. "What did you have in mind?"

"I'm not exactly sure." Noah hadn't thought it through before he dialed the number.

"Well, then, why don't you come by the marina next week. I'll be back in the States by then. Say Wednesday?"

"Absolutely." Noah regained some of his composure. "What time?"

"Come by around noon. We'll have some lunch, and I'll show you around."

"That would be great. Thanks very much. I appreciate it." Noah was stunned by the invitation. He truly did not expect such congeniality from a man of Ruffing's stature. Maybe he and his father had had a close relationship. Then he remembered how his mother squashed her breasts against Ruffing at the New Year's Eve party. Come to think of it, Noah couldn't recall his mother being so chummy with anyone. At no point in time, with anyone.

"My pleasure, Noah. By the way, will your brother be joining us?" Ruffing asked.

"No. Just me. He's preparing for exams. Thanks again. I'll see you next week." Noah got a rush of adrenaline. He was going to have lunch with the rich and powerful Daniel Josephson Ruffing. And if all went well, Noah would be gainfully employed after graduating. Next was finding an apartment for himself and Liam. He reminded himself not to start counting the money he hoped he could make. At least not until he nailed a job.

Fortunately, Ruffing obliged without too much convincing and made him a marina attendant. A fancy expression for dockhand. They were the people responsible for fueling boats and assisting boaters with whatever their needs. And there were always lots of those. But it was a start. A start in a very lucrative business, surrounded by very wealthy people.

In the beginning, it wasn't as glamorous as Noah had anticipated. He didn't get the royal treatment. The staff viewed him as a rich kid who wanted more spending money. They weren't too far from the truth. The difference was that Noah wanted *lots* more spending money. He wasn't about to let the ruin of his father become his legacy. He had often thought about changing his last name, but that would require too much paperwork. Besides, most people in South Florida had no idea who Bernie Madoff was, let alone Sidney Westlake. It was extremely rare for anyone to make a connection.

Noah was doing well financially. This pattern continued for a couple of years. He had gained more respect from his coworkers and was well liked by Ruffing's clients, which was evident by the large tips he would receive for simply tying up one of their boats. It wouldn't be unusual for someone from a foreign country to tip him two hundred dollars to tie a simple cleat knot.

It also helped that Ruffing had begun to give Noah some extra side work, for which he paid Noah, under the table, in cash. He felt he had achieved a lifestyle more to his liking than continuing to toil in academia.

In addition to selling yachts, renting slips, and running a robust bar and dining dock, Ruffing's marina provided an offshore supply service to day-boat fishing charters. With the ability to have goods delivered while out on the water, charter boats could offer bigger packages to their customers. The boats would take people out for big-game fishing, often spending one or two nights on the water. With the speed of the cigarette boat topping out at eighty knots, and with GPS, it was easy to arrange deliveries. Noah would be given the coordinates, then pack the high-speed craft with insulated boxes. Presumably, the boxes contained supplies, but Noah never packed them himself. Nor did he ever witness their being filled. The boxes were labeled and set on the dock, and he would put them on the boat and head out. When he arrived at the fishing boats, the boat captains would give him a banker's bag, seemingly filled with cash. Day-boat fishing was largely a cash business, so there was no reason for Noah to suspect anything was amiss. This pattern continued for a couple of years, and Noah was making good money. Very good money.

Noah continued to work for Ruffing while Liam pursued his doctorate in the area of cultural psychology. It was the study of how a set of ideas, behavior, and attitudes are formed in a group of people such as a family, and how that gets handed down from one generation to another. Liam was hopeful he would have some insight as to why his family was so messed up and hoped he could avoid the pitfalls in his own life.

After he completed the program, Liam applied for a grant to visit several countries and do research on the psychology of groups. He spent two years traveling to Tibet, India, and Peru, while Noah was banking the money he was earning with Ruffing.

When Liam returned to the States, he obtained a position as an adjunct in the psychology department at the University of Miami. Teaching wasn't his passion, but it provided his half of the rent and gas for the Jeep Grand Cherokee he had gotten as a high-school-graduation present. Noah had traded his for a newer, more expensive car. A Range Rover Sport. Liam often wondered exactly how much Ruffing was paying

Noah, but he never dared to ask. But something didn't feel quite right.

Most of Liam's old classmates in the doctoral program had gotten jobs with organizations that needed people to help them deal with the issues that arose from the increased presence of minorities, many of whom came from different cultures, in the workplace. Their doctoral program had focused on groups of people and cultural influences. Many were consulting with government agencies. Liam, on the other hand, was searching for spiritual significance in the cultural aspects of psychology.

Noah's take on all of what Liam found fascinating was that it was a crashing bore. He enjoyed the lifestyle that his income and rugged good looks afforded him access to, not staring at his navel contemplating the cultural divide.

Noah was always out late at night, and his friends were not always upstanding citizens. "Fast and loose" would be a good description. Liam needed to find his own group of like-minded people, even if he had to search beyond the walls of the university.

There were a number of health-food stores that attracted the "New Age" types and open-air markets that attracted a lot of drifters, people looking for free food. Liam would frequent these magnets for holdover hippies and lost souls, and began attending drum circles and several moon-worship festivals.

Still, it wasn't quite what Liam had in mind. When he had the opportunity, and there were plenty, he would converse with these (almost) kindred spirits. He discovered that many of them were simply lost in society. They had been drug abusers, alcoholics, prostitutes, and runaways. Many lived in shelters. Many of them were spiritually wounded. These were the people he wanted to connect with. Damaged souls in need of spiritual healing.

He found a park on the outskirts of the city limits. It was a remote area beyond the urban sprawl of Miami, at the edge of the Everglades. A perfect location. There they could meditate and chant without disturbing anyone or being mocked or hassled. Liam would read passages from Eckhart Tolle and Lao Tzu. Inspiring words like "eliminate everything that doesn't bring you joy" were part of the ritual. At one point, Liam was writing his own verses of encouragement.

Within weeks, his handful of low and powerless grew to over two dozen. Three months later, forty to fifty people would show up for his weekly sessions.

It was apparent that though they lived under the same roof, Liam and Noah were leading very different lives. They rarely spent any social time together, and when Liam would return to the apartment after one of his gatherings, Noah would tease him with, "So how was howling at the moon tonight?"

Since their childhood, Liam and Noah had been simpatico, as most twins would be, but the wreckage created by their father's financial crimes had changed both of them. In less than a decade, they had drifted apart in their approach to life.

The group of followers continued to grow, and Liam realized he needed something other than a mangrove swamp in which to hold his meetings. One afternoon, as he was scoping out a spot where the group could meet, he noticed a dilapidated building with overgrown foliage and a FOR SALE sign. The place needed a lot of work. But maybe he could get his group to pitch in. He jotted down the number of the real-estate agent.

"*Only* one hundred thirty-five thousand dollars?" Noah was dubious. "Where do you think we'll get that kind of money? The place is a disaster and needs thousands of dollars' worth of work. More like tens of thousands," Noah said, questioning Liam's idea of buying the old farm.

"Listen. Some of the people who come to my meetings are willing to help get it in shape." Liam had already anticipated his brother's resistance.

"And how are you going to pay them? And pay for the supplies?" Noah was dismissing the notion from the outset.

"They are willing to do it for free in exchange for housing."

"What are you talking about?" Noah's voice was louder than usual. *Has Liam completely lost his mind?*

Liam closed his eyes and took in a deep inhale. "Noah, these people I've met, well, they're just a little lost."

Noah immediately interrupted. "Oh great. A lost and found?"

"Noah, please. Hear me out." Liam was calm but determined. "The place is big enough to house a dozen people, maybe more if we can rebuild."

"Oh . . . no. I'm not going to be roomies with a bunch of cuckoo birds."

"Please don't call them that. As I said, they're lost souls," Liam continued. "The property has several outbuildings. Kind of like sheds. If they start on those, they could live outside the main house."

Noah furrowed his brow. "Are you trying to tell me you want to start some kind of ashram? With those weird tents and patchouli incense burning everywhere? What do you call those things exactly?"

"They're called yurts. And no. Not exactly."

"Then what exactly?" Noah prodded.

Liam motioned for them to sit down. "I have a vision."

"Swell." Noah groaned. "Not one of those again."

"Hey, remember when we were going to old man Coulson's, and I stopped you in the hallway and said I had a feeling something was off? And you accused me of having a 'woo-woo' moment?"

"Yeah."

"Well, this isn't one of them. A woo-woo moment, that is. Then again, maybe it is. Listen . . ." Liam proceeded to explain his vision for the property and a nonprofit sanctuary retreat.

The word *nonprofit* did not sit well with Noah—until Liam explained his idea further.

Chapter Five

Present Day
Washington, D.C.

Maggie used one of her chewed-up fingers to punch in the speed-dial number for Annie's cell phone. "Don't tell me the food truck ran out of hot dogs," Annie teased. Maggie was known for her voracious appetite. It was a wonder that she managed to stay in shape. "Are you biting your nails again?"

Maggie pulled her hand away from her mouth, looking to see if Annie was in her doorway. "Uh . . . um . . . well, yeah. But I have a good reason," she half defended herself.

"What's up?" Annie recognized the tone in Maggie's voice. Something was bothering her. Bothering her in a big way.

"Are you in the building?"

"Yes. Why?" Annie could hear the concern in Maggie's voice.

"Remember my college chum, Gabby Richardson?"

"Yes, the willowy, reserved blonde? Pretty girl."

"That's her."

"What about her?" Annie queried.

"Can we talk in person? I need to do some more digging."

"I'll head over to your office. Give me ten." Annie clicked off.

Maggie reviewed her notes. She racked her brain trying to remember the name of the place where Gabby was staying. She turned toward her computer and typed in *spiritual retreats, South Florida*. Over a dozen were listed. They included words like *moonrise, wellness, spiritual, meditative*. She tried another search: *retreats, uniforms*. There were dozens upon dozens of websites for clothing. Many of the shirts looked like what the flower lady described. *Well, that narrows it down to every spa, yoga studio, retreat, and hotel in the Miami area.* But it made sense. If the men were from the place where Gabby was staying, they would most likely be wearing that kind of garb.

She zeroed in on the most obvious sanctuaries when it hit her. *The Haven.* She added that to her notes as Annie walked through the door of Maggie's paper-infested office. One spark could start a bonfire. As much as the mess bothered Annie, she knew Maggie was a crackerjack editor. She didn't want to mess with Maggie's "flow."

"What's going on?" Annie moved a few piles of folders and clippings to clear a place for her to sit.

Maggie jumped right in. "About an hour ago, I got a message on voice mail from Gabby. She was calling from a florist shop in Miami."

Maggie dialed her voice mail and played the message to Annie.

"Play that again." Annie moved closer to the desk phone.

"I called the florist, and Gabby was gone. She was picked up by two men in a black SUV. According to the woman I spoke to, Gabby didn't put up a fight."

"A missing ticket. Missing passport. It sounds like someone definitely didn't want her to go anywhere."

"Sure does. Then two men pick her up at a florist's. I checked the distance from the airport to the flower shop. At least twenty minutes away. The creepy questions are, How did they find her and why were they after her?" Maggie filled Annie in with the rest of the information she had received from the woman on the phone. Then told her that she had discovered the name of the place. "It's called The Haven."

"Did you try calling them?" Annie asked, her wheels already turning.

"Not yet. I wanted to talk to you first. I thought I'd call under the guise that I was doing an article for our lifestyle section."

"Unless those places are open to the public, like a spa, they don't like people prying into their business."

Maggie pursed her lips. "I think it's private. The website doesn't have a lot of information."

"We should probably talk to Myra and Charles. Maybe Charles can get some intel on the place."

"Excellent idea." Maggie was starting to feel a sense of relief. If anyone could unravel this situation, it was the Sisterhood.

Annie pulled out her phone and pressed the button for Myra.

"Hello, darling." Myra's voice was clear and upbeat.

"Hello to you!" Even though the two women had shared breakfast only a few hours ago, each time they spoke on the phone, it was like long-lost friends speaking for the first time in ages. But that was the nature of their years of friendship. Loyalty. Support. Love. Affection.

"Everything all right?" Myra asked.

"Everything here is fine. Except for this mess of an office." Annie shook her head as she glanced around the spillage of paper. Maggie rolled her eyes.

"You must be in Maggie's office!" Myra laughed.

"Good guess!" Annie replied. "Do you recall meeting Maggie's friend Gabby? The tall, pretty journalism intern we had here for a while?"

"Why yes. They went to school together, right?"

"They did."

"So, what's going on?"

"Maggie got a disturbing message from Gabby. She left it on Maggie's office voice mail. She probably dialed in to the main toll-free number." Annie put her phone on speaker. "Gabby has taken up residence at a spiritual retreat outside of Miami. We think she may be at a place called The Haven. I'll let Maggie tell you the rest."

Maggie continued to give Myra what little information she had managed to acquire. Gabby had become a resident at a spiritual retreat. She had been getting depressed about the state of the world and wanted to give journalism a rest. Several months into her stay at the retreat, she was planning to visit her mother. But when she got to the airport, her ticket was missing, as was her passport. When Maggie had finished her recap, she added, "I have a bad feeling about this."

"Did you try to contact her through The Haven?" Myra asked.

"Not yet. I wanted to talk to you and Annie first. I'm not sure how to approach it, especially if Gabby is in some kind of danger."

Myra started stroking her pearls, a habit she had developed many years ago. "Why don't the both of you come over for dinner? I'm sure Charles can whip up something for all of us." She glanced over at Charles, who nodded his approval. "Annie, bring Fergus, too." Charles gave Myra a look. "I mean *send* Fergus over to give Charles a hand." She chuckled. Charles smiled. Charles and Fergus were a good team in the kitchen, as well as the Sisterhood's counterintelligence division.

"Sounds like a plan." Maggie was relieved. Two of the fiercest women she had ever met had her back. And Gabby's.

"Six thirty work for you?" Myra asked casually.

"Perfect. We'll see you then." Annie clicked off the phone. "We have a couple of hours. See if you can dig up any more information on The Haven. Who runs that place, do we know yet?"

"No, but I'll find out." Maggie turned to her computer as Annie stepped over another pile of clippings.

"Thanks, Annie."

"No worries. We'll get to the bottom of this. I'll swing by around five thirty. You can drive. I'll leave my car here and get a lift back tomorrow."

Maggie gave her a thumbs-up and dived back into the search engine, looking for more clues.

Chapter Six

Present Day
The Haven

When the two men picked up Gabby at the florist's, they spoke briefly. She knew not to ask questions. Her encounter with Noah a few weeks before had sent a chill up her spine. How odd. The chill had made her sweat.

She sat quietly in the back seat of the SUV. The dark-tinted windows made it hard for people to see inside the vehicle. Florida laws varied as to what windows could be tinted and at what percentage of light. Back-seat passengers could be completely hidden from onlookers. Gabby knew she was shielded by one of those. Even if anyone were looking for her, they would never see her through the dark-tinted window glass.

The traffic on the forty-five-minute drive back to The Haven was very light. During the trip, Gabby wondered what was going to happen to her. She didn't fear for her life, but she was baffled as to why her trip had been sabotaged. *I guess I'll soon find out.*

The SUV pulled in front of one of the garage doors. One of

the men opened the passenger door and motioned for Gabby to go into the main house. The garage housed several vehicles, including an airboat on a trailer hitch. No one was supposed to know about the boat, but Rachel, a friend of Gabby's, had first spotted it when she was wheeling the laundry carts to the parking lot. The shuttle van that took the group into town was pulling out of the garage. She pretended to look the other way and went back to the dormitory where the women slept.

One evening, when Rachel and Gabby were taking a walk around the center garden of the compound, Rachel mentioned it to Gabby.

"Why do you suppose there's an airboat in the garage?" Rachel whispered.

"Maybe it was owned by one of the members and they donated it when they joined," Gabby suggested.

But before they could continue speculating, they came upon another member and quickly clammed up. Maybe it was better to ignore its presence.

Gabby sat in the foyer of the main house. The living quarters and offices were located on the second floor. The main level held a room large enough to accommodate just under two hundred people seated in rows of chairs. There was a kitchen in the main house for Liam and guests, but the other residents took their meals in the dining hall, which had a large kitchen in the back where their meals were prepared. One side of the kitchen held a large pantry for dry goods, and the other side opened to a small garden for fresh vegetables. If nothing else, the food was nutritious, even if it was bland.

Gabby felt as if she had been sitting for an hour before Noah approached her. Gabby stood immediately.

"I don't suppose you know why you're here?" He gave her a menacing look.

Gabby gulped. "No. Not really."

"You were seen trying to board a plane. We don't allow Pledges to travel unaccompanied." Noah was cool and direct.

"Yes, but Liam gave me permission to visit my mother. She's in the hospital." Gabby could not hide her confusion.

"I'm sorry to hear about your mother, but as I explained to you when I caught you upstairs, the rules are the rules." Noah was almost mechanical in his explanation.

"I really don't know what to say. I apologize for any infringement." The word *infringement* made Gabby shudder. She had never thought she would be accused of such a thing. The Haven had very rigid rules for an organization dedicated to spiritual enlightenment. "But you can check with Liam. He said it was all right. My sister bought the ticket for me." She was almost pleading at this point.

"And that, too, created a problem. We had to track her down to let her know that you weren't going to be arriving on schedule." Noah seemed unusually peeved.

"What did you tell her?" Gabby was becoming agitated. *Why would they stop me from visiting my mother?*

"We sent her a text."

"With what?" Gabby was trying to remain calm.

Noah handed her the burner phone they had used and showed her:

It's Gab. Sprained my ankle on the way to airport. I'm OK but on crutches. Phone broke. This one is temporary. Sorry. Give Mom my love, Love you guys.

"I don't understand. Why?" Gabby was almost pleading at this point.

"I told you. It's the rules," Noah reiterated.

"But this is a lie. I didn't sprain my ankle. Why would you lie? What is this all about?" Gabby was distraught. Then Liam walked into the room.

"What seems to be the problem? Gabby, I thought you were going to visit your mother." Liam looked perplexed.

"She broke the rules, Liam," Noah admonished both of them.

"But her mother is in the hospital." Liam was irritated at what had happened. This was not the kind of refuge he envisioned for his followers.

"Liam, we'll discuss this privately. Meanwhile, Gabby, you go back to the dorm. And put on the appropriate clothes. Bring those to me later." He pointed at the jeans and hoodie she was wearing.

Gabby looked at Liam as if begging for help. Liam gave her a slight nod, but it wasn't much comfort. To either of them. She left the room, shaking like a leaf.

The walk from the main house to the dorm was slightly over a hundred yards. Not a terrible hike, but that day it seemed particularly long. The air was typical South Florida steam, with the mercury rising to ninety-four degrees. Gabby felt as if she had gone through the spin cycle of the washing machine.

When she arrived at the dorm, she noticed that the little bit of air-conditioning they were allowed made little difference. Maybe it was eighty-six inside. She clicked on a ceiling fan, hoping to move the hot, thick, stale air around.

Gabby sat on the bunk that served as her bed. The others were in town doing errands and chores. She didn't know whether to cry or scream. Something did not feel right. Not at all. A knock at the door startled her. "It's Liam. May I come in?"

Gabby got up slowly and walked toward the voice. Her hands were trembling. "Of course." She grabbed the handle, hoping it wouldn't slip out of her sweaty palms. When she opened the door, she noticed a sheepish look on Liam's face.

"I want to apologize, Gabby. I shouldn't be telling you this, but I think I can trust you."

"Is everything all right?" Gabby was getting nervous.

"Well, yes. But Noah thinks there has been a security breach. He's concerned that someone is pirating our manuals, videos, and programs." Liam gestured for both of them to take a seat. Gabby was still shaking.

"You don't think I have anything to do with it?" Gabby sounded crushed.

"Oh, no. Not at all. I suppose it's my fault. I forgot to mention your trip to Noah, so when he heard you had left in a taxi, he got suspicious." Liam cleared his throat. "I don't want you to worry about any of this."

"But what about my mom? I need to speak with someone in my family." Tears started streaming down Gabby's face. She began to stutter. "I . . . I . . . am so . . . so . . . sorry." She pulled a tissue from her hoodie and glanced down at her clothes. She wasn't wearing her *vastra*.

Liam noticed, too. "Perhaps it seemed suspicious because you're wearing civilian clothes." He waited for an answer.

Gabby didn't want to get her friend in trouble. Rachel had found a decent pair of jeans, a T-shirt, and a hoodie on one of the back trails of the property. According to the rules, you had to turn over items that were out of the ordinary, including clothing. No one was allowed to have anything that was not part of the program or that hadn't been approved. Even family photos were a no-no. Part of the teachings included releasing yourself from the past. Photos would only pull you back and off your path. Guitars were allowed only if you could play well. That went for anything.

There was a crafts cottage where members could make jewelry, paint, knit, crochet, decoupage, macramé. Liam thought it was good therapy. Noah thought it was a good source of revenue.

Gabby decided to take the fall for her friend and change the story a bit. She didn't want to venture a guess as to how women's clothing was out on the back trail, after all. "I found them under the table at the farmers' market." She looked up at Liam, hoping he would buy her story. "I kept them because I didn't want to travel in my *vastra*."

"I don't have to tell you that it's an infringement to have civilian clothes."

There was that word again. *Infringement.* Gabby was beginning to feel like a felon. The events of the day had her very confused. And more than a little paranoid. The thought had occurred to her that she might have wandered into some kind of peculiar, mind-controlling prison. She tried to shake it off.

Speaking of paranoid, it appears perhaps Noah is also teetering on the edge.

Liam had always seemed to be the sincere one. He always greeted everyone with a smile and was always full of encouragement. Prodding people to *move forward. Move up.*

Gabby shook her head in resignation. "I truly apologize." He still hadn't answered her question about what to do about her mother. "Liam," she said softly. "My mom? Please?" She looked deeply into his eyes, searching for that person she *thought* she had met just over six months ago. Maybe he wasn't who she had imagined him to be. This would be the real test.

Liam looked around the room. "I am going to assign you to office duty as a backup assistant. Answering the phone is one of those duties." He gave her a sly glance.

Gabby also looked around the room, and whispered, "So I would be answering your phone?" She was skeptical.

"Yes, the office phone. You will cover for Maxwell when he's on break. That's usually the same time I have lunch." Liam was all but telling her—and assisting her—to call her mother.

Gabby was in total shock. Why would Liam do this for her? Maybe he felt guilty about what had happened earlier that day at the airport. He had admitted that it was his fault.

Liam laid out the ground rules. "You will have three minutes, so think about exactly what you want to say."

"Well, what do I say? I assume I'm not going home?" Her voice was calm and matter-of-fact.

"I'm sorry. Not today. Maybe in a few weeks, after things are settled with Noah." Liam patted her hand. He looked at his watch. "It's time for Maxwell's afternoon break. I'll walk you up there and show you the ropes. It's only a fifteen-minute break, so there won't be any paperwork. Just be stationed at the desk. We'll get you some light filing or mailings when you cover his lunch break. He gets an hour. From noon until one. That shouldn't interfere with any of your classes. Right?"

She tried not to stutter this time. "No problem. Can I ask you a question?"

"Of course." Liam smiled.

"What about *my* lunch? I don't mean a break. Do I get to eat it at the desk?" She scrunched up her face.

Liam chuckled. "No. Sorry, no food at the desk. But you can have your lunch before or after. Fix it yourself when you have time."

Gabby couldn't believe this turn of events. "Sounds like a plan! Thank you!"

"Come on. We don't want to keep Maxwell waiting. You have no idea how grumpy he can get if he doesn't have his afternoon cookies."

She was finally starting to feel like she could breathe normally again. It was as if she had been holding her breath for hours.

They walked to the main house in silence and climbed the stairs to the open hallway. At one end of the hall was Liam's residence. It was a modest space, something akin to a small hotel suite. But not the Ritz-Carlton. More like a Courtyard Inn.

It had two rooms that formed an L. One area was where his queen-size bed and a low dresser stood. The other section had a small sofa and two club chairs. It was simple. Functional.

Private.

Chapter Seven

Present Day
Pinewood

As Annie and Maggie drove around to the back of the farmhouse, they could hear Lady and her pups yapping with delight. The women entered through the kitchen door. As far as anyone was concerned, *that* was the main entrance. They all gave each other big hugs, remembering to include the dogs. Maggie reached in her pocket and pulled out a few dog treats. "What?" She looked at everyone's puzzled face. "Oh, you thought if there was food in my pocket, I would eat it? Regardless of what it was?" She grunted. "I'll have you know I made a special stop to get these." She was almost whining. Maggie was known for her voracious appetite, and the group broke into fits of laughter.

"Seriously, love, if it's not moving, you'll usually have it for dessert," Charles taunted, using his best upper-crust British accent. Everyone knew he wasn't anywhere near the upper crust even though he had been a childhood friend of the queen, which made his comment even more amusing. Fergus roared, and the women chortled. It really didn't take much to get the gang into fits of laughter. That's probably because, when they were on a mission, it was often a matter of life and death.

"Hah. Very funny." Maggie was accustomed to being the brunt of jokes whenever it came to food. Human, dog, or otherwise.

Myra linked arms with Annie and Maggie, leading them to the atrium, where Annie and Maggie sat down on deeply cushioned chairs. Myra had opened a bottle of wine just before they arrived and poured some into a beautiful Baccarat decanter, giving it an opportunity to breathe. Myra wasn't a fancy person, but she appreciated fine things. She filled a glass for each of them and relaxed in her overstuffed chair. Myra raised her glass to the other two, who raised theirs in return. "To us! Now spill. Your guts. Not the wine!" The women cackled with glee. They took a sip of the fine cabernet sauvignon and commented on the sad situation in Northern California, where fires had charred thousands of acres of land. They sat in silence, then each voiced their thoughts on how lucky they were to be able to share a fine wine together.

Another sip, and they were ready to consider what Maggie had to say. Rather than pull out her laptop to show them onscreen, Maggie had printed out the information she had been able to gather and made copies for everyone. This way, Annie and Myra could take notes and no one was craning their neck to see the laptop screen.

Under normal circumstances, the group would meet in the War Room, located in the basement. Outfitted with the latest high-tech equipment, the War Room was like something out of a James Bond movie. The CIA and FBI would be green with envy if they could see what was in it.

Charles had been a member of MI6, though much of his background remained a mystery. Fergus had been a top official at Scotland Yard. Their connections with Interpol ran deep, as did their relationship with Avery Snowden, who ran an exceptional, and expensive, private surveillance agency. All of this was at the disposal of the Sisterhood should they need to right a wrong. But tonight's gathering was informal. Maggie wanted to be sure she had a good reason to worry about Gabby, and who better than Myra and Annie to put what she had learned into perspective for her.

Maggie handed copies to Annie and Myra and started from the beginning, when she had received the disturbing message from Gabby. Addressing Annie, she said, "After you left, I researched the ownership of The Haven. It's one shell company after another, leading me to an offshore bank in the Seychelle Islands. Naturally, they aren't handing over any info." She took a sip from her glass and continued, "I printed out The Haven's mission statement."

For the good of all. For the good of our planet. For the good of our souls. The Haven offers special programs for spiritual enlightenment and personal growth. Classes, seminars, and annual programs are available. Please call our center for more information on Yoga, Meditation, and Personal Development.

Costs may vary. 1-888-555-0292. Have a blessed day.

The Haven.

"Well, that says a whole lot of nothing." Myra stroked her pearls. "Do you know who runs the place?"

"Two brothers. Liam and Noah Westlake. It appears that Liam is the guru, and Noah is the general manager."

"Where did you find that information?" Annie asked.

"I called a local store, Betty's Health Foods. I figured if anyone knew of this place, it would be one of the granola-type folks. I told them I was thinking about spending some time in an ashram and that someone told me about one in the area, but I couldn't remember the name. And did she ever hear of something like that?" Maggie paused. "She said she was familiar with a place called The Haven, but it was more like a religious organization. Apparently one evening, when Betty was delivering food to the local shelter, she had heard Liam speak. She said he was very charismatic but she never considered joining his group of acolytes. She said that as far as she knew, they grew their own fruits and vegetables. They also made honey. She thought they were regulars at the farmers' market, selling produce, honey, and some handmade things." Maggie stopped to catch her breath.

"Sounds more like a hippie colony," Annie mused.

"Yeah, that's the thing that gets me about Gabby. I don't think she would have signed up for something like that, but who knows? It's the content of her message that is bothering me big-time."

"Do you want to go down there and check them out?" Annie offered.

"Maybe we should call in the sisters and see if Nikki can get more background information. And Charles and Fergus can check to see if they're on anyone's radar. Did you say their names were Westlake?" Myra furrowed her brow. She thought she recognized the name.

Annie snapped her fingers. "The Bernie Madoff of Chicago!"

"Right!" Myra concurred. "Whatever happened to them?"

"Sidney was convicted of a number of crimes, including securities fraud, wire fraud, mail fraud, and money laundering and is serving time at ADX in Florence, Colorado. It's considered the Alcatraz of the Rockies."

"That's a bit extreme, no?" Myra asked. ADX housed fewer than four hundred inmates. All were considered to pose a serious threat to the country.

"Not if you consider how many people he burned. They probably have him there for his own protection," Annie offered.

Maggie continued reading her research out loud. "Eleanor Adams Westlake has been residing in London. She left the country at the beginning of the year he was arrested."

"That was convenient." Annie snorted.

"Yep. And she also continues to claim she knew nothing about Sidney's criminal activity." Maggie was eyeing the cuticle of her right thumb.

Myra swatted at her. "Dinner will be served shortly." Maggie frowned, but Annie and Myra giggled with glee.

"Speaking of dinner, I am starving!" Maggie jumped up and stretched. And then placed her hands in a prayer position. "Please? Soon?"

Annie and Myra stood, then all three linked arms, and they trotted into the kitchen. The aroma of roasted chicken with fingerling potatoes filled the air. Charles once joked that he had learned from the queen of the culinary arts, Julia Child. With Charles's secret past, it was a very good possibility that it was true. Green beans almandine was also on the menu. Another Julia Child recipe.

Maggie went to the cupboard to fetch the plates as Annie pulled out the flatware and napkins. Myra plucked out fresh wineglasses, and, within minutes, the kitchen table was set. All that was left was to sit down and enjoy the sumptuous meal Charles had prepared.

The five of them sat around the table, said grace, and dug in. Naturally, Maggie was the first.

"When you were growing up, was there not enough food to feed your family?" Charles had asked this question dozens of times, as it always elicited laughter.

"Not enough for me!" Maggie held up a forkful of perfectly prepared food. Charles was a marvel in the kitchen.

That was only one of the many talents that Myra appreciated.

Dinner was filled with small talk, local and national politics, cheaters, and scams. The small group had certainly had their fair share of dealing with criminals. Perhaps they weren't convicted criminals, but they were morally bankrupt individuals, all of whom richly deserved their share of retribution even if the judicial system couldn't provide it.

After the table was cleared, they retreated into the study. Charles poured everyone a glass of port. "So, Maggie, tell us what's on your mind."

Maggie proceeded to reiterate everything she had told Annie and Myra. "I want to go down there and check The Haven out, but I think this is something the sisters should get involved with. I can't do this on my own."

"Of course not." Myra patted Maggie's knee. "I suggest we discuss this with the other sisters." The men looked at the women and nodded in agreement. "Shall we see who's available and set up a meeting the day after tomorrow?"

"If not sooner," Annie jumped in. "If Gabby is in trouble, we need to act on this fast." Fast was Annie's normal speed for everything. Especially driving. Myra was terrified to get into any type of automobile with her. Even if it was just to drive to the local grocers. It wasn't that Annie was reckless. She simply loved speed. She said it made her feel free. Myra, on the other hand, felt trapped in a bullet of steel, aluminum, copper, and rubber.

As soon as Annie would start the engine, Myra would shut her eyes, grip the handle on the door, and pray. It was probably the only time she wouldn't be fidgeting with her pearls for comfort. She needed to hang on with both hands!

Annie pulled out her phone, hit the SPEAKER button, and got several of the sisters on a conference line. "Hello, lovelies!" Lots of "hellos" "hey theres" and "hi-yas" echoed through the phone. "Any of you available to meet tomorrow evening?"

Alexis was the first to speak. "Count me in. What time?"

Kathryn had a long-haul run to Charleston but would be available the following week.

Yoko spoke next. "I'm good, too."

"I'm preparing for a trial," Nikki chimed in. "But I can make the meeting tomorrow. I'll know more about my schedule later this week." Nikki was a top-notch attorney who handled many high-profile and controversial cases. She was married to Jack Emery, a former federal prosecutor. The beginning of their relationship was fraught with suspicions and deception until Jack realized how much he loved Nikki and the importance of Nikki's extracurricular activities. Eventually, he came to respect what she and the sisters were doing and sometimes assisted them on a mission, or took on one of his own with the Men of the Sisterhood.

Isabelle was in San Francisco overseeing a building project she had designed for one of the supergeek billionaires of Silicon Valley.

Maggie wrote down who would be attending the first meeting:

> *Alexis, Yoko, Nikki, Charles, Fergus, Annie,*
> *Myra, Maggie*

"That's eight of us."

"Excellent." Myra clapped her hands. "Charles?" She looked at him wistfully, knowing full well he knew both the question and the answer.

"Yes, old girl. Dinner. Six o'clock. Fergus? You've got that, mate?" That was Charles's way of telling Fergus he was on duty to help with the kitchen detail.

"Right-o." Fergus nodded and gave him a thumbs-up.

"Splendid!" Myra responded, batting her eyes at Charles.

Annie ended the call with "Good night, sleep tight, don't let the bedbugs bite! Love you all!"

Air kisses and affectionate replies followed.

Maggie gave a huge sigh of relief. Her eyes welled with tears.

Annie put her arm around Maggie. "What's with the waterworks?"

Myra handed Maggie a clean linen handkerchief. "What is it, dear?"

"I'm just so grateful for everyone." She looked at Annie. "You." And then, turning to Myra, "And you." Then to Charles and, finally, Fergus.

"We're always here for you." Annie squeezed her hand affectionately.

"Yes. I know." Maggie wiped her tears and the dribble that was about to run from her nose. "I'm really worried about Gabby. She doesn't have people like you."

"Well, she does now!" they bellowed in unison, high fiving each other.

Maggie took one more swipe of her face. "Okay. So what are you making for dinner?" With that, the group hooted and howled. That was the Maggie they knew and loved.

Chapter Eight

When It All Began
The Haven, South Florida

Once Liam explained his intentions about using the property as a spiritual retreat to Noah, Noah's wheels started to turn. If they could set up a tax-exempt nonprofit, he was certain he could figure out a way to put money in his own pocket. He had been watching Daniel Ruffing continue to build his empire for several years. Noah had heard about the prime piece of real estate on the shoreline of Cuba that Ruffing had leased, but had never asked Ruffing about it. Nor did he intend to. Noah decided to seek some advice from his mentor. But he had to be careful how he approached him. Ruffing was slick. That was one thing Noah had learned from the beginning. And he was secretive. He also had a temper.

All the deliveries back and forth to the fishing boats were making Noah suspicious, but he didn't dare ask what kind of errand he was really running. He learned early on not to question anything Ruffing had him do. And that meant *anything*. But what he did know was that Ruffing was always pleased upon Noah's return from his fishing runs. He would often tip Noah a few hundred dollars. That alone made keeping his mouth shut worth it. Besides, he loved the whipping of the wind as he raced across the clear cerulean-blue waters off the coast of Florida. Depending on the time of day, his return trip to the mainland would be blessed with a spectacular sunset. If he had a few extra minutes, he'd cut the engine and gape at the glorious shades of orange mixing with red, then hues of purple. It was those occasions when he could understand Liam's desire for tranquility.

He would ask for advice as to how and where to start such an undertaking. At the end of the day, if everyone had completed their duties, the crew, dockmaster, and sometimes Ruffing himself would gather at the marina bar and have a few drinks. That's when Noah thought it would be a good time to discuss his brother's plan. *Be casual,* he kept repeating to himself.

There were about five people enjoying their beers and margaritas. Noah looked for signs of Ruffing, hoping he would show up. He didn't know if he'd have the guts to mention it if he thought about it much longer. From behind, he heard a familiar voice. "Ahoy, mates!" It was Ruffing's regular greeting. "Drinks all around." He motioned with his finger to the twentysomething blonde who was tending bar. She was wearing a T-shirt that said GOLDEN SHORES MARINA, modified by cutting off the sleeves, deepening the neckline, and trimming enough inches off the bottom that her midriff would show if she stretched her arms above her head. In reality, she didn't have to stretch too far for her upper lady-parts to be on display. The high-end liquor was on the shelf above her head. Not very convenient, but necessary for "the show" to continue. Her name tag said DAISY. She flashed a dazzling smile at Ruffing.

They probably go to the same dentist, Noah thought to

himself. He also got the impression that Ruffing and Daisy might have had a roll in the hay more than once.

This is a top-rated marina. Why would you want to have an employee who looks a bit trashy? Because . . .

After two beers, and a shot of tequila, also known as "courage," Noah had the guts to bring up the subject, as informally as he could muster.

"So, get this. My brother wants to start an ashram." He paused to see if Ruffing was remotely interested in discussing his brother's soul-searching mission. He waited a beat. "You know, one of those places where people sit around and meditate, chant, ring bells, burn incense, and who-knows-what-all."

Ruffing turned to him. "Yes, you and your brother seem to be vastly different. Considering you're twins." He took a pull of his fancy cocktail. "Except for the sandy hair, light brown eyes, and athletic build, you couldn't be any more different." Another pull.

Noah was almost sheepish when he offered up the family debacle as an excuse. But it wasn't very far from the truth. "It was because of Sidney." Noah refused to refer to the man who had put their family into bankruptcy as *Dad, Father,* or any other familial noun. "In addition to his having all his assets forfeited, being arrested, convicted, and hauled off to jail, our mother flew the coop to London before all that went down, taking the rest of the family money with her. That happened right after New Year's. She must have known something was going to happen even though it took months before he was arrested, when we were just about to graduate from college." Noah was pensive, recalling the shock of their fall into poverty. "Liam was always more sensitive and wanted to pursue his studies. At that point, I didn't give a crap about anything except trying to make money." Noah looked directly at Ruffing. "That's when I came to you for a job. The rest you know."

Noah signaled for another shot of Casamigos, the tequila brand that was founded by actor George Clooney. Noah stared at the bottle of distilled golden agave juice, recalling that Clooney and his partner had sold the company for one billion dollars. *Money makes more money,* he thought to himself.

He was startled back into the conversation when Ruffing said, "Liam seems like a very sincere, stand-up guy." Another swig. "So tell me about your brother's fantasy." Ruffing leaned his elbow on the highly polished teak bar and flashed his pearly whites at Noah.

Noah gave Ruffing the basic details. The spiritual goals. The property. The nonprofit.

Ruffing straightened up from his slightly lounging position. His interest was piqued by the last two concepts. Property and nonprofit.

"Where is the property?"

"At the far end of Homestead. Practically in the Everglades. It used to be a coconut farm, but after the Army Corps of Engineers messed up the Glades, the water table rose, so they lost a lot of the farmable area. There's a main building I assume was a residence, a large barn, and several other buildings."

"What's the acreage?" Ruffing asked, to Noah's surprise.

"From what Liam told me, the property itself is twenty acres, but it backs up against the national park." Noah squinted into the setting sun.

"Get the coordinates and meet me at the heliport tomorrow morning at nine. We'll be out of the local TV station 'chopper news' cycle by then." He used the air quotes to refer to the recent issues with airspace traffic.

Miami International Airport served over twenty million

passengers a year. Throw in Fort Lauderdale, Opa-Locka, and Key West, with their three executive airports, plus Homestead Air Reserve Base, and you had a jet propulsion circus only ten thousand feet above a thriving metropolis. It could get quite messy up there. There had already been two collisions, resulting in one death, over the past eight months. But Ruffing used his personal chopper daily and knew the best times to commute. And he paid through the nose for the finest gear and personnel, and whomever he had to pay to always be next in line at the helipads. Having the flexibility to get up and over the city within minutes was a time-saver, even if he had to pay through the nose.

Sometimes he would travel by water, up and down the Intracoastal. But a helicopter got him crosstown in under ten minutes. Traversing Miami Beach took even less time. But he usually used one of his boats to go from his marina to Star Island, on which he owned an elaborate forty-five-million-dollar waterfront estate. Star Island and two other exclusive islands, Hibiscus and Palm, were located in Biscayne Bay. The famous and infamous had resided there at one time or another. Celebrities like Gloria and Emilio Estefan, Shaquille O'Neal, and of course, Al Capone, who had owned a house on Palm Island. It was rumored that J. Edgar Hoover had bought a house on the opposite shore so he could keep a personal eye on the gangster. Ruffing loved to brag about his neighbors and the history, to whoever would listen. Which was pretty much everyone. This evening's cocktail hour was no exception. This time it was a complaint about some major hip-hop artists and unruly party guests who tried to trespass on his dock. "Man, you pay people to mind the fort, and they let anyone in." He was referring to the security guard and the gate that only allowed residents and their guests on to the small enclaves by car. "Musta paid them a chunk. But whatever . . ."

He knew full well it was easy enough to get people on and off the island. All you really needed was a boat. And he had plenty at his disposal. He was satisfied he had pleased his audience with another almost-celebrity-sighting and the pains of the enormously rich.

Ruffing stood and slapped Noah on the back. "See you in the morning." He nodded and winked at the bartender, indicating that she should put everyone's drinks on his tab, and left.

Noah was dumbfounded. *What the hell? Why would Ruffing give a rat's ass about some mucky dilapidated piece of junk real estate?*

That evening, when Noah informed Liam that his boss wanted to get a bird's-eye view of the land, Liam was astounded. "Really? But why?" Liam could no more figure out why Ruffing was interested than could Noah.

"Heck if I know, but what the hell?" Noah shrugged. "Get me the info. I'm meeting him tomorrow morning."

Liam pulled up a schematic of the area on his laptop and e-mailed it to Noah. "I'll print out a copy, too. Sometimes doing it 'old-school' isn't a bad idea," Noah said. He took the page from the printer and put it in his backpack. "Let's go over your plans again." He opened a blank document in his laptop, fingers poised above the keyboard. "Shoot."

Liam read from his notes. They were on one of those yellow-ruled pads, the kind that have been around for decades. There was something about writing your thoughts and ideas on a piece of paper. Paper you could keep or throw out. And it was in your face rather than having to search for it in an electronic box. Yes, Liam was an old soul. He also had a rough sketch of his idea. Clearly, he had given it a lot of thought.

"I've broken it down into segments," Liam said, continuing to explain his idea. He divided the agricultural development and the construction and reconstruction into two categories. The idea was to salvage the land and use it for farming. The buildings would serve as housing, classrooms, meditation rooms, and storage. The property would have to be cleared of the dead branches and overgrown grasses. The soil needed to be enriched, making it suitable for growing vegetables and fruits. Beekeeping was also on the list, which caused Noah to snort. "Bees? Seriously?"

Liam was not dissuaded. He maintained that not only would it be self-sustaining, it would also become a source of revenue. They would plant enough to feed the residents with a surplus they could sell at the farmers' market. The entire enterprise would be managed by members of the association. The Haven. People seeking enlightenment could join and live there in exchange for performing daily tasks. They would follow a routine, taking classes, meditating, preparing meals, doing laundry and housekeeping.

"And where, pray tell, do we find these schlubs?" Noah had to admit that the concept was good. Providing financing would be the biggest hurdle. Finding people wouldn't be as difficult as one might suspect. South Florida was a magnet for every type of antisocial, immoral, illegal, disenfranchised creature who walked the planet. It was warm and sunny most of the time. You could easily make yourself disappear with very little effort.

"Noah, have you seen how many people are showing up to my messaging meetings? There had to be over a hundred last week. If we got only ten percent of them, that would be ten. Ten people, Noah. Ten people can get a lot done." Liam looked at his brother pleadingly.

Noah had a wicked look in his eyes. "Let's not forget the prostitutes, homeless, drug and alcohol rehab people."

Liam did a double take. "What? Prostitutes? Drug addicts?"

"Yes, little brother. Aren't they just the right target for some spiritual enlightenment?" He was being half-sarcastic.

"I suppose, yes. But I was thinking more about people who were already on a spiritual path. Not a rehab facility." Liam looked at his brother curiously.

"First off, we need money. Second, we need bodies. We can wean out any wack jobs and weirdos up front. Keep talking, little brother."

Liam laid out the rest of his plan. There would be three levels of association among the general population. The newcomers would be called Tyros. After a six-month probationary period, they would move up to the status of Pledge. After a year, if they met all the requirements, they would be at the level called Luminaries. The next step was for Masters, but very few would ever get to that point. As they wrapped up their plan, they agreed that Liam would be the content manager, in charge of programs The Haven would mandate. Noah would handle the money. If Ruffing was interested in investing in the project, it would be natural for Noah to handle the finances.

Noah repeated everything back to Liam. "This sounds like it could possibly work, bro." He snapped the laptop closed. "This calls for a brew."

Liam still seemed a bit baffled at this sudden turn of events. But if he truly believed in manifesting one's life, this was a very good example as to how it can happen.

The letters DJH were emblazoned on the side of the Airbus H155 helicopter. A mere $10.2 million of spinning steel, titanium, and leather. Noah spotted Ruffing talking to the pilot. He jogged over, feeling the movement of the air being displaced by the whirling blades. Ruffing handed him a set of headphones and motioned for him to climb aboard.

Noah had been brought up in a wealthy household, but he

19YELLOW MOON ROAD   67

had never seen a display of this type of opulence before. As he stepped aboard, his jaw dropped when he saw the interior. *No wonder the other 99.9 percent of the population are pissed off.* Then he realized that, not that long ago, he had become a member of that segment of the population. It made him wonder if they had ever really been part of the moneyed elite. *Maybe it was simply Mother's delusion. If nothing else, she spent money as if we were. And where are we now?*

Noah gave the pilot the backup flash drive that contained the coordinates of the property, and Ruffing hopped in. Within a few seconds, they were a thousand feet above the ground, heading west. A few minutes later, they were hovering over the parcel that Liam was hoping to see become The Haven.

Liam and Noah were accurate in their description and location of the land. *It's perfect,* Ruffing thought to himself. He had been wanting to expand his business but didn't have personnel he could trust; nor did he have the time. He had a lot of balls in the air, and should any of them drop, a lot of people would go to jail.

Noah not only brought him a huge opportunity, he also brought with him people Ruffing could trust—Noah and Liam Westlake. Little did they know that their spiritual enlightenment enterprise would serve as cover for a great deal of sin.

Chapter Nine

The Haven

After that first helicopter ride, Ruffing arranged for funds to purchase and rehabilitate the property. The agreement was that Ruffing owned the land and the buildings. A second company would be formed, The Haven, and it would be a 501(c)(3) tax-exempt nonprofit. Liam and Noah would be directors and collect small salaries. The Haven itself would not pay any income tax as long as it complied with the rules governing 501(c)(3) nonprofits. Any money they took in would have to be used for their charitable work. Despite the difficulty of obtaining 501(c)(3) tax-exempt status for a quasi-religious institution after the debacle with the Church of Scientology, which had resulted in a payment of $12.5 million to settle a tax debt estimated to be around $1 billion, Ruffing's top-notch lawyers and accountants succeeded in making The Haven tax-exempt.

On paper, everything seemed to be honest and aboveboard with one exception: the transfer of funds. All financial transactions were in cash. Everything. Every single one, from the purchase of the land to the costs of construction, land rejuvenation, supplies, and interior furnishings. Everything. All cash.

Liam was a bit nervous about that aspect of the funding, but Noah was not concerned in the least. He was perfectly happy to hand out hundred-dollar bills to workers and suppliers. They, too, were happy to get the money in an untraceable form. It was a win-win for all concerned.

Noah kept meticulous records, though. He didn't want anyone questioning anything, particularly when dealing in cash. The initial investment by Ruffing was well over $500,000—a far cry from the original $135,000 to acquire the property. But Ruffing seemed unconcerned. He wanted The Haven to be nice enough to attract certain people but not luxurious enough to attract too much attention. Keeping a low profile was an essential part of his agenda. It was required to appeal to the unsuspecting chumps who would live and work at The Haven, including Liam and Noah, not to mention the saps who joined the organization seeking spiritual enlightenment, "fellowship," as Liam preferred to call it.

At present, The Haven had forty residents. There was a dormitory for women and one for men. Even husbands and wives had to sleep in separate quarters. Not that The Haven often had many married couples.

While outsiders looking in might consider The Haven a cult, Liam and Noah would vehemently disagree with anyone who made the accusation or even raised it as a possibility.

Nonetheless, all things considered, it certainly looked like one. Liam's initial vision of the community's organization was a bit hazy. To be sure, the program was intended to be stringent and disciplined, with a hierarchical structure. But it was Ruffing who suggested a particular type of discipline—very strongly suggested. The clear implication was that the money train would stop at the next station if Liam didn't organize The Haven the way Ruffing wanted it organized.

And so the community imposed something like a caste system on its members, segregating people from each other. Then there was the secrecy part. All contact with the rest of the world was prohibited; no one was allowed to speak to any outsiders unless they were on a recruitment mission or selling goods at the farmers' market. And even then, their conversations never strayed from the carefully selected language provided them by the Luminaries.

The Haven had different levels of programs. Each program was assigned a monetary value. The initial entry of ten thousand dollars was, of course, out of range for almost everyone there. The Haven took whatever cash they had, collected all their personal possessions, gave it a dollar value, then applied it against the entry fee. Whatever balance was left, the new members would have to work off by adding activities and chores to their daily programs of spiritual advancement.

As one progressed through the program, one would move on to the next level, which also had a monetary value—twenty thousand dollars. Of course, no one ever earned more money than they owed. So once they had paid off their debt, leaving them with no money and no possessions, they had no choice but to sign up for the next level, going into debt for another twenty thousand dollars. *Where else could they go?* For that twenty thousand dollars, they got a roof over their heads, three meals a day, and some personal development mumbo jumbo. What that meant was that The Haven obtained free labor in exchange for the various levels of "spiritual enlightenment" or "fellowship." One could only wonder what the Dalai Lama's opinion of The Haven's spiritual program would be. Or what the IRS would say if it knew exactly what was going on at The Haven, which resembled the goings-on at old-time company towns dotting the landscape of West Virginia coal country in the early part of the twentieth century.

Everyone dressed alike. They used similar jargon, as if they had been brainwashed. But all of them seemed to have a sense of bliss. Maybe it was because they had food and housing in a decent environment. Or maybe there was something in the food or water. Who knows. It was only very rarely that someone like Gabby Richardson would decide to enter into the life of The Haven. And if you had asked her about joining this sort of cult looking for spiritual enlightenment five years earlier, she would have vigorously denied that she would ever do so and would have probably said that places like The Haven should be illegal.

Just as with most of the followers, it was Liam who attracted her to the retreat. She had the assets to make the initial payment of ten thousand dollars in full and a money market fund with over one hundred thousand dollars that she could tap into if she wanted to continue after she completed the first course. Since she was able to pay the initial fee, The Haven did not require that she turn over any other assets or add chores to her daily routine. But she did have to turn in her cell phone, tablet, and all other electronic equipment. *No influence from the outside. One needed to look inside.*

The setup wasn't exactly what Liam had in mind, but he went along because he believed that he was doing good for the people who joined. If he wanted to continue to grow his community of spiritual wellness, then he had to play by Ruffing's rules. But at least Liam could control the message.

At The Haven, everyone was provided similar clothing to wear: yoga-style white pants, white shirts, and sandals. The ensemble was called *vastra*, a word that meant "clothing" in

Sanskrit. The clear intention of using a Sanskrit word was to create the impression that the teachings were similarly part of a tradition that the Western world associated with spiritual advancement. The only thing that distinguished the members of the community in regard to the level of "advancement" was the color of the scarves, or stoles, they wore.

The Tyros were newbies and wore green to indicate they were "green" to the organization. After six months of following the program, one would advance to being a Pledge. Pledges wore blue for loyalty. Depending on how hard they worked, which usually correlated with how much money they earned for the cause, it could take up to five years before a Pledge could advance to the next level and become a Luminary. Most managed to do it in under two years. The Luminaries wore purple, the color of royalty. When Noah was on the premises, his was stole silver. Liam's was gold. Both were handmade by the Pledges, interwoven with metallic threads.

The Tyros were responsible for the lowest of maintenance duties. They cleaned toilets, mopped floors, removed trash. Ruffing explained to Liam that it gave them humility. What Ruffing knew about humility was a mystery to Liam. But Liam didn't argue with his financier.

The Tyros' day would begin with morning meditations, followed by a breakfast of oatmeal and fruit. Chores came next. Midmorning, the Tyros would attend classes on philosophy and yoga. Then came lunch. All meals were served in the great hall, which had once been the barn. It had a dozen long wooden tables and seating was by levels. Only Tyros could sit with Tyros, Pledges with Pledges, and the Luminaries sat at a table set on a platform of risers in the front of the hall, where they could watch over everyone. There were also Guardians, employees of The Haven, not acolytes, who did that as well. They guarded the property when everyone was inside the compound and guarded the members when they went out in public. And they always moved in groups.

On a typical day, after lunch, Tyros would go to the farming area to see what work needed to be done or to run errands with the Guardians in The Haven's vans.

The Tyros were responsible for doing the laundry. The carts would be rolled into the parking area, where they would load the bags into a van. The number of bags determined how many Tyros were needed to do the laundry. The bags often had small padlocks of the kind one would use on luggage when traveling. While that seemed strange, no one questioned it. And if on a rare occasion someone did ask, the answer given was that they contained personal and private clothing for the Luminaries. They would also take Noah's and Liam's clothing to the dry cleaner next door to the Laundromat. Liam's and Noah's clothing were in black garment bags which also had padlocks on them. The half dozen or so Tyros would take carts from inside the Laundromat, unload the bags, and wheel the bundled laundry to a door in the back of the Laundromat. The words in red letters read PRIVATE. There was also a security keypad that prevented any nosy busybodies from entering.

The Tyros would knock on the door and someone in a black shirt and pants would open the door, revealing only a vestibule where another locked door would lead to a private room. Within a few minutes, the black-garbed person would return the carts to the Tyros, with the clothing in the carts no longer in the original bags. The Tyros would then begin the washing, drying, and folding routine. No one seemed to question what went on behind the closed doors. For all anyone knew, maybe they were counting the uniforms to be sure there were none missing? Possible?

One of the Tyros would be assigned to take clothing to the dry cleaner, which had a slightly different routine. The Tyro would drop off the garment bags and be handed different ones to return to The Haven.

This all happened twice a week. On the weekends, the

Tyros would load the vans with tables and whatever the Pledges would take to sell at the farmers' market. It was a collection of produce, honey, zucchini bread, and carrot cake they called Heavenly Foods. Other items for sale included handmade pieces such as macramé plant hangers and belts, crocheted vests, and a few decoupage boxes.

They placed a small CASH ONLY sign on the table. And the Guardians watched every transaction like hawks. People sometimes grunted when they were told they couldn't use debit or credit cards, but most people had enough cash to buy a few eggplants, or fennel, baked goods, or a jar of honey. The handmade items were never more than thirty dollars, an amount most people had in their purses, or combined in pockets with their friends or spouse. At the end of the day, the Guardians would put the cash in a locked box and secure it in the front of one of the vans. The Pledges and Tyros would gather whatever remained, fold the tables, and return everything to the van, including themselves. No one ever seemed to want to sneak away. For most of them, it was a way to avoid sleeping in a cardboard box and scrounging for food.

It was common knowledge that both the Laundromat and the dry cleaner were operated by other members of The Haven. They were supposedly from a different but connected faction. But no one asked. In truth, no one was allowed to ask questions of a superior outside a classroom. Not even a "How are you?" was permitted.

The Pledges were on a similar schedule but attended more advanced classes. When not studying or meditating, Pledges would pick vegetables, prepare meals, and sew. Once the main chores were complete, they were allowed to go to the arts and crafts cottage and make something that could be sold at the market. There were no days of rest. If a Pledge was lucky enough, he or she would be asked to work in the office to assist Liam or Noah. Those were highly coveted spots and caused some jealousy among the women. Ruffing would remind Noah and Liam that jealousy was a great motivator. Pledges were constantly trying to outdo each other for attention.

That's when Liam took special notice of Gabby. She wasn't like the rest of them. She was genuinely interested in evolving, and jealousy was not an asset when it came to one's spiritual development.

Gabby made it through the Tyro phase easily. Paying the ten thousand dollars enabled her to avoid the unpleasant tasks used to take care of the entry fee. Still, she understood the importance of doing a job well, no matter what it was. Her spiritual compass seemed to be out of kilter. Perhaps she had become jaded from covering horror stories in the dark alleys of the city.

When she first arrived at The Haven, she considered doing light housework a promotion from covering crime scenes. She had been at The Haven just under six months when she became eligible to move up to Pledge status. She felt she had decompressed and was ready for some serious enlightenment. She had emptied the polluted vessel of her mind and released the past. She was open and ready to receive and gladly spent the twenty thousand dollars to take the position and the opal ring that came with it. It was the only piece of jewelry allowed.

Several weeks before Gabby was to fly home to see her mother in the hospital, she overheard part of a conversation between Liam and Noah.

It had sounded a bit heated, with Noah raising his voice, and saying, "We have to deliver whatever he wants before the end of the month, and it doesn't appear that there are any possible candidates."

Liam sounded frustrated. "You know I don't approve of any of these secret rendezvous or whatever else he has on his agenda. I don't know why you insist on dealing with those people."

"Listen, little brother. If you want this spiritual mumbo jumbo gig to survive, we need his funds to keep the place going. We simply can't survive on free labor and a vegetable garden." Noah sounded gruff.

"Noah, I want to spread a message of brotherhood and sisterhood and connecting with a higher power. I believe we can get there through our work. We can get more people and maybe some other benefactors. Becoming a global institution is not a priority."

"Yeah. Whatever. You always had reality issues," Noah snapped back.

Liam took a deep breath, intoned, "Peace, brother," and retreated to his private quarters.

As Noah briskly left the room, he literally bumped into Gabby and gave her an annoyed look. "I don't believe you are allowed on this floor, Gabby."

Gabby shrunk in embarrassment. "I'm very sorry. I was told to retrieve the platters from this morning's breakfast."

"Fine. But in the future, know your place," Noah added sternly. "We have a hierarchy for a reason."

"Yes, sir. I know that spiritual growth comes in steps," Gabby readily responded with the appropriate answer.

"Very well. See that you remember those words." Then Noah turned sharply and walked away.

Liam overheard his brother admonishing Gabby and went out to the hallway. "Are you all right?" he asked her kindly.

Gabby was still shaken from the brusque encounter with Noah. "Yes. Yes, sir." Her hands were trembling. The last thing she wanted to do was get on Liam's bad side. If there was such a thing.

"Please, call me Liam." He looked her straight in the eye, causing Gabby's stomach to flutter. But it wasn't a bad kind of flutter, which made her even more nervous.

"I, uh, the rules?" Gabby's eyes looked directly into his, pleading.

"I didn't make up the rules." Liam smiled. "It has to do with our founders." That was the best word they could use to explain how The Haven was originally financed.

The "official story" was that three men had retired from major religious organizations, pooled their money, and backed Liam. Their names were Devin Marlow, Christopher Giamelli, and Isaac Greenstein. It was said that these founders believed organized religions were too constricting and divisive and that a new ideology needed to be shared. Shared by someone who was authentic. They chose Liam to deliver the right words and the right message. It was close to the truth, but not quite. Liam had the charisma, and the right intentions, but in order to accomplish his goals, he had inadvertently made a deal with the devil.

Gabby blinked several times before she could speak. "Oh, yes, the founders." She hesitated again. "What would the others say if I called you Liam?"

"Let's keep it our secret. Okay?" He smiled once more.

"Yes, of course. Thank you." Gabby was able to get the words out without stuttering. She nodded, turned, and hurried down the stairs, forgetting the reason for her being on the third floor. *What is wrong with me? I interviewed serial killers, rapists, and drug dealers. Why does this man make me nervous? Perhaps it was the very lean diet of The Haven, combined with the heat? Or maybe that encounter with Noah?* She tried to shake it off. She listened for footsteps before she began her climb back up the stairs to retrieve the platters she had been sent to get. All quiet. She scurried up and as softly as possible, grabbed what she had been sent for, and bustled back down. As she entered the kitchen, Rachel gasped. "Are you okay? You look all hot, red, and sweaty." Rachel grabbed a kitchen towel and traded it for the platters in Gabby's hands.

"I'm okay. I think." Gabby wiped the perspiration from her forehead.

"What do you mean, you *think*?" Rachel put the plates in the large kitchen sink, turned, and put her hands on her hips. "You look like you seen a ghost."

Rachel Steward's grammar wasn't the best. Before she fled the backwaters of North Florida and came to Miami, she had lived in a trailer park, with her crack-smoking, beer-drinking parents. They paid no attention to her. None at all. That's probably why she had gotten involved with someone recently out of jail for armed robbery. *He* paid attention to her, an underage girl. That was not only a parole violation, it was statutory rape. Back in the slammer he went, and Rachel took a pregnancy test. She was relieved to find that she wasn't going to have a baby. She tried to be careful, but she was also an easy mark for someone who showed her affection. If you could call using her body a show of affection.

After a year of working the night shift at a convenience store while suffering from depression, Rachel left for good. She packed what few clothes she had and the couple of hundred dollars she had been able to scrape together, bought a one-way bus ticket, and headed to Miami. She landed a job as a waitress at a Denny's outside Homestead, where she met two other young women who needed a third roommate to split the rent. The rent in that area of South Florida was much cheaper than in Miami proper, so with three of them contributing, they could afford a decent place. Decent enough meaning it wasn't covered in graffiti, and you could actually walk on the street at night, which was a good thing since she didn't have a car. Walking and riding the bus were her only means of transportation.

One evening, when she was walking home from work, it dawned on her that it had been five years since she had bolted from that tin can of drugs and foul smells. Her situation wasn't perfect, but she got along well enough with her roommates and made enough money to pay the rent and her bills and buy a used bicycle. In another year, if she saved enough, she might be able to buy a car. And pay for the insurance. It might not have been a picnic, but she lived a clean, if boring, life.

The weekends were split between work and chores. She usually had either the Saturday night or Sunday morning shift. If she had to run errands, she would ride her bike. It was totally retro, complete with a basket, a bell, and streamers on the handle grips. Rachel stopped at the local farmers' market and was approached by a young woman, approximately the same age, wearing a white yoga-type outfit. She said her name was Ginny, and she handed Rachel a small jar of honey. "This is raw organic honey. We keep bees on our farm. We guarantee it is one-hundred-percent organic." Rachel was about to say, "No, thank you," but before she could utter a word Ginny pulled out a spoon, dipped it in the jar, and said, "Here, please try it."

Rachel followed the young woman over to the produce stand, where there were many jars of honey for sale. It was then that she first met Liam, who totally charmed her. The dozen or so people who were minding the stand were equally affable, and she engaged in what she thought was a very heady conversation. For the first time in her life, she was discussing something other than reality TV shows, what latest celebrity had gotten liposuction, and who was doing what to whom in Hollywood. It was almost too much for her hitherto-unchallenged mind. The following week, she returned to the produce stand for more insight. After several visits and chats with the people in white, Rachel was invited to attend one of Liam's talks. She was both nervous and excited. Before the evening was over, Rachel wanted to be a part of this group. This organization. *This*, whatever *this* was.

The next day she gave her roommates notice that she wanted to move, and it took only two weeks to find her replacement. South Florida was full of transients. Some good. Some not so good. Rachel had been lucky to this point with the company she kept, but now she was moving on to join a different set of people. For the first time in her life, she felt genuinely optimistic about the future.

When she arrived at The Haven, she had to turn over her material possessions, including her bicycle. She was surprised when she got a little choked up giving it over to the man in the black shirt and white pants. It was the first thing she had bought for herself after putting a deposit on the apartment. Sure, it was secondhand and as old as the hills, but it was hers. Until then. The man kept smiling but said nothing and handed her the clothes and scarf she was to wear. She couldn't tell if he was Latino, Filipino, or just a well-tanned black-haired dude from Florida.

Two more years passed, and Rachel moved from Tyro to Pledge, where she remained. She preferred it. Even though she was much more serene than she had ever been in her life, she still felt that she didn't have the brains or the interest to learn more. She kept to herself when they had free time, which wasn't often. Their days were filled with chores, errands, and classes, or creating something to sell at the market. Her life was mundane, but Rachel was content. It sure beat riding her bike in monsoons to a job serving chicken-fried steak and mashed potatoes to cranky customers. But even that life was way better than living in the meth-cooker she had escaped from. Life wasn't so bad although she felt lonely, even with all the people around her.

They had no spunk. They were like the Stepford Wives. She couldn't remember the last time she felt a flicker of gaiety.

Contentment, yes. Exhilaration, no. Not for a while. Maybe never. Maybe it was because Liam was less visible. Many of his lectures were being given by the Luminaries, most of whom had no charisma.

Rachel finally felt a sense of delight when a new member joined. Perhaps she could make friends with someone who still had a flicker of emotion. Her name was Gabby. There was something about Gabby that Rachel liked. Even though Gabby was more than ten years older than her, Rachel felt in sync with the newbie.

"So? What? What are you so flushed about?" Rachel prodded.

"Oh, it's silly." Gabby wiped her forehead again.

"Silly don't look like that." Rachel pointed to Gabby's forehead. That's when Gabby explained about her encounters with Noah and Liam.

"Yeah, Liam is a good guy, but Noah can be a bit of a prick sometimes. Wasn't always that way."

Chapter Ten

Pinewood

Myra was awakened from her nap by the cacophony of dogs yapping, women laughing, and squeals of delight. She had been reading in the atrium when she dozed off. Barbara, her dead daughter, had appeared in a dream. Or was it a dream? It wouldn't be the first time Myra had a "visitation" from her daughter. At least that's what some psychic folks called it: a visitation. She swore she could smell Barbara's perfume, Miss Dior by Christian Dior. Myra tried to shake off the fog before she met the rest of the group gathered in the kitchen. When she entered, instead of greeting everyone with a high five or a hug, she stood silently. She could still smell the perfume. Barbara's perfume. Charles put his hand on her shoulder. "Are you all right, love?"

Myra perked up, and asked, "Does anyone else smell perfume?"

She realized it was a silly question considering there were several women in the room. Yoko was the first to speak up.

"I am trying out a new one. I wanted something that went with all the flowers in my greenhouse. Something that would complement me without conflicting with the other blooms. It's Miss Dior."

Myra's knees went weak. Thankfully, Charles already had his arm around her. She blinked several times at Yoko. "Were you just in the atrium?"

"No. Just walked in the door. Why?" Yoko looked perplexed.

"Did you know that that was Barbara's favorite perfume?"

"Oh my goodness. No. I had no idea. Myra, I am so, so sorry." Yoko was mortified.

Myra smiled at Yoko. "No need to apologize." She looked over at Nikki, who had tears in her eyes. "It's a sign," Myra said wistfully. With that, she hugged Yoko, then hugged everyone else. The atmosphere quickly turned jovial again.

In her usual fashion, Maggie was the first to ask, "What's for dinner? It smells scrumptious."

Charles had a glimmer in his eye. "Toulouse-style cassoulet and fresh loaves of sourdough bread."

Maggie put the back of her hand to her forehead, pretending she was about to faint. "You're channeling Julia Child again?" She pretend-swooned.

Myra touched her pearls. "Is there some kind of psychic theme happening here?" Everyone looked perplexed. "I should have mentioned that just before you arrived, I had a dream about Barbara. I could have sworn I smelled the perfume in the atrium. Then Yoko appears with the same perfume Barbara wore, but she was nowhere near me. Now you used the word 'channeling.' I find it very interesting considering that what we are going to be discussing tonight is a spiritual retreat."

They all glanced at each other, wide-eyed, then started to giggle. "That *is* a bit spooky, eh?" Fergus chimed in with his British accent, except his was a bit more refined than Charles's.

Annie hooted. "Then I guess it *is* the theme! Woo-hoo for Woo-woo!" Fits of laughter broke out until Charles whistled, bringing the roar under control.

"Ladies. Please. We're not about to have a séance," he joked. "But yes, I dialed up Julia on my bat phone." More whooping followed his comment.

Fergus leaned into Charles. "I think they may be suffering from hunger. Better get some food into them to quell the hysteria." That comment just brought more howling.

Annie stifled a laugh. "I think Fergus may be right. Let's get the table set and indulge."

As if they had done it a hundred times, as they probably had, the women knew what their duties were and moved about the kitchen like a dance ensemble. Within minutes, each place setting was on display and awaiting another one of Charles's magnificent delights.

Maggie waited until everyone was seated to sit down, which surprised all of them. "Are you all right?" Annie asked, half-serious.

"I am." Maggie approached the table. "I guess I'm a little verklempt. I know, I went through this last night, too." She nodded at Annie and Myra. "But I wanted to let the rest of you know how much I love all of you and appreciate you very much." She was about to wipe her nose on her sleeve when Annie reached over and handed her a napkin. "See? This is what I mean. You all look out for each other, not to mention the countless people you've helped. And you look out for me, too."

"Dear girl, can you stop the blubbering and sit your arse down?" Charles winked at her. "This cassoulet is not waiting."

Maggie dabbed her eyes with the napkin and began to giggle. She took her seat and hugged Yoko and Alexis, who were sitting on either side of her.

"That's better, dear." Myra reached across the table and patted her hand.

"I believe that has to be the first time you were the *last* one at the table." Annie chortled, asked Maggie if she would say grace, and when that was done, passed the fresh-from-the-oven bread.

Myra looked up at Maggie. "You've been a bit weepy. It's not like you."

"Yeah. Hormones, maybe?" Maggie snorted, the women roared, and Fergus and Charles rolled their eyes.

"Or maybe it's because you're concerned about your friend," Myra offered.

"What friend?" Yoko asked.

"That's why we're here tonight," Annie announced. "One of Maggie's college friends seems to have gone missing."

Everyone stopped eating. "Well, that's the thing," Maggie interjected. "I'm not sure if she's really missing."

"Rules, girls. We'll take this up after dinner." Charles lifted a glass of wine. "Here's to those who have seen us at our best, and seen us at our worst, and can't tell the difference!"

Alexis almost choked on her drink. Maggie's came out of her nose. The women couldn't seem to get control of themselves.

Fergus looked at Charles, begging for an answer. "Is it a full moon, old chap?"

Charles raised his glass again and made a circle in the air, indicating to the women, who were all in hysterics, "It's always a full moon when this bunch gets together here."

At this point, Myra and Annie were doubled over. Even the dogs were howling. "Oh, Maggie, I'm so terribly sorry." Myra was brushing her hair away from her face. "I don't know what's gotten into all of us tonight." She took a short inhale. "All right. Let's enjoy our dinner before it gets cold. We certainly don't want to insult the chef!"

"Certainly not," Charles added. The rest of the dinner was relaxed in spite of Maggie's bouncing her knee. That was something she did when she was nervous. A habit she couldn't seem to break. She had gained some control over her nail biting, but the restless knee was yet to be conquered.

"Charles, that was delicious." Myra gave him a peck on the cheek as she handed her dish to Nikki, who was helping to clear the table.

"Yes. Fantastic!" Maggie added. Alexis and Yoko expressed their appreciation as well.

Within the usual thirteen minutes, the table was cleared, dishes done and out of sight, and not a crumb to be found.

They marched down the old dungeon-like steps to the basement of the farmhouse. In the mid-1850s, during the struggle between the North and the South, Pinewood had become part of the Underground Railroad. Many of the tunnels and outer buildings remained.

Tonight, as in many nights before, the women entered the space where they would investigate, explore, and examine a situation, then establish a plan for righting a wrong. It was called the War Room. It was, indeed, one of the most highly sophisticated technological hubs outside of the military. The missions they had been able to pull off were highly complex, sometimes having to deal with high-ranking people in the government and at other times having to outwit law-enforcement authorities trying to stop the infamous vigilantes. So far they had been able to stay one step ahead, leaving nothing in their wake. It was some kind of magic trick. Or so it seemed.

As the women entered the room, they saluted the statue of Lady Justice, a ritual they engaged in on every occasion. Coming and going.

The women took their seats, and Charles powered up the large TV screens that covered the walls. Maggie uploaded her notes onto the screens, and onto everyone else's laptop.

All of them had met Gabby on several occasions when Gabby was an intern at the *Post*. She was sweet, bright, and lovely. Those qualities could easily work against her in the world of journalism. Evidently, they had. Maggie reiterated the story about Gabby's looking for a higher purpose and moving to an ashram-like community. If it qualified as a community. There was little information about who owned the property. There were shell companies up the wazoo. The brothers came from a once-wealthy, now-disgraced Chicago family. Prep school, father gone bad and in jail, mother ski-doos to Europe, boys have to fend for themselves.

"I'll have Interpol do a check on the shell companies," Charles offered.

"We'll do a poke around for the mum," Fergus added.

"Do you think we should send Avery or one of his people down there to check it out?"

Myra stroked her pearls. It helped her to think. "Let's wait until we gather what intel we can. Once we get a clearer picture, perhaps we'll know enough about the outfit to give Avery some direction."

"Nikki and Alexis, see if you can find out more about the brothers. Where were they between the time their father was hauled off to jail and now? Where did they work? Live? Study? Who are their known associates?" Annie started writing a list. "Nikki, I know you have a trial coming up, so whatever you can't handle, send it over to me and Maggie," Annie instructed.

"I thought I should go down there and check it out," Maggie offered.

"Not until we have more information. If they can make Gabby disappear, then we don't know what we would be walking into."

"Gotcha," Maggie had to agree. "Okay. I'll dig up some of the family history. It's good to get background."

"Yoko, get in touch with some of your botanical friends down there and see if they have any info," Myra directed.

After everyone stopped jotting down notes, or entering information into their laptops, Myra and Annie stood. "When should we meet again?"

"The sooner the better." Maggie was almost begging.

"I can get on this first thing," Alexis said.

"Ditto," Yoko added.

Nikki chimed in with, "Let's plan to meet late tomorrow afternoon. Say five o'clock. War Room first, then dinner. We'll work with what we can find and keep digging."

Fist pumps filled the circle. "Woo-hoo!" they chanted.

"And woo-woo, too-too," Annie couldn't resist saying. Once the giggling had stopped, Annie reminded them that, technically speaking, they hadn't voted. "Can I assume we're all in?" In unison, fists were pumped in the air with each of them declaring "All in!" Then high fives went around the table.

Maggie tried to hold back her tears of gratitude, but they dribbled down her cheeks. Annie took one look at her, and said, "Girl, you better stop all that blubbering. We have work to do!"

You could feel the energy in the room. The sisters had a mission—find Gabby . . . and uncover what unsavory situation she had stumbled into.

As the women left the room, they saluted Lady Justice and climbed up the stairs. Lady and her pups were waiting in a straight line, tails wagging. The dogs loved having the sisters around. Besides the good vibrations, they got lots of treats.

table near the door. He stood immediately. "May I ask the purpose of this visit?" He sounded like an automaton.

"I am here to cover for Maxwell's morning break," Gabby answered nervously.

The Pledge looked at his clipboard. "Name?"

"Gabby Richardson." She surreptitiously looked around the main hall while the gatekeeper scrutinized his list.

"Please sign here." He handed her the clipboard. "Remember, you are only to go to the desk. Nowhere else on the floor is permitted."

"Yes. Understood." She signed the paper and climbed the staircase leading to the private floor of offices and living accommodations. A small desk with a landline telephone was the only piece of furniture in the hallway.

Maxwell was locking the desk when she arrived. "As I mentioned yesterday, you answer the phone and take a message. No one is ever available. Got it?"

"Got it," Gabby responded.

"I'll be back in a half hour." Maxwell put the keys in his pocket and headed down the hallway leading to the front staircase.

Gabby sat nervously at the desk. *Is this a good time to try to make a call to my family? Will they know if I place a call? And what about Maggie? I have to get word to her as well.* Listening very carefully for footsteps or voices, she jumped when Liam flung open the door to his office.

"Good morning." Liam was in a fine mood. "You ready?"

"I . . . I think so. How hard can this be?" Gabby mustered a smile.

"Give it a few minutes and it will be ringing off the hook." Liam looked at his watch. "Ten o'clock. That's usually when the calls come in. Remember, just take a message and give them to Noah. He fields all the calls."

"Roger that." Gabby smiled back at him. She watched

Chapter Eleven

The Haven

After the incident at the airport the day before, her surprise encounter with the Guardians at the florist's, followed by the confrontation with Noah, Gabby realized that she was on unannounced probation. She needed to be cautious going forward. If she even wanted to go forward. She certainly did not want to arouse Noah's ire again. She hoped that Liam had told Noah that she would be covering for Maxwell during lunch and his breaks.

The dozen new Tyros were on the lawn, learning rudimentary tai chi moves, and the Pledges were attending their morning classes. Gabby was trying to keep a very low profile, and as she walked toward the main building, she didn't slow her pace to speak to anyone. A simple nod was all she felt was necessary. She wondered if anyone knew about the episode from the day before. Rachel tried to chat with her, but Gabby gave her a gesture that indicated "not now" and kept walking.

When Gabby entered the main building, she found a very tired-looking Pledge whom she did not know seated at a

Liam's back as he disappeared down the back staircase. She listened again. Nothing. Gabby pulled the phone under the desk. If anyone should enter the hallway, she would say she tripped and knocked it over. She quickly dialed her parents' house, where her sister was staying to look after everything until their mother got out of the hospital. Three rings. Four rings. *Pick up, damn it!*

"Hello. Richardson household," the voice of her seven-year-old nephew answered. He was a bit mature for a boy his age, and well mannered.

Gabby whispered, "Jake, it's Aunt Gabby. Where's your mom?" She knew she didn't have time to chitchat.

"Hey, Aunt Gabby! How come you didn't come home? You hurt your foot or something?"

"I'm okay. Jake, please put your mommy on the phone. It's really, really important."

"She's not here. She went to pick up Grammy. Grammy's coming home today."

"Who else is home?" Gabby wondered who was minding Jake.

"Grandpa, but he's in the basement looking for some stuff. Want me to go get him?"

Gabby knew she didn't have much time if she wanted to get in another call. "No, just tell him that I'm okay and will try to call again tomorrow? Okay? You got that?"

"Yes, ma'am! Aunt Gabby is okay and will call again tomorrow!" Jake was proud to be trusted with a message.

"Okay, great. Now go tell Grandpa right now. Okay, honey?" Gabby was starting to get nervous. Someone could walk up either flight of steps any minute. "I've gotta go. Love you!" She quickly hung up, placed the phone back on the desk, and took her seat. She was trembling. *Calm down. Deep breaths. Light in . . . dark out.* She had repeated the sequence several times when the phone rang and scared her half to death.

She regained her composure, and answered, "Good morning. Thank you for calling The Haven. How can I help you?" *There. That wasn't too hard.*

"Dry cleaning is ready for pickup," a voice with an unusual accent said. Gabby couldn't quite put her finger on it, but it wasn't Hispanic, which was common in that area.

"Thank you." Gabby jotted down the message as the person on the other end of the phone hung up without saying another word.

Another call. This time it was from the local car wash. "Need to reschedule detailing job. Maybe tomorrow." Another odd accent, another abrupt end of the call.

Gabby made a note in the message book. Within a few minutes, Maxwell returned. *That was a quick half hour,* she said to herself. But she was relieved that she had been able to get off a message to her family. Next was Maggie. *Do I dare try another call at lunch?*

"How did it go?" Maxwell asked dryly.

"A few messages." She handed the book over to Maxwell. "Men with peculiar accents."

Maxwell responded with, "Come back at noon. There's a lunch meeting in Liam's office today, so mind your place."

A lunch meeting. That would quash her hope of reaching Maggie. *Maybe during Maxwell's afternoon break.* Gabby got up and headed down the stairs. She would be able to make her morning class on Vishnu, the Hindu god known as the preserver of the universe. After her class, she went to the kitchen and fixed a sandwich of tempeh, caramelized onions, coconut bacon, and cashew cheddar sauce on grilled millet bread. It was actually quite tasty if you didn't know the ingredients. The coconut bacon was a good substitute provided you didn't let it sit around too long; otherwise, it would get soft and start to taste like coconut. She ate her sandwich quickly and headed back to the main house, nodding at Rachel as she passed by. Rachel gave her a curious look. Gabby, again, gave her the "not now" sign. She would figure out a good time to bring Rachel up to date. But then she wondered if she should mention any of it to her friend. Gabby had no idea why her trip had been interrupted, and now, with the new assignment at the main house, perhaps saying nothing was a better choice. Then a thought occurred to her. *Maybe I'm being tested. But by who? And why?* She made a mental note to be careful.

Gabby entered the main house and got the same greeting from the same weary Pledge, as if he had never seen her before. "May I ask the purpose of this visit?"

Gabby smiled and repeated the same words she had spoken earlier that day. He handed her the clipboard, and after signing it, she proceeded to her station. As she was dashing up the stairs, she almost bumped into Noah. Sensing someone behind him, he turned. "Whoa. Take it easy," Noah exclaimed. Then he realized it was the same woman he had reprimanded the day before, and several weeks before that. "Oh. it's you," Noah said sourly. "I understand my brother has entrusted you with phone duty."

"Yes, sir." Gabby wasn't about to offer any other chatter.

"I don't understand why he would, but this is your last chance to prove you can be trusted." Before Gabby could say a word, he turned around, continued up the stairs, and went into his office, slamming the door behind him.

What is up with this guy? she asked herself. *Could he really be related to Liam? A twin no less.* Shaking her head in bemusement, she watched Maxwell lock the drawers, then took her place behind the desk. No covert calls this time. She knew that Maggie would be worried. She had, after all, left a cryptic message from a flower shop phone.

Several ominous-looking men approached the desk. "Liam and Noah please." She recalled the accent she had heard earlier that morning. It was the same. *Russian? Ukrainian? Romanian?* Somewhere in that part of the world. They all sounded like Dracula to her.

She buzzed Noah's and Liam's offices. "Three gentlemen are here to see you." They hadn't given Gabby their names, and she knew well enough not to ask.

"Send them into my office," Noah snapped.

"I'll be right out," Liam replied. He was smiling when he exited his office. "Gentlemen." He offered his hand and led them to Noah's office. "This way, please."

The three men entered Noah's soundproof office and closed the heavy door behind them. She strained to hear any conversation, but the only sound was the hum of the ceiling fan above her head. It was then that she realized that the night she had overheard Noah and Liam arguing, the door to Liam's private quarters had been ajar. *So much secrecy.* Gabby was getting a lot more cynical about this place, which was purportedly a haven. *A haven for what?* she wondered. She was startled out of her reverie when Liam exited Noah's office.

"That was quick," Gabby said, belatedly realizing that she shouldn't have said anything and putting her hand up to her mouth.

Liam smiled at her. "Noah said he could handle the meeting and that I should plan a trip to Tibet." He shook his head and went into his office.

The meeting ran past Maxwell's lunch hour. When he returned, she gave him the messages she had taken and left. She had no idea how much longer the meeting went, nor what it was about. But the whole thing certainly seemed strange to her. Why would well-dressed foreigners be interested in The Haven? They definitely didn't look like anyone she had seen before. And those accents. Again, she tried to pinpoint it.

On her way back from lunch hour duty, she spotted Rachel heading in her direction. Rachel looked elated. "You are not going to believe this." The excitement in her voice was palpable.

"You know about the other sects to The Haven, right?"

"Not exactly. I thought this was it. No?" Gabby was intrigued, her misgivings growing.

Rachel explained what little she knew. "Apparently, there is another branch of The Haven. It's an elite group that travels to other places to spread the word."

"I wasn't aware of it. Tell me more." Gabby feigned excitement.

Rachel looked around. A dozen or so Pledges and Tyros were milling about. She gestured for the two of them to take a path far enough away from the center of the compound so no one could hear.

"Well . . . it seems that every so often they pick someone or several someones to join the traveling staff."

"Does Liam go with them?" Gabby tried to sound interested, not suspicious.

"No. We're like recruiters, I guess. We meet with people and discuss the teachings and the programs. From what I've heard, some of the people we meet with have a lot of money and The Haven wants them to become benefactors." Rachel's elation was growing. "They told me that there is one person in particular who is interested in funding a local cable program for Liam's work. Isn't that exciting?"

"Yes. Yes, very." Gabby was now even more dubious than earlier in the day. "So, tell me. What does this mean?"

"They send us to a special seminary to teach us exactly what to say. They also give us civilian clothes to wear."

"How many people at The Haven know about this? Tyros? Pledges? Luminaries?"

Rachel shrugged. "Definitely not the Tyros or Pledges. I dunno about the Luminaries. It's very hush-hush. I didn't know about it until Noah told me this morning. He also said I wasn't to discuss any of it with anyone. But I had to tell *you*! You've been such a good friend to me."

"Your secret is safe with me. I promise." Gabby gave Rachel a hug, but she had a feeling of foreboding that this might be the last time she would see her friend.

"I have to get ready. Not like I have anything to pack," Rachel said with a big grin. "Although I will miss my bicycle. Even though I haven't used it since I got here, I knew it wasn't far away. Silly, I know, but that bike got me around for a long time."

"If I see it, I'll let it know." Gabby chortled.

"Thanks for being such a pal." Rachel gave Gabby a big hug and hustled to her dorm to pack the few items she had made in the crafts shed.

After stopping to talk to another Pledge, Gabby was walking to her dorm when she noticed Noah pulling his car around near the garage. It was a black Cadillac Escalade with tinted windows. Just like the one the Guardians were driving when they picked her up from the florist's shop. A few minutes later, Rachel joined him, got into the vehicle, and they drove off. Something didn't feel right to Gabby, but whom could she ask? Obviously, no one.

After her afternoon class, she walked toward the main house to relieve Maxwell for his break. She got the same routine from the Pledge on duty in the foyer, signed her name, and went up the stairs. The hallway was empty except for

Maxwell standing ready to retreat for his break. "You're on your own. Liam is teaching a class, and Noah has left." Maxwell turned and walked away.

Gabby waited a few minutes, listening for signs of life. All quiet. Once again she pulled the phone under the desk and dialed the *Post*'s toll-free number. Luckily, they had a real human answering the phone at the newspaper. Someone could die waiting for all those prompts people are forced to endure before they can press the right button. Annie, the newspaper's owner, knew the importance of technology. Probably better than most. But when people are calling a newspaper, it was usually something that needed immediate attention, and it was necessary to speak to a person who could put them in touch with the right people. Pronto.

"The *Post*. How may I direct your call?" The greeting was almost as familiar as what she said during her part-time phone duty, but for different reasons.

"Maggie Spritzer, please," Gabby whispered. The line went directly to voice mail.

"Hi, this is Maggie. I'm away from my untidy desk. Please leave a message. I'll get back to you as soon as I crawl out from under the mess."

Gabby was crestfallen but she recovered lickety-split.

"Mag. It's Gabby. I'm okay. Back at The Haven. Strange happenings." It dawned on her that her nose for a story hadn't completely deserted her. She knew she was smack-dab in the middle of something. "I'll try again, maybe tomorrow." Heavy footsteps were climbing the stairs. Maxwell. He had forgotten to lock the desk. Maggie clumsily staggered to her feet, dragging the tangled phone from the floor.

"What the hell?" Maxwell bellowed.

"I tripped over the phone cord," Gabby said sheepishly.

"Give me that thing." He angrily reached for the phone.

Gabby handed him the jumble of wires, receiver, and the phone with the lights blinking. She thought she heard him mumble "stupid bitch." She was getting the feeling that she wasn't well liked by some of those on the second floor. Still, she wanted to believe Liam had good and forthright intentions. The rest of the group was another matter.

Gabby apologized profusely, to no avail. Maxwell was annoyed. He untangled the wires and put the phone back in place. Gabby blushed and apologized one more time. Maxwell gave her a disgusted look. "I'll be back in a half hour. Try not to break anything while I'm gone." He turned and left. She thought he might report her. At the very least, he would complain about her. Maxwell didn't like her, and Noah didn't trust her. Her dismissal from phone duty was imminent. She had to get one more call in to Maggie before she was discharged from her duties.

Gabby realized the phone bill would arrive at some point, and she wondered who would be scrutinizing it. There was a bookkeeper who had a tiny office next to Noah's. The bookkeeper wore a purple stole, indicating he was a Luminary. A high-ranking member. Would he question the calls? And how long would it take before they realized it was her family's landline? If it was Noah who viewed the bills, she knew she would be out on her ass, or worse. Her hope was that she had a few weeks before her secret call was exposed. She doubted they did anything online, such as banking and paying bills. There were no laptops in sight. The only computers were in Noah's and Liam's offices. And those were always behind locked doors. No, technology wasn't a *thing* at The Haven. Even the messages she took were written down on a pad of paper. It seemed like everything was on paper.

Including financial transactions. CASH ONLY except for some of the bills. But she knew there was a checking account. One morning, a plumber had arrived to fix a leak. She had instructions to give him the envelope that was tacked to the corkboard. When the plumber finished, he opened the envelope to see if the amount was correct. Gabby was standing next to him at the time and couldn't help but notice the payer information in the upper left corner wasn't THE HAVEN. It was TRIDENT ENTERPRISES. She hadn't given it another thought until now.

Chapter Twelve

Pinewood

In less than twenty-four hours, the sisters were able to cobble together some information about The Haven. Nikki followed several transactions from one shell company to another. There had to be a half dozen of them, incorporated in Delaware, Wyoming, or Nevada. Nikki knew full well that it is very easy to open a shell company in the United States. A good lawyer can do it in less than half an hour. The über-wealthy use them, together with offshore accounts in places like the Cayman Islands, Switzerland, Singapore, and Belize, to hide money and assets. A second use is to launder money as it moves from one shell company to another, helping to obfuscate the original source. A staggering seventy billion dollars are secreted away in foreign countries.

In 2016, there was a massive leak of 11.5 million documents at what at the time was one of the largest law firms in the world, Mossack Fonseca, headquartered in Panama City with branches in forty different countries. The leaked documents were aptly named the Panama Papers. It revealed that there were over 210,000 separate entities juggling billions of dollars in offshore accounts. The information was astounding, and The Haven appeared on the list.

With the help of her staff and her good friend Lizzie Fox Cricket, one of the most brilliant lawyers in the country, Nikki was able to trace the shell companies associated with The Haven. That was the easy part. The not-so-easy part was tracing the money passing through the shell companies to the offshore bank accounts in which they were stashed. And that is exactly why the very wealthy and the very corrupt, who were sometimes the same people, used those banks—to avoid paying taxes. For the very corrupt, however wealthy they were, it was also to hide the illegal nature of their money-making activities. The bankers' lips were sealed. The sisters hoped that Charles or Fergus could pry them open.

Late that afternoon, the group returned to Pinewood, each with whatever information they could find.

Yoko had called her distributor of exotic flowers in Miami. Whenever the distributor had excess, or the shelf life of the flowers was ending, he would take them to the farmers' market to sell at a fraction of what it would cost at a flower shop. Freddie, her contact there, said he recalled seeing "Moonie-type" people at one of the farm stands. He had never had any interaction with them, but they stood out because of their "costumes," he said, and how they all looked as if they had just drunk some spiked lemonade. Yoko then called the florist shop from which Gabby had made the phone call. Still no more information.

Charles and Fergus offered up the most intriguing tidbits.

"There is a connection between the Westlake twins and the billionaire Daniel Josephson Ruffing. At one time, Noah Westlake, who is now the general manager of The Haven, worked at Ruffing's marina," Charles continued. "Apparently, Ruffing was involved in some business deals with Sidney Westlake, who is now serving fifty years in prison. But

Ruffing broke ties before the old man checked into the gray-bar hotel." Everyone hooted at his reference to prison. "Ruffing's visible assets include several pieces of real estate."

Fergus chimed in. "In addition, he leases a parcel of land on the coast of Cuba."

"Is that legal?" Yoko asked.

"Not if he'd bought it," Nikki replied. "Cuban law forbids selling land in Cuba to foreigners, but there is no prohibition on leasing to them. Ruffing's leasing the land is a boon for both him and Cuba. Cuba gets foreign currency and Ruffing can pull out anytime he wants."

"Wouldn't Ruffing lose whatever money he had to invest in the property?" Alexis asked.

"Doubtful," Annie jumped in. "Ruffing isn't the type of guy who would do a deal that could hinder him in any way. Besides, we don't give a hoot about what happens to him. At least not yet." Annie looked at Myra, who looked at Nikki. Side glances went around the table as if they were all reading each other's minds. Giggles followed.

"I have a feeling Daniel DJ Ruffing is going to come up covered in dog poop once we start digging," Fergus said. More laughter ensued.

When Maggie's cell phone beeped she checked and found that her assistant at the *Post* had forwarded her a recent voice-mail message from Gabby. After listening to it, she held up her hand to indicate everyone should listen. She clicked the SPEAKER button on her phone:

"*Mag. It's Gabby. I'm okay. Back at The Haven. Strange happenings. I'll try again, maybe tomorrow.*"

But instead of the call being disconnected, they could hear the noise of the phone being fumbled and a faint exchange between Gabby and a man. A man who sounded very annoyed.

Myra jumped in. "Play that last part back, please."

Through the noise of the phone being juggled, she heard

the man say *stupid bitch*. "Again." Myra leaned in to listen closely.

"Did you hear that?" She was appalled. "He called her a 'stupid bitch.'" Boos and hisses filled the room as all eyes looked in Charles's direction.

Charles looked at Maggie. "Let's see if we can trace it back." Charles hit a few buttons on his computer keyboard, typed in the main number of the *Post*, then Maggie's extension. Within seconds, Charles's monitor brought up a list of phone numbers. "Let's isolate the Florida area codes 305 and 786." Four numbers came up. Maggie recognized the one from the florist. "With any luck, one of these is where Gabby is." Charles uploaded the list to the monitors on the wall.

"Although I don't think it's a good idea to call them. We don't want anyone to be aware that they are under scrutiny."

"Agreed." Myra leaned closer to the screen and fingered her pearls. "Annie, I think Maggie should go down there and do some digging."

"Yes, but not alone. Alexis? Yoko? You said you had some free time?"

"Yes!" Yoko said with enthusiasm.

"Right on for me!" Alexis added.

"We tried to contact Avery, but he and his people are working on a project for the men right now. They may be able to help us next week. In the meantime, he is going to send a colleague down there to scope out the perimeter," Fergus informed them. "The rest of the surveillance will be up to the three of you until we can get more assistance from Avery's people."

"As long as it isn't a stakeout, I'm fine with that." She hated stakeouts.

"I think we need to approach it like this," Annie began. "Yoko, get in touch with your distributor. Tell him you want to visit the farmers' market. You'll even help.

"Alexis, you'll pretend you're a tourist and attend the

farmers' market. Take a look at what they're selling and see what you can find out about the members and what else they may be pitching.

"Maggie, you go to the *Miami Herald* offices and see what you can dig up about The Haven, Ruffing, and the Westlake twins. See if there's any ink on them. I know we can do it from here, but a face-to-face always gets better results," Annie observed. "I'll have my crew get the plane ready. Plan to leave tomorrow afternoon. Does that work for everyone?"

"Yeps!" "Yeses!" and "You betchas!" filled the room. High fives all around, and a salute to Lady Justice. And then they all went up the stairs for a belated dinner.

Chapter Thirteen

South Florida

The smell of the leather interior of the Cadillac Escalade was intoxicating. Rachel had never ridden in such an opulent vehicle in her life. She was sitting in the passenger seat next to Noah. She stroked the fine upholstery. "Is this one of The Haven's cars?" she asked innocently.

"It's part of our fleet. We get a good deal because we lease several at a time." Noah was being unusually pleasant. "It handles well. Drives like a dream."

"It sure is dreamy." Rachel laid her head on the headrest. "So where are we going?"

"Too many questions," Noah reminded her.

"Oh. Sorry. I'm just a little nervous." Rachel's face was flushed.

"No need. I think you are going to enjoy your new job." Noah patted her knee. That, too, was out of character for him. But Rachel wasn't thinking about Noah as much as she was thinking about her new assignment, even if she had no idea what it entailed. She had been picked to be a spokesperson for The Haven. How bad could it be?

They drove for almost an hour until they reached Fort Lauderdale. The car pulled into the underground parking lot of a very fancy high-rise. Rachel resisted the temptation to ask where they were. She kept telling herself she was on an adventure.

"Remember, do not speak to anyone." Noah's tone was more like what she was used to. Stern.

She nodded, fearing that if any more words came out of her mouth, she would be sent back to The Haven.

He guided her through the elevator doors and pushed a button for the fifth floor. When they emerged from the elevator, they were standing outside a dentist's office. Rachel was about to protest. She hated dentists. Hadn't been to one since . . . well, she couldn't remember when. She started to tremble. Noah touched her elbow. "Don't worry. This won't hurt a bit. You will be pleasantly surprised."

Rachel thought the words *not hurting* and *dentist* did not belong in the same sentence. She took a deep breath as they entered the reception area of the very posh office. The receptionist smiled at Noah. "He's ready."

Noah led Rachel down the hall to a procedure room. "Relax. You are going to love how you look after this."

Rachel was on the verge of hysteria and started to hiccup.

Dr. Stenhouse greeted her. "I see we have a nervous Nellie on our hands." He was an older man with a kind face. "Here. Sit." Rachel took a seat in the patient chair. "Give me a big smile." Rachel almost winced. "Bigger," the dentist instructed her. He held her chin and turned her head to the left, then to the right. "This shouldn't be too difficult. We'll be done in a jiffy." Rachel wanted to scream, *Done with what?* But she was frozen in place. The dentist gave her a big smile. "Don't go away. I'll be right back." He nodded for Noah to join him in the hallway.

"Looks like she did a lot of smoking at one time," the dentist said. "But I think we can do the front, top, and bottom, in about two hours."

"That's fine," Noah replied. "Thanks. Text me when she's ready."

"You got it." The men shook hands as if this were not the first time they had met.

Dr. Stenhouse returned to the procedure room, where Rachel sat in a cold sweat. "Okay, dear. We are going to put your nerves to rest. I am going to be performing a veneer treatment on your teeth. In a couple of hours, you will have a magnificent smile. How does that sound?"

To Rachel, it actually sounded pretty good except for the pain. "Will it hurt?" she had to ask.

"Not at all. You will be in a twilight state. You won't even know what's going on." With that, he took a syringe that had been prepared in advance. First a little valium, then the propofol. Within minutes, Rachel was in lullaby land.

This particular dentistry center specialized in one-day veneers. It was state-of-the-art. And why not? DJ Ruffing owned a piece of it. They used a computer-generated camera with a wand that captures thousands of images. The images are sent via interoffice e-mail to a computer software program, then on to a milling machine, where the patients' personal restorations are carved. *Voilà.* A new set of choppers in a few hours. Ruffing was a silent partner in a number of enterprises. This one explained his gleaming white teeth.

A few hours later, Rachel came out of the anti-anxiety and local anesthesia fog. A tall, exotic woman stood in front of her. She was smiling. Another dazzling smile.

"Rachel?" The woman had a refined Caribbean accent that indicated she was well educated. "Hello. I am Simone. How are you feeling?"

Rachel blinked her eyes several times, trying to get reoriented. She squeaked out a soft, "Hi. Okay. I think." She wiggled her fingers and moved her head side to side. The dentist's office. *But who is this woman?*

"So very happy to hear it." Simone's voice was sultry and lyrical. "Would you like to take a look at your beautiful new smile?" Simone handed Rachel a mirror.

Rachel blinked again. "Is this me?" Rachel recognized her eyes and her nose, but her smile looked like it had come from a fashion magazine. "Holy smoke. Wow." Rachel started making faces, trying out different expressions. "I can't believe it!"

Simone pulled up a side chair and sat across from Rachel. "Now, my love, as soon as you get your equilibrium, we are going to the Bal Harbour Shops to get you into something appropriate to wear." Rachel wasn't sure if she was still buzzed from the drug or if the words *Bal Harbour* had sent her into a tizzy. She had never been there, but she had heard about it. She knew she could never afford it. Bal Harbour had shops that sold luxury goods. Gucci, Brunello Cucinelli, Dior, Fendi, Chanel, just to name a few.

"But I don't have any money." Rachel was finally coming around to full awareness.

"Oh, no, my love. Money is not an issue," she said in her singsong accent. "Getting new clothes is part of your preparation." Simone's voice was soothing. "Come. Here, put this on." Simone handed Rachel a floral jumpsuit. "There is a bathroom over there." Simone pointed to a small room with a toilet and sink.

Rachel sat up and took Simone's hand. "I guess yer the boss," Rachel said plainly.

"Tomorrow we will go to Salon Ethos for hair and makeup. There is one thing, though, we have to work on immediately."

Rachel started to get nervous. "What? What's wrong?"

"Your grammar, love. You use words like 'seen' when it should be 'saw.' For example, 'I seen a good movie the other night.' " She continued, "It should be 'I saw a good movie the other night.' "

Rachel cocked her head. "I know. Yer, I mean, you are correct." She smiled. "How's that?"

"We'll keep working at it." Simone smiled, got up from her seat, and helped Rachel out of the dental chair.

Rachel remembered a scene from *My Fair Lady* and recited it to Simone. "The rain in Spain stays mainly on the plain."

Simone chuckled. "You are going to do just fine, my love. Come." She put her arm through Rachel's and guided her back to the elevators. "We'll get something to drink in the lobby."

They stopped at a drink stand and got two Cokes.

Simone directed Rachel to a waiting vehicle. Another black Cadillac Escalade. *Can it be Noah?* Rachel thought. But it wasn't. It was a man dressed like a Guardian. White pants and black shirt. He opened the rear passenger doors for the women to climb in. Rachel sheepishly looked at Simone. "Do you happen to have a mirror?"

"Of course, love." Simone reached into her cream-colored Louis Vuitton hobo bag, which was on the floor between them. That was when Rachel took a good look at her new companion. She couldn't help but notice Simone's long legs as she pulled the mirror out from the leather bag. Simone had straight black shoulder-length hair with heavy bangs. It framed her high cheekbones, emphasizing her large, almond-shaped eyes. Her skin was a pretty pecan brown. She wore a zebra-print pencil skirt with a white tank. Simple yet elegant. "I like your outfit," Rachel offered.

"Thank you, love. Maybe we can find something like it for you."

"Seriously?" Rachel was about to pinch herself. *What in the world is happening to me?*

"Yes, love. We are going to have to buy you several out-

fits. There are a lot of different occasions you must be prepared for."

Rachel was afraid to ask any questions, but Simone didn't
seem like the others. She surely wasn't dressed like anyone
she had personally encountered, certainly not at The Haven.

"Can I ask you a question?" Rachel squeaked.

"I am sure you *can*. But the question should be, '*May* I ask
you a question?' "

"Got it." Rachel took a hard swallow. She wished she had
been paying closer attention in grade school. "May I ask you
a question?"

"You may ask. But I may choose not to answer." Simone's
tone was even, as if to say, *If I don't like the question, you're
not getting an answer.*

"Understood." Rachel nodded. She might not have paid
attention in grammar school, and she might be a high-school
dropout, but she was no dummy. "Can you tell me how long
this preparation process is going to take?"

Simone tilted her head. "It really depends on you, my
love."

"How so?"

"Now that you have a wonderful smile, we are moving to
the next steps of your transformation. The only thing that
will hold you back is if you cannot hold a conversation without falling back to a trailer-park vocabulary."

Rachel was stunned. How did Simone know about her
trailer-park history? Did it matter? And if so, to whom? "I
shall do my best to articulate with good grammar and grace."
There. She knew she could do it. Hanging around Gabby for
all those months must have rubbed off on her. Gabby's speech
was meticulous.

"That's excellent, my love." Simone looked out the window of the car. "We're almost there." The Cadillac pulled
into the upscale area. "You can drop us in front of Neiman

Marcus," she instructed the driver. He pulled to the curb, got out, and opened the doors for the two women. "Thank you. I'll text you when we're done."

Simone looked over at Rachel. "I think we need to get some food into you before we do anything else." Simone took Rachel's elbow and led her to Le Zoo. She didn't want Rachel to faint in any of the boutique stores.

Rachel didn't have much of an appetite, but as soon as she saw the menu, her salivary glands kicked in. "I have absolutely no idea what to have." She combed the menu.

"Hello, Jacques," Simone greeted the maître d'. Apparently, she was a regular.

"Bonjour, madam. Lovely to see you." Jacques nodded at Simone, then at Rachel. "We're between lunch and dinner menus, but I am sure the chef can accommodate you."

"Jacques, we don't have a lot of time. We have much shopping to do before the stores close. Can you ask the chef to make a salad niçoise for us?"

"*Tout de suite.*" Jacques bowed and went immediately to the kitchen.

"Oh, love, I hope you don't mind that I ordered for both of us? It will be just enough to fill you up and perk you up. A little fish protein is good, and it should be easy for you to eat." Simone looked around the opulent restaurant.

"May I ask another question?" Rachel inquired with a slight hesitation. She didn't want to blow it.

"Of course, love." Simone smiled, a smile that virtually duplicated Rachel's new one. "I am here to help you prepare. And as I said, if I do not feel the question is appropriate, I will not answer it."

"I understand." Rachel continued, "After we finish shopping, where will I be staying tonight? Will I go back to The Haven?"

"No, love. You may never return to The Haven. But not to

worry. You will be well looked after. As for tonight, you will be staying in an apartment in Miami Beach. It belongs to one of The Haven's benefactors."

"A benefactor? I don't think I'm ready for that." Rachel's nerves woke up.

"Oh no, love. They don't live there. They simply own it. The Haven has use of it for circumstances such as this. We need to keep you on track, and it's much more convenient this way. Plus, you and I will be able to spend more time together preparing you."

Rachel was still confused, but she was enjoying the attention and the new smile. She was practically drooling over the idea of real, good food. Not that the food at The Haven was bad. It was just outright boring.

Within a short time, a waiter brought their salads and a bottle of Perrier. "No bread. *Oui?*"

"*Oui,* no bread." Simone smiled back at the waiter.

"One more question, if I may?" Rachel was catching on quickly.

"Yes, love?"

Rachel looked down at the hand Simone was touching. "My ring. Do I get to keep the ring?"

"Of course, love." That's our secret way of recognizing each other," Simone reassured her.

"But you aren't wearing one." Rachel immediately regretted saying those words. "My apologies. That was not an appropriate statement."

Indeed a quick study, Simone thought. "That is true. I'm in a different part of the organization." Simone brought that conversation to an abrupt halt. Rachel knew when to quit.

After they finished their meal, Simone nodded at the waiter, who cleared their plates. "Shall we?" Simone rose from her chair.

"I am ready! And you were correct. I feel much better.

Thank you." Rachel was working very hard at speaking well. She also noticed that the waiter never brought the check. She was about to remind Simone that they hadn't paid their bill, but she thought better of it. Simone was the woman in charge. She must have known what she was doing.

For several hours, they moved from one luxury boutique to another, creating a new wardrobe for Rachel, complete from head to toe. The clothes would be delivered the next day to the condominium where they were spending the night. Rachel felt like Cinderella. She just hoped she didn't turn into a pumpkin at midnight.

Simone sent a text to their driver to pick them up in front of Saks Fifth Avenue. "Tired, love?" Simone asked.

"I am," Rachel replied. "This has been quite a day."

"There's more tomorrow, so you will need a good night's sleep." Simone waited for the driver to open the doors for them and assist them into the SUV. "We should be there in about twenty minutes."

The drive down Collins Avenue was spectacular. Rachel was mesmerized by the glamour and the glitter. As promised, the SUV pulled into the drive of a very modern luxury building. It was Faena House, one of the most exclusive and expensive condominium buildings on the beach. Rachel stared up at the curved façade of the balconies. This time, she actually pinched herself. "We are here," Simone stated as she waited for the driver to open their doors.

Rachel tried to contain her excitement. The cool air and the scent of something expensive filled the lobby. It was a heady experience.

The gentleman at the reception desk greeted them. "Good evening, Miss Jordan, Miss Steward." Rachel was taken aback that he knew her name.

"Good evening, Bentley," Simone responded. Rachel echoed her as they made their way to the elevators. Rachel resisted the temptation to say, "Wow!" as she took in the atmosphere. It exuded money. Lots of it.

Simone pressed the elevator button that said PENTHOUSE. Rachel was holding her breath. She wasn't sure why, but the entire day had been one incredible surprise after another. *What can be behind those doors?* she asked herself, as Simone clicked open the security locks.

Simone entered as if it was something she did on a regular basis. A small remote control was sitting on a table next to the front door. She clicked it several times, which brought up the lights and the shades. Another two clicks, and soft jazz music started to play throughout the rooms. Rachel could no longer contain herself. She spoke in a hushed voice, "Oh my God. This is spectacular."

"Yes. Quite," Simone agreed. She picked up her phone and sent a text to someone but didn't say to whom. Her phone beeped a few seconds later. She read the reply and placed the phone back in her Louis Vuitton bag. "Come. I shall show you your room."

Rachel was trying not to gawk, but there were so many things to look at. The breathtaking view was the perfect backdrop for the fine art, sculpture, and lavish exotic flower arrangements. It was another magazine reference for Rachel. During her waitressing days, she had seen copies of *Architectural Digest* several times when she was checking out a newsstand. By the looks of the cover, she knew it represented a world completely different from her own. She didn't dare to peruse it.

Rachel followed Simone down the hallway to a large bedroom with a queen-size bed, a large walk-in closet, a lavish bathroom, and a view of the Miami skyline. Simone opened the closet and pulled out a pair of pajamas. "These should probably fit you." She handed Rachel the silk garments. "There is a robe and towels in the bathroom." Rachel stood and stared at her blankly.

"This is where I am sleeping?" Rachel was all atwitter.

"Yes, my love. Now go get yourself cleaned up and get some sleep. Tomorrow will be another busy day for you. I will be right across the hall if you need anything."

What could I possibly need? Rachel thought. "I am sure I will be fine. Thank you. Thank you so much for today. It was wonderful."

"You are very welcome. Good night." Simone turned and closed the door behind her.

Rachel went into the bathroom. The tub was big enough to fit two people comfortably. She wondered if she should take a bath. *Why not? Simone didn't say I can't.*

Rachel gingerly approached the tub, waiting for someone to bring her fantasy day to a crashing halt. She glanced around the opulent space. It was very quiet except for the soft music coming out of the speakers. Returning to the bedroom, she looked around for some indication as to how to turn off the music when she spotted a panel on the wall. She peered at it. It controlled the music, air-conditioning, and lighting. All very high-tech. She scrutinized the buttons, trying not to make a mistake, and decided the button with the musical note must be for the sound system. *Here goes,* she thought as she pressed the down-facing arrow. Silence. She breathed a sigh of relief, returned to the tub area, and prepared a bath. There were several jars of bath salts on the ledge. Eyeing the jars, Rachel lifted the lid off each one and sniffed. She picked the lavender one.

Rachel immersed herself in the deep tub, soaking away her anxiety about what the next day would bring. So far, it had been a whirlwind, but she reminded herself of that old expression: "All good things must come to an end." Then she remembered Liam's teachings about manifesting. Paraphrasing him, she recalled the message: *If you think negative thoughts, then you will attract negative energy. If you think positive thoughts, you will attract positive energy.* That's when it dawned on her that she had not seen Liam to say good-bye. He of all people should have given her some insight as to what to expect. *Oh well. I'm here now.*

Rachel drifted off to sleep until the water in the tub reached an uncomfortable temperature. She bolted upright and tried to get her bearings. When she remembered where she was, she quickly exited the tub, wrapped herself in a velour robe, and headed to the bedroom, where the pajamas waited for her on a chaise lounge. She slipped into the pajamas, then into the bed. She relived the events of the day until she finally fell into a deep slumber.

The next morning, there was a light tap on her door. It was Simone. "May I come in?"

"Oh yes!" Rachel jumped out of bed and hoped she didn't look too disheveled.

Simone was already dressed in a peach jumpsuit with a wide belt. Her handbag and shoes completed her outfit. Rachel couldn't help but notice what a stunning and exotic beauty Simone was. "You look beautiful."

"Thank you, my love. And today you, too, will look your most beautiful best." She made a hand gesture, indicating for Rachel to get up. "Come. We have much to do. There is breakfast waiting."

"Should I wear the same thing I wore yesterday?"

"No, my love. Most of the clothes were delivered. Take a quick shower, and I will bring them in here." Simone left the room and fetched the dozens of shopping bags, garment bags, and shoe boxes that were piled in the foyer. She called into the bathroom, "Wear a tank top with one of the cargo pants. You want to be comfortable."

When Rachel finished her shower, she returned to the bedroom. Her mouth was agape, seeing the dozens of boxes, and bags of clothes. She knew they had done a lot of shopping, but since they hadn't carried anything home, she had no idea how much had been purchased. And by whom? She shrugged and began to peek into the shopping bags. It could take her an hour to find the cargo pants, but then she remembered they were from Dolce & Gabbana. It was the leopard tank top that had caught her eye. She picked out a pair of Stuart Weitzman thongs to go with it. She quickly got dressed and met up with Simone on the balcony, where a fruit platter, yogurt, and herbal tea awaited.

"You look lovely," Simone commented. "By the end of the day, you should be ready to move on to the next step."

Rachel didn't dare ask what that was. At the moment, she was just along for the ride.

After they finished breakfast, they met the driver who would take them to Salon Ethos on the other side of Biscayne Bay. As they crossed the Julia Tuttle Causeway, Rachel could see the massive estates on the private islands. One of them belonged to Daniel J. Ruffing. But Rachel had no idea that there was a billionaire funding most of The Haven's properties. But it wasn't because he was altruistic. Not in any way, shape, or form. He was a businessman. A very rich and crafty one.

Salon Ethos was all abuzz with loud music, people laughing, blow-dryers humming. Simone was greeted once again as if she had been there a hundred times. A flamboyant young man with streaked-blond hair and leather pants that looked like they had been spray-painted on greeted them with, "Simone! Darling!" and air kisses.

"Trigger! Nice to see you." Simone air-kissed him in return. "Meet Rachel."

"Hello, sweetness! Welcome to the magic!" Trigger waved his hand around the room. "Let's have a look at you." He escorted Rachel to a chair in the back. He looked at Simone. "So, sister, what did you have in mind?"

"Trigger, I am going to leave it up to you, my love. Hair, nails, pedi, and makeup."

"Any particular occasion?" Trigger tilted his head to the left, then to the right, sizing up the day's challenge.

"She is starting a new position. She needs a bit of polish and style. I have every confidence you will know what to do." Simone gave him a nod and looked over at Rachel. "I'll be back later."

By the end of the session, Rachel had gone from mousy-brown hair to a ginger shade of red. Her unruly curls became a straight bob, with her hair lightly brushing her neck. Her nails were polished in a French manicure, with matching toes; and the makeup was striking but not freakish. She barely recognized herself when he was done.

Rachel stared into a full-length mirror. *If the girls at the diner could see me now. And the other Pledges?* They would be green with envy. Except for Gabby. How she wished she could share this with her. Then Simone's words echoed in her head, *You may never return to The Haven.*

Chapter Fourteen

Myra was pacing the floor, stroking her pearls as if she were waiting for a genie to appear. In fact, she was waiting for Maggie, Alexis, and Yoko to arrive, so they could get their instructions.

Charles approached her from behind and placed his arms around her waist. "What are you fretting about, old girl?"

Myra turned into his arms and placed her head on his shoulder. "You know I always get concerned when the girls are away from our home base."

"And I must say, you do a marvelous job of concealing your worries." Charles nuzzled her neck. "But it's the pearls that always give it away. It's your 'tell.' "

"Oh, Charles, I don't think I'm over the time when Annie went missing." Myra sighed.

Charles lifted her face to his. "But she *is* back. And she *is* safe. Do I need to remind you of your credo? 'Whatever it takes.' You know we shall keep them safe."

Myra looked up at him and smiled. "Or someone is going to be in very big trouble!" She laughed. Myra knew that when it came to their missions, the sisters were as adept as any special ops team. The Sisterhood had some of the deepest connections and access to information, people, places, and things. Whenever things did not go according to plan, they would change the plan. They were *that* adaptable. They had to be. Too often, circumstances would require a switch in strategy. Winging it wasn't a preferred method, but the group was swift, stealthy, and ingenious. Plus, they had each other's backs. Always. Myra hoped that things would progress smoothly and nothing go awry. First and foremost, they had to locate Gabby. Once she was safe, they could begin to take on the crew that had put her in peril.

Lady and her pups announced the arrival of Nikki with yapping, barking, and tails wagging. Just as soon as the ruckus subsided, it began again when Maggie pulled in. Over the next few minutes it would be a cacophony of yelps, hugs, and treats. The hugs weren't limited to the pooches, either. High fives, hugs, and smooches were the typical greeting among the sisters. They acted like teenagers, including pulling stunts like sliding down the banister. Once the commotion was over, everyone took a seat at the kitchen table.

Before the women had arrived, Charles had set out a tray of scones, croissants, and muffins, along with a large bowl of fruit. Maggie was the first to dive in. "Oh, Charles, you always know what to serve."

"As if it mattered!" Annie chortled.

Fergus stifled a laugh, trying not to choke on his coffee.

As they munched on the fine baked goods, Charles handed them burner phones and a flash drive with the latest information they had, while Annie gave them the rundown. "Maggie, you will go to the *Herald* and talk to a few of your colleagues while we try to unravel the shell companies The Haven is associated with." Maggie nodded in response. "Yoko, you will go to the flower district and meet up with your distributor. He will bring you to the farmers' market and have you work at his stall, so you can keep an eye on The Haven's comings and goings. Alexis, you will go to the farmers' market as a tourist and check them out front and center. Buy a few items, engage in conversation with them. See what you can find out about this woo-woo crew."

Fergus informed them that even though Avery's people weren't available, he had asked a colleague who lived in Miami to scope out The Haven for any obvious security. "There doesn't seem to be much. The area is fenced in, but more as a property marker than a deterrent. There are security cameras at the front entrance, the main house, and over the doors of the outbuildings. It's simple loop video. It tapes over every twenty-four hours, so in essence there is no video-security history. All that's on tape is the last twenty-four hours."

Myra interjected, "We don't want any of you approaching The Haven until we have more background information. We don't want you walking into something we know little about."

Charles added, "Fergus and I are looking into the shell companies. It still may take a few days before we can get banking information. Interpol is always closing the back doors to their technology. It doesn't stop hackers but slows them down a bit." A few guffaws filled the air. If anyone knew about hacking it was Charles, Fergus, and the Sisterhood. "We're waiting for new Internet routing system codes." Charles's eyes scanned the room. Annie was biting her lip, trying not to laugh.

"What?" She looked at Charles, hiding her mouth with her hand to stifle a giggle.

Charles cleared his throat, and continued, "We'll conference in tomorrow evening at nineteen hundred hours."

Lady was barking at the arrival of the car that was to take them to the airport. "Good luck, be safe."

"Whatever it takes!" they cheered in agreement, high-fived, and hugged.

Annie pulled Maggie aside. "You will need this." She

handed Maggie a bottle of fifty SPF sunscreen. "Those freckles don't have a chance in Miami! Be sure to use it."

"And wear a hat!" they said in unison. They chuckled and hugged one more time before the girls headed to the car.

The plan was for Yoko, Maggie, and Alexis to take Annie's Gulfstream jet to Miami Executive Airport. Once they landed, they would each rent a car and drive to the Biltmore Hotel in Coral Gables.

Miami-Dade County sits at the southeast corner of Florida, covering over two thousand square miles, one-third of which is part of Everglades National Park. Coral Gables provided easy access to the spiderweb of expressways they would have to travel to Downtown Miami, Homestead, or wherever their leads would take them.

It was almost noon when they arrived in Miami. The drive to the hotel had taken almost an hour. By the time they checked into their suite with adjoining rooms, it was close to two o'clock. Maggie checked her watch. "It'll take me about a half hour to get to the *Herald* building. I'm meeting up with an old friend for coffee at four."

"The flower market is also about thirty minutes from here. I told Freddie I'd stop by to grab a drink after work," Yoko informed the others.

"I'll review the files again while you're both out," Alexis offered. "I'll order room service."

"Ooohhh . . . room service," Maggie cooed.

"Girl, don't you ever *not* want to eat?" Alexis chided her.

Maggie shrugged. "At least I haven't bitten my nails in a while!" She grabbed the room service menu. "Just doing research." She let out a big grin. "Depending on what I find out, I may not have time for dinner, so I want to know what I can plan on for later." She gave Alexis a wink.

Yoko pulled out her phone and dialed Annie's number.

Alexis and Maggie could only hear one side of the conversation. "We're here. Yes. All Checked in. Uh-huh. I won't. Yes, I will. Thank you. You too!" She snapped the phone shut.

The other two women placed their hands on their hips. "Well?" "So?"

"Myra made me promise not to let you leave the building without the sunscreen, and to make sure you took your hat!"

Maggie gave Yoko a salute. "Understood!" She grabbed the tube of cream and lathered her face with it. "Happy?"

"I am. Thank you." Yoko smiled.

"Okay, ladies, time for both of you to shove off before you get stuck in rush-hour traffic." They all high-fived each other and went on their way.

On the way down the elevator, Maggie said to Yoko, "I'm really worried about Gabby. I want to go over to The Haven and see if she's there."

"Oh no you don't. We have strict orders. Don't be one of those nitwits in those thriller movies where the babysitter hears a noise in the basement and goes down to investigate."

"I'm not an idiot. I am, after all, a journalist," Maggie said in protest.

"I'm not saying you're an idiot, but I know you are very concerned about your friend. Sometimes we do foolish things when our emotions are involved."

"I know you're right." Maggie sighed. "I need to put my head in journalist mode and not friend mode."

"Exactly." Yoko gave Maggie's arm a squeeze. "Don't worry. We'll find her."

The women parted in the lobby, each off in a different direction.

Maggie pulled out a paper map of Miami and traced her route to the *Miami Herald*. Yoko did the same in her car. They did not want to leave any electronic footprints in any GPS.

Much to Maggie's surprise, traffic was light on her way there. When she arrived, the parking lot was crowded, forcing her to leave the car at the far end of the lot. After a few hundred feet she realized she had left her hat in the car. "Dang," she admonished herself. She knew she had to go back and get it. The sun was blazing hot, and the humidity was like a steam bath. She could see the thunderheads forming in the west. Like clockwork, every day the skies would fill with cumulonimbus clouds over the Everglades and move east across the city. More often than not, they would cause downpours, creating havoc on the roads. Rain would come down in sheets, making it impossible to see. The entire episode would last for less than an hour, unless you were traveling in the direction of the storm. If the hat didn't protect her from the sun, it might be some help if she got caught in the deluge. She hurried to the main entrance as the clouds began to burst behind her.

When she arrived at the front security desk, she flashed her press credentials. "Good afternoon. Maggie Spritzer to see Jimmy Griffin." The security guard scrutinized her identification and dialed a number. "Maggie Spritzer to see you," a short pause, then, "Elevator banks are to your right. Second floor."

Maggie smiled. "Thanks!" She realized she had been sweating when she entered the building and pulled out a tissue to wipe her face. Miami was certainly hot.

When the elevator doors opened, Jimmy Griffin stood waiting for her. He wrapped his arms around her, lifted her off the floor, and gave her a spin. "Maggie Spritzer! How's my favorite Ping-Pong pal?"

Maggie laughed. "After losing that match in Dallas?"

"Heck, it was better than standing around waiting for the results of the primary."

"Yeah. Fun times." Maggie remembered all the traveling she had done a few years before, following all the presidential primary elections. "Glad I'm not on that beat anymore. A lot of hostility."

"Politics and hostility. Kinda redundant, doncha think?" Jimmy snickered. "You must get a boatload of that stuff up there in the Beltway."

"Puh-lease. You can only imagine what isn't covered in ink," Maggie joked back.

Jimmy Griffin was in his late thirties. He had been in journalism since college. He had hopped around the country, working for several of the two dozen newspapers owned by the McClatchy family, mostly covering political races. But he wanted more of the nitty-gritty and took a job at the company's *Miami Herald* news desk. He and Maggie used to cover many of the same stories, so they would often find themselves in the same "dumpy motels" following the many hopefuls on the road to the White House. They would usually grab a bite to eat or have a beer, but there had never been any romance. None of their contemporaries could figure out why. Maggie would respond with "It's just *not* one of those things."

"Come. Let's go grab a coffee. There's a bunch of places just a few minutes from here." He grabbed one of the dozens of umbrellas in a stand just outside the newsroom door.

"Is that yours?" Maggie asked.

"Huh? This? Maybe." Jimmy chuckled. "Everyone throws their chutes in here. You grab one and bring one back. Doesn't matter."

"The honor system." Maggie smiled. "I'm impressed."

They made their way to a Cuban coffee stand. Jimmy ordered two café cubanos, sugar included. Maggie spotted something that looked like cake. "Mmmmm . . . grab me one of those!" She pointed to a *pastelito*.

Jimmy burst out laughing. "Well, I see that your appetite hasn't changed one little bit!"

Maggie giggled as she wiped some of the flaky crust from

her lips. "I'm waiting for all of it to catch up with me. I must have a wicked-fast metabolism."

"I'm in awe." Jimmy beamed at his friend. "So what brings you to Miami? It can't be a story about The Haven. They are boring. B-o-r-i-n-g. Boring. A bunch of miscreants who otherwise would be in a shelter, work camp, jail, or rehab. And the guy who is their 'leader,' "—Jimmy used air quotes—"is another snooze festival."

Maggie stared down at her coffee, debating how much she should tell Jimmy.

"What?" Jimmy prodded. "I know that pensive look."

"They profess some sort of spiritual enlightenment, but it seems more like a cult." She decided to give him some information. "It appears that they are funded by several shell companies."

Jimmy's eyebrows furrowed. "You mean it's not all peace, love, and do you want to buy an eggplant?"

"Not from what I've learned." Maggie still hesitated.

"So why is that of interest to you?" Jimmy was a top-notch reporter, in the same league as Maggie.

"Don't you find that a little suspicious?" Maggie leaned in. "A spiritual retreat that is hiding behind shell companies?"

"Good point. But why are you interested in them? Certainly there must be a lot of more pressing issues for you to be tracking down."

"Let's just say it's personal." Maggie hated to be secretive with her longtime friend.

"Oh no you don't." Jimmy sat up tall. "You're not pulling that with me."

Maggie looked around to make sure no one could hear her. "I got a disturbing phone call from my friend Gabby."

"Gabby Richardson?" Jimmy asked.

"Yes, Gabby."

"What kind of disturbing call? I know she wanted to take a break from the crime-scene stuff, but what does she have to do with The Haven?"

"Apparently, she saw the leader, Liam Westlake, at a few venues and was impressed. She said she was on a soul-searching journey and signed up for a program there."

"Wow. I didn't know that normal people went there."

"Not every person on a spiritual quest is a loser."

"I didn't mean it that way. It's just that they have a reputation for taking in people who can't seem to survive on the outside."

"So, it's really not such a bad thing," Maggie noted.

"But suspicious?" Jimmy asked.

Maggie decided to bring Jimmy in on some of the details, just in case she needed his help going forward.

"Okay, but you have to promise me this goes nowhere else. We're talking off the record. Capisce?"

"Capisce."

Maggie proceeded to tell Jimmy about the two messages Gabby had left on her voice mail.

"That is a bit creepy. So what do you plan to do?" Jimmy asked. "Go to The Haven?"

"That's just it. We're kind of at an impasse. We don't want to storm the place before we have more information about the setup. The shell-company stuff is what's making this situation ominous. Why would a place like The Haven have to hide behind shell companies?"

"Good question. Knowing you and your boss, I'm sure you tried to trace the shell companies."

"We have. There are several, which lead to a dead end when we get to the offshore banks."

"Yeah, that's tough. If the countess can't get the goods, I don't know who can."

"Exactly." Maggie picked at the crumbs on her plate.

"How about this. I'll go through the archives to see what stories have run about The Haven and the Westlake twins. Maybe we can find some strands leading to something or someone."

"Jimmy, that would be great. It would save me a lot of time." Maggie was relieved that she hadn't made the trip only to find herself locked in a room of archival information.

"And I will keep it under my hat," Jimmy assured her.

"You are the best!" She reached over and grabbed his hand. "Let's make a plan to have dinner in a couple of days."

"How long are you in town?"

"As long as it takes." *And whatever it takes.* She reminded herself of the Sisterhood credo.

"Okay. Cool. I'll do some digging when I get back. It's a quiet day on the desk. Well, so far. But it's Miami, anything can happen. New York may have invented the phrase 'in a New York minute,' but here we say '*un minuto de Miami.*"

"Thanks, Jimmy. I appreciate this very much. Especially the *pastelito.*" They both rose from their chairs, and Maggie gave him a big hug. "I have a new temporary phone number." Jimmy knew exactly what she meant. It wasn't unusual for a reporter to carry a burner phone in case they had to ditch it in a hurry.

They parted ways, Jimmy promising to get in touch in a day or so. Maggie was relieved that she had some backup boots-on-the-ground help.

That same afternoon, Gabby reported to the main house to relieve Maxwell for his break. He was in a foul mood. "Try not to break anything today." Gabby resisted correcting him. She hadn't actually broken anything, but arguing with Maxwell would not be good form. Instead, she apologized one more time.

Maxwell continued. "Liam is on leave, so it's vital that you take copious notes. Understood?"

"Yes. Understood." Gabby was not thrilled that she would have to deal with Noah, but maybe Maxwell would return before she had to interact with him. Unfortunately, that wasn't what happened. Like one of the storms of South Florida, Noah arrived in a bad mood.

"Oh, you again." Noah's greeting was terse.

"Good afternoon." Gabby smiled as if she hadn't heard him.

"Yeah, whatever." Noah stomped into his office and slammed the door.

Hard to believe they're brothers. Even though he was behind closed doors, Noah was a very short distance from where she sat. There was no way she could sneak a phone call today. She sat at the desk and tapped her pencil, trying to figure out another way to get another message to Maggie.

Yoko met with Freddie, her flower distributor. They had a quick glass of wine while Yoko explained that she was doing research on farmers' markets and wanted to see how he ran his stand. She thought it was an excellent way of selling off excess inventory. "Meet me here at eight o'clock. Sharp. We have to get our vehicles out of the way before nine."

"Thanks, Freddie. I appreciate this."

"No problem. I can always use the help. Even though my people are used to the temps in the greenhouse, they really hate sitting outside with the sun beating down on the canvas as the humidity increases. When they are in the greenhouse, they can walk around. At the farmers' market, all they can do is sit and bake."

Yoko smiled. "Well, I'll see you in the morning."

"*Mañana!*" Freddie smiled back.

Once the three women were back at the hotel, they brought each other up to date with what they had accomplished.

"Listen, I had to give Jimmy some information," Maggie informed them. "I know I should have checked with Annie first, but he can be a great resource for us. I didn't mention anything about anyone else except I was worried about Gabby. Remember, he worked with her, too. Besides, he and Annie know each other, and I trust him. We were on plenty of stakeouts together, except we didn't carry guns. I knew he always had my back."

"That sounds reasonable, but you should let the others know right now," Alexis said.

"Of course! I was just waiting until I got back here. They don't kid around with the torrential downpours. I didn't want to be distracted. It was scary out there." Maggie's eyes widened. She pulled out the phone and punched in Annie's number.

"I trust you are using your sunscreen?" Annie chided as she answered the phone.

"Yes, ma'am," Maggie replied. "When I'm not dodging buckets of rain."

"Good girl. What's the latest?"

"I met with Jimmy Griffin today to see what he might know about The Haven. He said it was 'boring . . . b-o-r-i-n-g.' He wanted to know why I was interested, and I mentioned Gabby. He worked with her for a while, so I thought he might have some insight."

"How much did you tell him?" Annie asked very calmly. Annie knew that Maggie could be kooky at times, but she was sharp as a tack.

"Just that I knew she had signed up for some spiritual enlightenment stuff at The Haven and I had received two odd messages. I told him I was concerned but was hesitant to go there in person. He offered to help out if I needed it."

"Glad to know we have some backup down there. We're still waiting on Avery to give us some assistance."

"I'm glad you're okay with this." Maggie breathed a sigh of relief. She would never want to put anyone in danger or jeopardize a mission.

"I was worried that you were too close to the situation," Annie confessed. "But I also know how resourceful you are, and now you have Jimmy Griffin to help out. Good work for just a couple of hours," Annie continued. "This could work well in our favor because we need some intel on Daniel Josephson Ruffing."

"The billionaire playboy?" Maggie asked.

"Yes, the very one. It took some digging by Nikki, Fergus, and Charles, but they found that Ruffing is connected to a multitude of the shell companies, one of which is connected to The Haven."

"Wow." Maggie's jaw dropped. "How were you able to find out?" As if she really had to ask.

Annie chuckled. "As I said, it took a lot of digging, but there is one shell company, Trident Enterprises, that has been paying the bills for The Haven."

"Why would Ruffing be involved in a spiritual retreat? Or whatever it is?" Maggie asked, puzzled.

"That's exactly what we have to find out." Annie paused. "As soon as we find Gabby."

"Do you think there is some coincidence? Foul play?" Maggie scribbled some more on her pad.

"We've barely scratched the surface. Maybe Ruffing needed another tax write-off," Annie offered as an explanation.

"Maybe, but why would Gabby leave such a cryptic message?"

"Perhaps she didn't like the way the place was being run."

"But it sounded rather menacing, beginning with the phone call from the flower shop, to what the florist told me about her getting into a car with two men, then her latest message." Maggie replayed the scenarios in her head and out loud.

"If she didn't like how the place was being run, then they may have been concerned about bad publicity. She was a reporter before she signed up with them," Annie suggested.

"Good point," Maggie agreed. "So what's the next move?"

"Ask Jimmy to get you as much *real* background on Ruffing that he can find. We know he pays dearly to control his public persona in the media, as well as what is *not* covered in the media."

Maggie was taking copious notes.

"His public persona is easy to find. He owns a very large marina-boatyard in Downtown Miami, near Miamarina, a colossal estate on Star Island. Helicopter, private jet. The works. He also leases property in Varadero on the coast of Cuba, which seems a bit shady and suspicious. I don't think he goes to Cuba just for the cigars, and it's rumored that it's a playground for the rich and powerful. We need to find out who he hangs out with when the paparazzi aren't lurking about."

"Got it."

"Maggie?" Annie lowered her voice.

"Yesss . . ." Maggie dragged out her answer, recognizing the tone in Annie's voice. It was the voice that said, "You may have to go out on a stakeout."

"Aw, c'mon. You know I hate stakeouts." Maggie started to whine like a four-year-old.

"I didn't say you *had* to, I said you *may have* to." Annie didn't want Maggie on a stakeout any more than Maggie did. It would be a last resort if they couldn't get more information using all their other resources. "Let's just keep that door open."

"Yeah, but just a crack." Maggie thought about the heat and humidity sitting in a car all night. It gave her the willies.

"Don't get all wired up about it. Yet." Annie was trying to be reassuring.

"Okay. I'll try not to."

"Good. Meanwhile, I'll let the others know about Jimmy. We weren't expecting your call, so everyone is out and about."

"We're going to the farmers' market tomorrow. Yoko is going to work at the flower stand, and Alexis and I will arrive as tourists. We plan on going separately and pretending we don't know each other."

"Excellent. We'll talk again tomorrow evening. Be safe and behave!"

"We will." Maggie hit the END button on her burner phone.

She turned to the others. "I'm famished!"

They burst into laughter and passed around the room service menu.

Chapter Fifteen

Gabby was usually one of the Pledges who attended the farmers' market. Her smile and charisma were a winning combination. But this day she was asked to cover for Maxwell the entire morning. While she didn't mind, she was disappointed that she wouldn't experience the atmosphere of the market. With so many people selling their wares—exotic fruits and vegetables that could only be grown in private gardens; handcrafted clothes; toys; and accessories—she loved the experience of seeing and meeting many different people. Not only was it a haven for excess inventory for florists, it was also a place where artists could make a few dollars selling paintings, sculpture, jewelry, and much more. Gabby loved the eclectic ensemble. It was inspiring—free spirits enjoying life, expressing their passions—even if she was only allowed to watch from a distance. On the one hand, she was disheartened about not going, but on the other, it might present an opportunity for her to get a message to Maggie. That was only if Noah, with his grouchy personality, wasn't around.

Gabby looked on as the van was being loaded with the week's cornucopia of goods. *Maybe tomorrow,* she thought.

She made her way to the main house to answer the same stupid question from the same dolt as she had done three times a day, every day since she had begun filling in for Maxwell. *Guess he's just doing his job.*

As she climbed the steps, she noticed that Noah's office door was open. That was a bad sign. It meant he was on the premises.

Her angst increased when he stepped into the hallway. "Good morning, Gabby." His voice was calm and even. Not like the past few times, when he had been abrupt and downright rude.

"Good morning." Gabby nodded and went behind the desk to take her seat.

"Maxwell tells me you've been doing a decent job with the messages. They are clear and detailed."

Gabby was stunned at the sudden congeniality, especially the comment coming from Maxwell. "Thank you." She had been a journalist, after all. Accurate note taking was a necessity for doing the job well. She wondered how much Noah knew of her background.

"Keep up the good work." Noah turned and went back into his office, closing the door behind him. Gabby irritated him. Perhaps it was because she was bright, or maybe because Liam had taken a liking to her. But as Noah slouched in his large leather chair, he reminded himself of the real reason he tolerated her. In just a few months, she would begin to have access to the principal in the trust fund that her grandparents had established for her. Noah understood the importance of keeping Gabby content. But not overconfident. It was a fine balancing act. For most members, The Haven was a big step up from the lives they had led beforehand. According to Liam's way of thinking, The Haven was indeed a refuge for everyone who participated. For Noah, it was nothing more than cheap labor to keep up the façade. Ruffing was expanding his business and putting more pressure on Noah. Besides running the business end of The Haven, Noah was still called on to make runs to the fishing boats for "special deliveries." Those deliveries were always made well past midnight. *"Ran out of booze,"* would be Ruffing's explanation.

After working for Ruffing for more than a decade, Noah knew that he was in good standing with his boss. It was a solid professional relationship. One couldn't call them friends. It was always business, with the exception of interacting with people at the marina. Those exchanges were casual. Noah was very careful not to fraternize with the überwealthy customers. But there were loads of other people who had money, just not in the same league as the überwealthy billionaire.

The events Ruffing threw at the marina were monumental, and Noah would attend them as "perimeter staff." Noah was allowed to mingle and enjoy the amenities, but with the understanding that if something needed to be taken care of, he was on call. But when it came to the private soirees at Ruffing's Star Island mansion, only the elite of the elite were invited. That particular guest list included foreign dignitaries, multinational banking executives, shipping tycoons, and a smattering of royals from all over the world.

Out in the hallway, seated at the desk, Gabby was perplexed. *Why is Noah suddenly being nice to me?* she wondered. *Is it possible he's interested in my trust fund?* She could believe that was Noah's ulterior motive, but Liam's? Surely not. But her journalistic instincts had been awakened. She knew there was something sinister about The Haven though she could not figure out what it was. The people who came and went on the second floor were always on edge, which seemed decidedly odd for a community that touted itself as being a spiritual retreat. Plus, the men who came and went didn't look like they were part of any religious sect or seeking spiritual enlightenment. No, they looked more like gangsters, hit men, thugs as far as she was concerned. And those accents. Eastern European and Far Eastern. It was like the Tower of Babel.

She pulled out one of Liam's Daily Mindfulness books and started to read. It was filled with the verses of some of the great spiritual leaders of all time, with anecdotal notes from Liam. He had self-published several on the subject, and they were part of the package you received when you signed up for the program. As one advanced through the steps of the program, one had to buy the more advanced edition. Or, for most members, do more labor to pay down the debt.

Copies of the basic books were also sold at the farmers' market. Next to the incense. The Haven had started with only one stall at the market. Now they were up to five, dividing them up by products. It had developed into a fine cash-flow business.

Gabby was engrossed in a passage from the book *The Art of Happiness* when the phone rang. Gabby bounced from her chair. "Good morning. How may I direct your call?"

"Good morning." A sultry-sounding woman with a Caribbean accent greeted her in return. "Please tell Noah the package is ready for delivery. Thank you."

Gabby wrote it down, word for word. Then she cocked her head. She didn't recall ever having taken a message from a woman.

Yoko had reported to Freddie at eight o'clock in the morning. Yoko noted how many boxes and their contents were being loaded into the truck. Freddie wanted an accounting at the end of the day. It wasn't that he didn't trust anyone. He wanted to be sure he included the proper amount as profit for his tax return. Freddie had been one of the lucky ones to escape Castro's regime during the airlifts. He was only five years old at the time, but he remembered how terrified his mother and sister were, hoping that his father wouldn't be too far behind. It took almost a year before the family was reunited and settled in Miami. Freddie had the utmost respect for America. He never wanted to put himself or his family at risk. Playing by the rules was essential, especially in the hotbed political climate of immigration reform. He and his family were legally documented immigrants, but the prejudice was real nonetheless. A lot of people assumed that if you looked different or had an accent, you were an illegal alien. He was adamant that everyone in his family speak proper English without a hint of an accent. As he loaded the last box of birds of paradise into the truck, he turned to Yoko. "Thanks for helping out today. It's my granddaughter's first holy communion this afternoon. It will give me a couple of hours to clean up and get there on time." He hoisted a thumb at the three young men who had loaded the trucks. "The boys here will do all the lifting. All you have to do is collect the money and count it at the end of the day."

"Oh, Freddie, I appreciate the opportunity to see how you run things. I promise to keep my calculator in my apron pocket at all times." She smiled, jumped into the passenger seat of one of the trucks, and headed to the farmers' market.

Back at the hotel, Alexis and Maggie got ready for their own journey to the market. Alexis, being a master of disguise, exited the bedroom and twirled in front of Maggie. "Wah gwaan?" Alexis said in her best Jamaican accent. "Every ting is every ting." She tossed her head from side to side, swinging the blond dreadlock braids that hung from her head wrap. "Mi agwan easy."

Maggie was practically rolling on the floor. "You are too much! That is one of your best disguises."

"Ya mon!" Alexis replied.

"I especially like the native garb." Maggie was referring to Alexis's colorful blouse and skirt, a traditional outfit worn by

Jamaican women. "And the extra padding!" Alexis wanted to hide her lithe figure, anticipating a different disguise in the future if necessary. Or none at all. No one would be able to recognize her once she shed that day's outfit.

Reverting to her normal speaking voice, Alexis asked Maggie, "So what are you going to wear today?"

"Besides sunscreen and a hat?" Maggie joked.

"Yes, clothing would be a good idea," Alexis teased. "I have a short blond wig you can borrow and a camouflage jacket. It's got padding, so you could look a little heftier."

"Won't I sweat?" Maggie hated to play dress-up and preferred light khakis and a T-shirt.

"No, it's vented."

"You got anything else in your bag of tricks?" Maggie was dubious about a jacket in eighty-plus-degree heat.

"I have a caftan and a black wig."

"Jeez . . . then my head will sweat."

"Quit whining. You'll wear a big straw hat." Alexis went back into her room and returned with an outfit that no one would ever suspect Maggie Spritzer would wear. Satisfied they could pull off being tourists, they headed to the market in separate cars.

When they arrived, they each stopped at the flower stall. Alexis approached Yoko. "Wah gwaan?"

Yoko looked up from her calculator. "Good morning." She had no clue it was Alexis. Alexis wandered through the booth, looking at the variety of blooms. "Dis be-u-di-ful," she said in her Jamaican accent, giving Yoko a sideways glance. Still nothing. Alexis was thrilled she had been able to fool one of the sisters.

She circled back to where Yoko was standing and held out her hand, in which she was clenching several anthuriums. It was only then that Yoko recognized Alexis's bracelet. It was a simple gold-link chain that Alexis wore very often.

Yoko smiled. "Those are lovely." She calculated the amount, and continued, "That will be fifteen dollars, please."

Alexis dug into her sack and pulled out a twenty-dollar bill and handed it to Yoko. Yoko handed her a five and said, "Thank you. Hope to see you again."

Alexis replied with another "Ya mon!" Yoko had to stifle a laugh.

Alexis continued to wander through the market, stopping and looking, as any other tourist or shopper might do.

Several minutes later, Maggie arrived at the flower stall, trying not to trip over the caftan. It was a bit long on her, but she had put on wedge sandals to help make up the difference in height between her and Alexis.

Maggie was a little easier to recognize. The freckles with the black wig seemed incongruous, but Alexis had covered most of them up with some stage makeup. Maggie didn't quite look "Goth," not with her pale skin and black wig, but the fake tattoos made her borderline. Yoko greeted her with, "Good morning. Looking for anything special today?"

"Nah. I'm waiting for something to jump out at me," Maggie replied. "I'm trying to do a Zen kind of thing."

One of the other workers had been standing nearby and chimed in. "If you're into that kind of stuff, there are a bunch of . . . I don't know what you'd call them . . . but they sell incense and junk like that."

"Oh really? Where?" Maggie looked around.

"About five stalls down to your right. You can't miss the smell." The worker made a facial expression that said, "weirdos."

"Thanks. I'll check 'em out." Maggie turned to Yoko. "Do you think you could save me a couple of those orangey-looking things?"

"You mean birds of paradise?" Yoko pointed.

"Yeah. I don't want to be carrying them around."

"Certainly. We'll be here until four o'clock."

"Thanks!" Maggie turned on her wedged heel and strolled toward The Haven's group of stalls. The smell of patchouli almost knocked her over. She scanned the first booth, hoping to spot Gabby. Nothing. A young woman approached Maggie. "Hi, I'm Cassie."

Maggie was expecting some kind of sales pitch but got none.

"Hi, I'm Melissa." Maggie used one of her pseudonyms. "Wow, that incense is certainly intense."

"It's actually resins," Cassie explained. "We make them at The Haven." She waved her arm, indicating all the items on sale. "In fact, we make pretty much everything you see."

"Really?" Maggie pretended to be intrigued. "Do you do it together?"

"Some raise the vegetables we sell at the far booth; the beekeepers make the honey; and we have an art cottage where most of the other things are made."

"We? Is it a club?" Maggie wanted to sound totally uninformed.

"Oh no. We are members of The Haven," Cassie offered.

"The Haven?" Maggie queried.

"Yes. It's a spiritual retreat."

"Spiritual retreat? Sounds interesting. I've read some of Deepak Chopra's stuff, but I never really got into it, if you know what I mean."

"Yes, learning and understanding a different philosophy can be challenging. Deepak is very good about explaining it in Western terms. We've been taught several of his ideals. Liam, our Master, is very fond of his writings, as well as . . ." She was about to continue with a list of philosophers when Maggie interrupted her.

"Liam? Master?" Maggie leaned closer to Cassie.

"Liam is the Master teacher at The Haven. He started it

several years ago. He's helped many people get another chance at life."

"Wow. That sounds pretty heavy." Maggie relaxed her stance, hoping to get more information.

"Yeah. I was in a bad way when I heard Liam speaking at a park outside of Kendall. He made me feel like my life was important."

"Seriously?" Maggie sounded casual enough to solicit an affirmative answer.

"For sure. I had lost my job and was sleeping on the couch at my brother and sister-in-law's tiny apartment. I felt like I had no purpose, but now I am happy to get up every day," Cassie said wistfully, as if she were recalling a dream.

"That's beautiful." Maggie looked into Cassie's blank stare.

"Sometimes I feel like I have no path. Ya know what I mean, right?" Maggie continued. "Ever since I flunked out of college, I can't seem to figure out what I want to be when I grow up." She let out a giggle, trying to evoke a connection to this lost young woman.

Cassie smiled. "Follow me." She led Maggie/Melissa to a table covered in books, pamphlets, and flyers. Almost all of them had the kind-looking face of Liam Westlake on the cover. The book jackets resembled those of the motivational speaker Anthony Robbins, except Liam had more of a halo effect on his. Some of the other publications had the symbol of Om.

Maggie pointed to the symbol. "What does this mean?"

Cassie was quick to respond. "It's a universal symbol that represents peace, tranquility, and unity. When we meditate, we say it out loud. 'A-um.' "

"Oh, is that what that is? I always thought it was some kind of humming. Duh." Maggie feigned ignorance.

"Well, it sorta is. I mean, it's to help you vibrate on a certain level."

Maggie gave her a stupefied look. "I'm really ignorant about this kind of stuff. I must confess I only thumbed through those Deepak Chopra books."

"No worries. I was totally ignorant of anything spiritual before I joined The Haven."

"Join?" Maggie pressed, trying hard not to go into reporter overdrive.

"Well, there are different programs you can sign up for." Cassie had memorized the speech quite well. She had repeated it hundreds of times. She went on to explain the study programs, ascending levels, and the Tyros, Pledges, and Luminaries. But of course, there was a fee structure.

Maggie was taking mental notes, then asked, "How does the fee structure work?"

"I'm not the best one to explain those details, but I can introduce you to someone who can."

"Sounds interesting." Maggie wasn't ready to commit. "I have some stuff I need to get, and I'm meeting up with a friend later. Will you or someone be here tomorrow?"

"Fer sure!" Cassie beamed. "Do you have any particular time in mind?"

"Not yet."

"No problem. We are here from nine to four." Cassie handed Maggie a pamphlet with symbols and quotes from some of the greatest minds in spiritual enlightenment. "Read this over when you get a chance. These are some of Liam's favorites."

"Would I get to meet Liam?" Maggie asked.

"Not this week, I'm sorry to say. He's away doing an immersive retreat. But if you decide you want to take some classes, you will get to meet him and hear him speak. He's awesome."

"Thanks, Cassie. I will certainly read this and stop by tomorrow." Maggie held out her hand, but Cassie gave her a big hug instead. For a quick second, Maggie felt the wig shift slightly, and she grabbed the brim of her hat and stepped back. "It was very nice meeting you. Have a great day!"

"Thank you. Namaste," Cassie replied.

Maggie was pleased that she had gotten a smattering of information. Liam was out of town. Cassie was not specific as to his whereabouts, but at least they knew where he wasn't. That was good intel she could share with the others.

Maggie strolled a little farther to check the rest of The Haven's stalls. No sign of Gabby. Maggie was jazzed that she had gleaned a hint of what The Haven was about. Her journalistic sense was telling her she was getting closer.

On her way back to the flower booth, Maggie passed by Alexis carrying her anthuriums. They gave each other a polite nod. Alexis made her way to the vegetable part of The Haven's stalls. She set down her flowers to inspect some of the produce. "Where get you dees strawberries?" she asked in her best Jamaican accent.

"Excuse me?" A young man dressed in the same garb as everyone else approached her.

"Dis? You grow? You buy?" Alexis sounded stern.

"Oh, we grow. We grow on farm." The poor guy was inadvertently imitating her. Alexis almost burst out laughing.

Instead, she pulled out some cash. "You grow. *I* buy." She opened her shopping bag and pointed to the berries, and green beans, "Dis much," and handed him a ten-dollar bill.

"Yes, ma'am."

Alexis gave the stalls a quick scan. No Gabby.

He quickly filled her bag with two baskets of strawberries and a pound of green beans. "Here you go. Thank you very much."

"Thenk yuh," Alexis replied, and walked to the other end of the market. It was almost noon. She texted Maggie and Yoko when she got back in her car:

In car. No sign of GR.

In less than a minute she got a reply from Maggie:
Ditto. Got some intel. Heading back to hotel.
Alexis responded:
OK. C U soon.
And Yoko texted:
C U around 6:00. Don't forget flowers.
Throughout the day, Yoko kept one eye on the five stalls The Haven manned, and the other eye on the cash box. It was an easy-breezy day, minus the humidity. Fortunately, she was used to spending a lot of time in a greenhouse. Besides the obvious clothing and robot-like personnel, the only odd thing she noticed about The Haven's area were the men who appeared to be standing guard. They had been hanging around the perimeter. All day. She would certainly bring that up during their conference call later that evening.

For Gabby, the day ran long. She wasn't used to sitting in one place for six hours, not counting her breaks. The stiff hallway patrol guy who asked her the same question every day, three times a day, was actually her understudy for phone duty. She thought it was a bit humorous. Maybe after covering for her, he wouldn't ask that same stupid question anymore. *Doubtful. He seems like an automaton. Huh. So many of them do,* she said to herself. She really hadn't paid much attention to most of the others. She was on her own vision quest, not an afternoon social. Gabby stretched and rose from her chair. She would be happy to do some yoga. As she was about to walk down the stairs, Noah came out of his office. "You've done a good job today."

Gabby almost tripped on the step. "Thank you. I am happy to do it."

"Glad to hear it. Maxwell isn't feeling well, so you're going to have to cover for him tomorrow as well." Noah sounded much too cheery.

"Yes, of course." Gabby tried to hide her disappointment. It was bad enough she wasn't going to the market, but with Liam's upbeat energy missing, it was like being in a cell. No one spoke to anyone. Liam would always stop and say hello and ask how you were, although lately he had been behind closed doors. And now was away. Gabby's gut was screaming at her that something wasn't quite right.

Chapter Sixteen

Pinewood

The sisters started arriving around five o'clock. They planned to have something to eat before the seven o'clock conference call with Alexis, Maggie, and Yoko. Like with any other arrival, Lady and her pups greeted their guests with yelps and tails wagging, as the sisters hugged one another, patted the dogs' heads, and gave them treats. Myra hugged everyone hello and feigned scolding them. "Too many treats! They're going to get fat!"

"Speaking of eating," Charles interrupted the boisterous gathering. "We should get started if we want to be finished by seven."

Setting the table was like synchronized swimming. Everyone knew her task, and the table was ready in minutes. With a minimum of eight people and several dogs in the kitchen, it was a wonder no one tripped, bumped, or dropped anything. "Kitchen choreography," Charles had once called it. If only the rest of the world acted with such competence, cooperation, and precision.

The women took their seats while Charles and Fergus carried the large bowl of fettuccine carbonara, Caesar salad, and garlic bread to the table.

"Smells divine," Myra exclaimed. They all held hands and said grace.

With Maggie absent, Charles asked, "Who's going to be first?" Everyone looked around the table.

"I guess I'll go," Nikki offered.

"I'm sure Maggie will appreciate your taking the lead," Annie said gleefully. Snickers and giggles followed. "But I can tell you, she is not going to be happy that we're having one of her favorites tonight while she's eating hotel food."

Charles reddened. "I hope she doesn't get her knickers in a twist. I should have remembered."

Myra patted his hand. "I'm sure she'll understand." Then she lowered her head, and whispered, "Unless we don't tell her."

"You know she's going to ask," Annie reminded her.

"I suppose you're right." Myra sighed.

"I'll vow to make it again the next time she's here," Charles promised.

"Whew." Nikki grinned. "I'd say to freeze some of it, but that would be gross."

"No such thing. It has to be fresh or not at all." Charles waved his fork like a symphony conductor's baton.

They passed the bread, chatted, and polished off the two pounds of fettuccine. "Good thing Maggie wasn't here! We'd have run out of food!" Nikki noted gleefully.

"Not in my kitchen," Charles protested. "I would have tossed something together." Everyone giggled, knowing how proud Charles was of his culinary accomplishments.

Myra stroked her pearls. "Shall we?" With that, everyone stood and cleared the table, dishes, pots, and pans. It was similar to the ballet they had performed getting the table ready. Complete and total organization. Just like everything else they did.

With the kitchen spotless in under thirteen minutes, they descended the stone steps to the War Room, each saluting Lady Justice as they passed by. The sisters took their seats while Charles and Fergus powered up the electronics. No matter how many times they convened in the War Room, they still stood in awe of the technology at their fingertips. It was like being on the set of the television show *NCIS*, except this was their own private MTAC.

In addition to the large screens and the audio equipment, a large electronic map covered one wall. With the flick of a finger, they could bring up a map of almost anywhere in the world. It would put Google to shame. Fergus pressed a few buttons on the screen, and Miami-Dade County glowed like a wall mural. A yellow dot designated the location of The Haven.

At exactly seven o'clock, everyone who was available called in on the secure conference-call line.

One by one their images appeared on the various screens. It was as if they were all in the same room.

When the greetings were complete, Nikki began.

"There is some information regarding the relationship of The Haven to the shell corporations. They are funded by Trident Enterprises, a shell company that is connected to several others. But the most interesting thing we've discovered is that Daniel Ruffing is also connected to Trident. To what extent and in what capacity, we haven't been able to ascertain, but the proximity of his other properties to The Haven is something to be suspicious of once you ask yourself why someone like Ruffing, with no noticeable spiritual or philanthropic chops, would want to be affiliated with a spiritual retreat and own property with such a low real-estate value." Nikki paused for any comments.

"That does seem a bit odd," Isabelle came through on the video screen. "I tried to find some back doors to their website but came up with nothin'. Even their website is lame. It's almost as if they haven't entered the twentieth century, let alone the twenty-first."

"Thanks for checking, Isabelle. I know you're on a job," Myra said.

"No problem. I had some free time. The fog was rolling in, and we had to knock off early. Besides, I needed the practice!" Guffaws filled the room. In addition to her talent as an architect, Isabelle was becoming a crackerjack computer hacker.

Nikki continued, "We checked out the names of the original founders, who are listed on their site. I couldn't find any information about the three men. It's as if they never existed.

"Maggie, want to give us a briefing?" Charles asked.

Everyone cringed, expecting the most obvious question.

"Hey, I can still see you guys! What's with the faces? Oh . . . I bet you thought I was going to ask what you had for dinner?" Maggie retorted.

Annie held out her hand, waiting for Fergus to pay up on his five-dollar bet. "You really didn't think you were going to win that one. Haven't you met Maggie?" The room was vibrating from all the cackling going on.

"Hello? I said I can see you! What's so darn funny?" Maggie pouted.

"The old girl bet me that 'what did you have for dinner?' would be the first thing out of your mouth!" Fergus snorted.

"I have a reputation to maintain." Maggie grinned.

"And so you do!" Annie exclaimed.

"Can we please get down to business?" Charles pressed forward.

"Not until you tell me what you had." Maggie cocked her head, waiting for a reply.

"I'm terribly sorry to report that I made fettucine carbonara tonight." Charles ducked his head as if Maggie could swat him. "But I promise I shall revisit that recipe upon your return."

"Everyone? You heard him," Myra jumped in. His fettuccine was one of her favorites, too.

"Can we please get on with this?" Annie pushed. "Maggie, what did you find out?"

Maggie explained her interaction with the young woman at the market. She described the enthusiastic Cassie, the Pledge she had met, and the various books, pamphlets, and flyers on display. Most had Liam's face plastered on the cover. "The market is massive. About a hundred vendors. The Haven has five stalls, each selling a different product. There was no sign of Gabby. The booth I spent the most time in was the one with Cassie. She half explained the course setup. Said someone would be there tomorrow to explain the various tiers, costs, et cetera."

Yoko was next. "They all dress similarly. The only difference is the stole around their necks. Seems like they're color-coded. It reminded me of some kind of cult you would have seen in the seventies. Aside from looking like a throwback to Moonies or Hare Krishna, they looked perfectly banal. However, one thing struck me as quite odd. There were three men hovering around the perimeter of the booths. It was almost as if they were standing guard. They were expressionless. If it weren't for their outfits, you would have thought they were Secret Service agents. They looked like professional security. Earbuds and all."

Myra touched her pearls. "Why would an organization like that need security?"

Nikki chimed in. "And why would they be funded through a shell company that is also tethered to one of the many Ruffing holdings?"

Annie started to write notes on one of the electronic boards. "This is what we know:"

1 SECURITY GUARDS
2 SHELL COMPANY – TRIDENT ENTERPRISES
3 DANIEL RUFFING – TRIDENT ENTERPRISES

"What we don't know is where Gabby Richardson is. Fergus is still trying to sort out the source of her second call. We already know the first was from a florist. The second call also went through our toll-free line, so we need another day to zero in on the origin." Annie looked up at Maggie's monitor. "I hate to say this but . . ."

"I'm already planning on it." Maggie sighed, acknowledging she was going to have to go on a stakeout. "It's the only way we'll get a glimpse of the comings and goings at The Haven."

"Do you think you can get Jimmy to accompany you?" Myra stroked her beads. "I wouldn't want you skulking out deep in the woods alone."

The electronic map on the wall indicated that The Haven was on the far west side of Homestead, butting up against the Everglades. "The only issue could be traffic. If there's too much, then there's a problem. If there's too little, we'll look conspicuous," Maggie mused aloud. "But that hasn't stopped me before! I'll call Jimmy right away. When should we start?"

"Since we have little to go on, I suggest you start tomorrow morning. Early," Annie said.

Maggie groaned. "I'll bring plenty of bagels. Oh wait. Do they have bagels in Miami?"

Giggles filled the room. "You're near the University of Miami. A third of the student body is from the New York metropolitan area. I'm sure there's a law," Annie added.

Charles turned to the screen displaying Alexis. "Anything you noticed, gleaned, surmised?"

"Everything was cash-only. No credit or debit cards. They

were cordial. Almost zombie-like. I wore my Jamaican disguise just in case I needed to go back."

"Excellent," Charles added. "Sit tight until we get some intel from Maggie. Maggie, you okay with this?"

"Yep! I'll be there at the crack of dawn."

"Does anyone else have something to add for now?" Myra asked.

Shrugs and "nopes" went around the room.

"Okay, all. Keep in touch and be safe!"

Before they logged off, all the women, whether they were in the room or phoning in, saluted Lady Justice.

It was literally the crack of dawn when Maggie and Jimmy meandered their way to the back roads of Miami-Dade County.

Maggie had a bag of bagels on her lap. A cooler filled with water and sandwiches sat behind her seat. She knew she was going to have to use Mother Nature's bathroom at some point and had brought a roll of toilet paper. Her biggest concern were bugs and snakes, not necessarily in that order. They went past the entrance, turned around, and pulled onto the side of the road several yards before the entrance to The Haven.

Jimmy had borrowed a beat-up truck similar to one that a gardener would drive, including a wheelbarrow and some rakes in the flatbed. The rig was much less obvious in that area than a clean, polished SUV would be, which was confirmed when he saw one pull up to the front gate. "What the, what the . . . ?" He elbowed Maggie and jotted down the number on the license plate as it was going through the gate. The SUV was a black Escalade with tinted windows.

Maggie looked at her watch. It was barely five thirty in the morning. Maggie opened her door. "Where are you going?" Jimmy hissed.

"I want to see who is coming and going in that vehicle."

"Okay. Be careful. I do not want to incur the wrath of Annie if anything happens to you."

Maggie jumped from the cab and slipped her burner phone into the front pocket of her chinos. If anything did happen to her, Charles would be able to get the coordinates off her phone and send help. But she didn't think that would happen. It was a spiritual retreat, after all. Okay, maybe more a cult. But they all seemed rather harmless. Harmless except for the disturbing phone calls she had received from Gabby. But Maggie was optimistic that Fergus would sort it out sooner rather than later.

Between the insect repellant and the sunscreen, Maggie was a slimy mess. "If anyone catches me, I'll just slither out of their hands!" She gave Jimmy a wink and dashed across the road. She made her way along the perimeter of the chain-link fence, using the foliage to conceal her from view. She listened for the vehicle and followed the sound, which led her to a building. It appeared to be a garage. She could hear voices in the distance. All she could make out was a woman with a sultry voice speaking to a man in Spanish. "*Diecinueve camino de la luna amarilla.*" She couldn't hear anything else they said. She peeked through the huge ferns and saw an impeccably dressed, tall, honey-toned woman with straight jet-black hair. She could almost double for Alexis. There was another woman with her. Maggie guessed her to be in her early twenties. She, too, was perfectly dressed and had a stylish ginger bob haircut. *Wow. They surely don't look like any of the people I saw yesterday.* She sent a text to Jimmy, describing the women and the only words she heard, "*Diecinueve camino de la luna amarilla.*" She had silenced her phone and turned off the vibration feature.

Just as she was shoving her phone in her pocket, she heard the snap of a branch behind her. Before she could steady herself, she felt the cold barrel of a rifle on her back. She immediately put her hands in the air.

"What are you doing here?" a deep voice demanded.

Maggie didn't make a move. "I, I was looking for my dog."

"Here?" The voice sounded impatient.

"Yes. I stopped down the road for him to go, you know, pee-pee, and he broke from the leash. I've been looking for him for over an hour." Maggie sounded convincing. "May I please turn around?"

"No. Walk forward along the fence." He gave her a nudge.

She tripped on a root of a banyan tree and fumbled with her phone. She was able to hit the DUMP button before it hit the ground. She decided to leave it there under the leaves. All things considered, she decided that it was better if they didn't confiscate it. It would seem very odd for someone to be walking around with something other than a Samsung or an iPhone, which could raise serious suspicions. At least Charles or Fergus would know her latest location if she couldn't get out of this situation. Whatever kind of situation it was.

The man grabbed her arm and yanked her up, not noticing the "breadcrumb" she had left behind. "Move it." He gave her another shove.

"I'm just looking for my dog," Maggie pleaded.

"Yeah. Whatever. Keep moving."

Maggie walked slowly ahead of the armed man. She didn't want to cause any more trouble and kept her mouth shut.

As they approached the entrance to The Haven, she heard the sound of an airboat nearby. She glanced at her watch and made a mental note. She knew Jimmy would be worried, but there was absolutely nothing she could do about it. Jimmy would know to call Annie and inform them of her disappearance if she was gone too long.

As they entered the property, Maggie saw the tall, honey-toned woman get back into the SUV. She was alone. Another mental note. *What happened to the other woman?*

The man with the gun spoke again, but not to Maggie. "I have an uninvited guest in the driveway." She couldn't hear a response. He was probably wearing a headset. Maggie recalled that Alexis had said there were men in strange clothes who looked like Secret Service agents. "Says she's looking for her lost dog." Another few seconds went by. "Roger that."

Within minutes, a young man in a white outfit came out of the main building. "Follow me." Maggie obliged. He led her up a flight of stairs and into a small room that had only a long table and two chairs. It looked just like the interrogation rooms you see in movies.

"Wait here."

As if I have a choice, Maggie thought glumly. She took a seat and heard the door lock behind her. *This is too weird.*

Jimmy checked his watch. Maggie had been gone for over an hour. He had responded to her first text but heard nothing back since. He debated whether or not he should call Annie. *Give her a little more time.*

Chapter Seventeen

Simone had helped Rachel get ready very early that morning. She picked her outfit and labeled the others for different occasions. Not that Rachel wasn't bright enough to figure it out, but Simone found it a useful tool for newly indoctrinated "spokespersons." After all, most of them came from seedy backgrounds. They wouldn't know the difference between a clutch and a satchel, or a Valentino and a Versace. Whenever Simone thought of Gianni Versace, she wanted to cry. They had become social acquaintances when she had first arrived in Miami Beach. After all these years, people were still reeling from the senseless murder of the famous and generous designer. As the SUV pulled out of the driveway, Simone pushed the power button to roll down her window. She needed some real air. Not recycled, interior car air. She noticed a sorry-looking pickup truck parked across the road a few yards from the gate and shook her head. She muttered to herself, "What a shame. I'd bet he can barely feed his family." She knew all too well the struggle to become an educated person of color. Especially one from a different country. Occasionally, she regretted getting involved with the people she now worked for, but doing so had been too tempting to ignore. When it came time to choose what to do with her life, she had had the choice of becoming a teacher at an urban high school or the private concierge to one of the richest men in the world. So . . .

Rachel was a little confused when Simone had awakened her at such a very early hour, but she was ready for this next big step in her life. Simone had helped her get ready and pack her bags, giving Rachel a list of what accessories went with each outfit. She told Rachel they would first go to The Haven, where she would meet up with her transportation.

It all seemed on the up-and-up, and Rachel was over the moon with her makeover. It instilled a confidence she had never felt before. She guessed the phrase "dress for success" had been invented for a reason. Yes, Rachel felt that she was about to spread her wings and be the best spokesperson The Haven had ever had. She promised herself that she would make Liam proud.

When they arrived at The Haven, Rachel realized that no one would be up at that ungodly hour. Only maintenance workers would be moving around at five thirty in the morning. Meditations started at seven, which is when almost everyone was in the middle of the compound. She was disappointed, knowing that no one would see her in her new garb, hair, and makeup. Not even Liam. Then she brightened. *I'm sure he'll be at some of these fundraisers. He has to be! He is the Master!*

Before Simone left, she handed Rachel a light poncho, sunglasses, and a hat. "Here, put these on."

Rachel thought it was a bit odd since it wasn't raining, but she complied. One of the Guardians escorted Rachel to the path that led to the farthest point of the property. She was starting to get nervous. *Why were they walking toward the*

Everglades? As soon as they passed a large banyan tree she spotted the airboat. She didn't ask any questions. She had been taught not to.

The Guardian helped her onto the boat and put her suitcases between the aircraft-type propeller and the last row of seats.

He helped her buckle herself into a seat in the second row. The boat was equipped to carry at least six passengers. Today, it was just Rachel and the boat driver. The roar of the engine startled her, and she instantly clutched the armrest. It was a wild ride, something Rachel had never experienced before. Not even at an amusement park.

They skirted the cypress swamps and the mangroves as they skimmed over the water. It was spectacular to see. But why would The Haven have her travel like this? At least part of the mystery was solved. Sort of. She had spotted the airboat in the garage and wondered why it was there. Now she had a partial clue. They actually used it. The reason why they used this unconventional mode of transportation was the rest of the mystery.

Rachel tried to guesstimate how long they had been gliding over the River of Grass, a name used to refer to the Everglades, sixty miles by one hundred miles of moving water. It was certainly a day of many firsts for Rachel.

When the boat began to slow down, Rachel could swear that she saw a helicopter sitting in the marshes. She blinked several times until she was convinced it wasn't a mirage. The boat driver gently glided the front of the boat onto a helipad. Rachel blinked again. This was the second time she had had to pinch herself in the past several days. The whirring of the helicopter blades echoed the sound of the airboat, only it was much louder. A man wearing headphones greeted them and indicated for the driver to put Rachel's bags in the compartment. He gestured for Rachel to climb in, which she did, but she stopped suddenly when she saw how luxurious the aircraft was. She glanced around quickly and boarded. She didn't know where to sit until another man showed her to one of the deep leather seats. It was then that she noticed the logo for Hermès. That raised another question: *Why would The Haven use a helicopter? And why one this plush?*

Chapter Eighteen

Myra was jolted awake from a deep sleep. The scent of Miss Dior filled the room. She elbowed Charles. "Do you smell that?"

"What love?" Charles was only half-conscious.

"Barbara's perfume." Myra scooted out of bed and took in several big inhales. "Something is wrong."

"What on earth are you talking about?" Charles was shaking himself awake.

"Can't you smell it?" Myra asked again, but this time, she was more insistent.

"I do. But where do you suppose it's coming from?" Charles was perplexed.

"It's a sign." Myra clutched her pearls. "I need to call Annie."

Jimmy ducked when the Escalade passed by. The rear window was down in the Escalade and Jimmy caught a glimpse of the passenger in the rearview mirror. He recognized her as a socialite connected to Daniel Ruffing. *What is she doing at The Haven?* He checked his watch. Maggie had been MIA for almost two hours. It was time to call Annie.

"Jimmy Griffin, I hope you have some interesting news for me," Annie chided him.

"Well, yes and no. Maggie's gone missing."

"What do you mean she's gone missing?" Annie gasped. She checked her watch. It was only eight o'clock in the morning.

"We were on the stakeout down the road from The Haven. A black Escalade entered the place around five thirty. Maggie wanted to get a look at who it was and was skirting the perimeter. She sent me a text, but when I replied, she didn't respond. I haven't heard anything since." Jimmy was trying to keep his voice calm.

"What was in her text?" Annie asked calmly, trying to quell her concern.

"The only thing Maggie could hear were the words: '*Diecinueve camino de la luna amarilla.*' I have no idea what that means." Jimmy shook his head. "I shouldn't have let her leave the car."

"As if you could have stopped her," Annie said with resignation. "I'll have Fergus get the location of her phone. Hang tight."

"There is one other thing I discovered."

"I hope it's something we can use." Annie's voice was even.

"There was a woman in the Escalade. Her name is Simone Jordan. She works for Daniel Ruffing. I thought her being here so early in the morning was very strange."

"We knew there was some kind of relationship between Ruffing and The Haven but didn't know the extent." Annie was fumbling and rushing to get dressed. "There is a shell company that has been funding The Haven. Ruffing is connected to the shell company. We just can't figure out why he would be involved with a spiritual enlightenment group," Annie explained further.

"Ruffing is an extremely powerful dude. Not well liked, but people manage to overlook assholes when they're loaded." Jimmy knew about the billionaire's reputation for lavish, over-the-top spending. The *Herald* covered all of Ruffing's extravagant events. But only those they were invited to attend.

Annie had to chuckle at his remark. To be sure, Ruffing was a certified billionaire, but even so, there was no comparison between his wealth and hers. One thing she did know however: she, at least, was not an ass. "For now, stay where you are just in case Maggie returns. Meanwhile, we'll try to locate her phone.

"Roger that." Jimmy wasn't comfortable sitting around, but he knew it was the only option.

Annie's phone rang again. This time it was Myra.

"Annie. I had another message from Barbara. Her perfume filled my bedroom. Charles smelled it, too. Something's wrong. I'm worried."

Annie held the phone away from her face and gave it a dubious look. She, too, had encountered what some would call "paranormal experiences," especially telepathy between herself and Myra. She also knew that Myra had "visitations" from Barbara, usually in a dream.

"You are spot-on, my friend. I just got a call from Jimmy. Maggie's gone missing."

"Oh dear Lord!" Myra clutched her pearls. "What happened?"

Annie recounted what Jimmy had said to her a few minutes before. "Fergus is working on locating her phone, but we need the wall map."

"Okay." Myra knew that was the first step in finding Maggie.

"We'll head over to you and Charles in a few minutes."

Annie pulled her shoes on and went to fetch Fergus. They climbed into the golf cart, which was their usual means of transportation between the two houses. Annie put the pedal to the metal, causing Fergus to hang on for dear life. "Bloody hell, woman! This isn't the Indianapolis 500!" While most carts traveled at a speed of fifteen to twenty miles per hour, Annie's was custom built to get up to fifty. Annie ignored his comment and drove as fast as she could.

The cart swung around to the back of the farmhouse, kicking up stones and dust. Fergus staggered out of the cart and almost keeled over.

"I think you broke your own record." Annie didn't answer and dashed into the kitchen, leaving Fergus to fend for himself, where Myra and Charles were waiting.

When Fergus staggered in, all four stomped their way down the steps to the War Room, instinctively saluting Lady Justice.

Charles fired up the wall map while Fergus logged into their private GPS system. Within a minute, a small dot flashed on the screen. Charles increased the size of the map so they could get a closer look. "It appears that her phone is just outside the perimeter of the property. She either dropped it by accident or on purpose. Obviously, we can't be sure which."

"Maggie knows to ditch the burner if she gets caught." Annie tried to keep the fear out of her voice.

"You don't think she tried to trespass?" Myra was almost yanking at her pearls.

"It's not like Maggie to put herself in jeopardy. According to Jimmy, she was only going to see who was getting in and out of the Escalade."

"Where is Jimmy now?" Myra asked.

"I told him to sit tight until he either heard back from us or Maggie." Annie was still keeping her cool, but everyone in the room was feeling anxious.

Charles took the lead. "I'll let Jimmy know we tracked the phone but not her. Maybe he's spotted something we can work with."

"The woman in the car who works for Ruffing should give us some kind of lead, no?" Myra asked.

"Most definitely." Charles nodded in agreement as he dialed Jimmy's phone and put it on speaker.

"James, it's Charles. We located Maggie's phone. It's sitting just outside the perimeter of The Haven. She obviously dropped it because she hit the DUMP button." Their phones were equipped with a button that would erase all calls but still allow for the phone to be tracked by Charles and Fergus.

"I warned her to be careful. I could strangle her." Jimmy was exasperated. He rarely felt helpless, and this was one of those rare occasions.

"James, I want you to stay where you are. Do you have the means to look into that woman you spotted?" Charles added.

"Yes, I have a tablet with me. Her name is Simone Jordan. She's often seen at Daniel Ruffing's fundraising events. She does some kind of concierge work for him. I'll send you a photo from our archives. It'll just take a few minutes."

Fergus typed the name *Simone Jordan* into one of his Internet search engines. But this wasn't your typical Google, Bing, or Firefox. This accessed a deep website that only the highest level of international criminal investigators could connect to. It was a little going-away present Fergus had given himself when he left Scotland Yard.

Maggie sat in the sterile room, waiting for something to happen. It had been almost two hours. She was glad she had stuffed a bagel in her pocket. When the security guard patted her down, that was all he could find on her, and he let her keep it. She was relieved that she had ditched the phone after hitting the DUMP button. The information on the phone could be extremely revealing if anyone outside their group got their hands on it. If they found the phone now, it would have no data on it. If nothing else, the sisters would know approximately where she was. Darned if *she* knew her whereabouts. The room was very uninviting and odd for a retreat. A few minutes after ruminating as to how she would be rescued or escape, the door swung open with a bang. She almost flew out of her seat.

"Who are you, and why were you snooping around?" Noah's voice was menacing.

"My name is Melissa Logan. As I tried to explain to the gentleman who escorted me here, after some creepy guy threatened me at gunpoint while I was standing on public land, I was looking for my dog." Maggie sounded very convincing. She figured that any ordinary citizen would be outraged at the treatment she had received and played up her annoyance. "He was getting restless in the car. I figured he wanted to go to the bathroom, so I pulled over, and he broke from his leash."

"Oh really?" Noah wasn't buying it. "Where's your car?"

"About a mile down the road." She was still confident she could convince him. "I was running after him when he took off into the woods." There. Done. She looked up at him.

Noah peered deep into her eyes. She didn't blink. "We haven't seen or heard any dogs around here." Noah wasn't sure he was buying the story. "And where is your phone?"

Maggie pretended to check her pockets. "I . . . I must have lost it when I was in the woods."

"You seem to lose a lot of things," Noah said sharply.

"Mr. . . . ?" she asked, waiting for a response but not expecting one. She was pretty sure she was dealing with Noah Westlake.

"Never mind who I am."

"Okay. But can you please let me go? My dog has been missing for a couple of hours." She bit the inside of her lip, hoping to draw some tears.

"Fine. We'll have someone escort you off the property. But if we see you snooping around again, you'll have to answer to a higher authority." Noah wasn't referring to a deity or the police. He knew it would be one of Ruffing's thugs. "Follow me."

Noah looked down the hall and saw Gabby organizing the desk for her phone duty. He did not want anyone to know about this odd encounter. He stood with his back to Gabby and led Maggie in the opposite direction, to the back stairs. Neither woman could see the other. Maggie heard the phone ringing in the distance. She strained to listen. "Good morning, how may I direct your call." Then she froze.

"Is there a problem?" Noah barked at her.

"Uh, no. I just thought of something. My dog has a microchip. Maybe I can find him that way." She resisted the urge to turn around to see whose voice it was that she had heard. But she didn't have to. She knew it was Gabby's.

Once they reached the ground floor, a guard walked her to the front entrance and waited for her to walk until she was out of sight. That meant going in the opposite direction from Jimmy in the truck. She shook her head, indicating that he should not come after her yet. Let her keep walking. There was a bend in the road about a half mile from the entrance. Once she got past that point, she could move into the bushes until Jimmy could drive around. He waited a few minutes, then started the rattletrap and moved slowly down the road. Once he made the bend, he saw Maggie's neckerchief on a bush and pulled over.

"Thank God! What the hell happened? Are you all right?" Jimmy was vacillating between anger and relief.

"Drive!" Maggie bellowed. She sat back and took a few deep breaths. "I know where Gabby is."

"Where? Is she okay?" Jimmy was trying to focus on the road and on Maggie's words.

"She seemed okay. Give me your phone, please."

"Well? What did she say?" Jimmy was getting increasingly irritated. Maggie wasn't talking fast enough for him.

"Nothing. At least not to me."

"You are going to have to be a little clearer. Explain."

"Let me call in so I don't have to repeat myself." She dialed Annie's number.

"Jimmy Griffin, you better have some good news for me!"

"Annie, it's Maggie. I'm okay. I found Gabby."

"Is she with you?" Annie asked.

"No. She didn't see me."

"If you found her, then why isn't she with you? And what do you mean she didn't see you?" Annie was holding on to her patience as best she could. She put her phone on speaker so Myra, Charles, and Fergus could hear.

"There was an Escalade that entered the property. I saw two women get out, both very well dressed, then I was caught staking out the perimeter by one of the guards. Even though I was on public land, on this side of the fence, he put a gun in my back and forced me to enter The Haven. I ditched the phone after dumping its contents. But while I was being escorted up the driveway, I saw only one of the women, the older one, get back into the SUV."

"Yes, we know about the phone," Myra chimed in. "Fergus was able to get its location."

Maggie continued. "The guard turned me over to another dude, who took me to the main house and up to a space on the second floor that was as austere as a police interrogation room. Very odd." Maggie took a deep breath before she went on. "They had me in there for about two hours. And then a guy came in to actually interrogate me. He didn't give me his name, but I'm pretty sure it was Noah Westlake."

"What did you tell him?" Myra asked as she was stroking her pearls.

"I told him that I was looking for my dog and acted really pissed at the way I was being treated. I figured that any solid citizen would be. I gave a good enough performance that he let me go."

"Thank goodness for that. But how does Gabby fit into this?" Annie asked.

"When the guy led me out of the room, I heard a voice at the far end of the hallway answer the phone. It was Gabby's voice."

"I'm still not quite clear about what you're saying," Annie nudged her.

"The guy was standing between me and the person answering the phone. He was blocking my view and hers. He led me in the opposite direction to a back set of stairs. But I know the voice that answered the phone was Gabby's." Jimmy handed Maggie a bottle of water from the cooler.

"So she didn't know that you were there," Charles surmised.

"Correct," Maggie answered. "We have to get her out of there."

"Yes, but we need to get to the bottom of all of this. Gabby was right when she left you that 'strange happenings' message," Charles added.

"Gabby could probably simply walk out of there. She must have a reason for sticking around," Annie commented.

"I'm not so sure about that, Annie. Remember this all started when she was prevented from flying home to see her mother in the hospital. I think we should call a meeting for tonight and see how many pieces of the puzzle we've managed to assemble," Charles suggested.

"Good idea," Myra agreed. "I'll get everyone who's available to phone in or show up by seven. Does that work for you, Maggie?"

"Right now, a gallon of espresso would work for me." Maggie was starting to come down from the adrenaline. She felt around for the bag of bagels and gave Jimmy the stink-eye. "You ate *all* the bagels?" Laughter came through the phone lines. Everyone was relieved that Maggie was safe and back to normal.

Chapter Nineteen

Rachel watched out the window of the luxury chopper. The color of the water below was changing by the minute. It went from deep blue to turquoise as they skirted the Florida Keys to the east.

It was a spectacular view from where she sat. They had been in flight for just over an hour, barely skimming the water. She still had no idea where she was headed and didn't dare ask. She spotted an island ahead as the helicopter moved even closer to the ground. She feared they were going to crash. Within minutes, the aircraft was on the ground. But where?

The pilot cut the engine. Rachel sat frozen in her seat until a young woman climbed in and introduced herself.

"Hello, Rachel. I'm Yvonne. Please follow me." Yvonne instructed the pilot to bring Rachel's luggage to an awaiting Jeep.

"I'm very excited to be here," Rachel squeaked. She still wasn't sure what to say or to whom.

"We're happy to have you. Here, climb in." Yvonne gestured for the man wearing camouflage and brandishing an AK-47 to assist Rachel. Another man dressed similarly hoisted Rachel's bags into the back. Rachel tried not to act concerned. *Why on earth am I being greeted by men who looked like they're part of a militia group?* Even more reason not to ask questions.

From the surroundings, it appeared that they were near a beach resort, with a private road that led from the helipad. As they approached the elaborate property, Rachel could see several scantily dressed women on a veranda. There were also two men wearing traditional Middle Eastern clothing, smoking cigars, and laughing.

Her thoughts were running amok until the Jeep stopped at the foot of the terraces surrounding the elaborate swimming pool.

"Welcome home," Yvonne said easily.

"Excuse me?" By now Rachel thought this must be one big misunderstanding.

"*Diecinueve camino de la luna amarilla.* This is where you will be living from now on."

"There must be some kind of mistake. I'm supposed to be a spokesperson for The Haven," Rachel said halfheartedly.

"Of course you are," Yvonne humored her. "Let's just say you will be entertaining guests."

"I don't understand." Rachel was more confused than ever.

"You will shortly. Follow me." Yvonne escorted Rachel to the main house. It reminded her of Vizcaya, former villa of industrialist James Deering, which had been built on Biscayne Bay in 1916. Vizcaya was now a historical landmark on ten acres of beautifully landscaped gardens. Thirty-two rooms had been restored to their original splendor and were open to the public. Rachel remembered the few times she had brown-bagged her lunch and sat among the fountains and sculpture. It was a spectacular architectural achievement. She would fantasize what it would be like to live amidst such splendor. Was her dream coming true? Only if one's dreams were nightmares.

As they walked through the main hall, Rachel was awestruck by its size and opulence. They climbed the grand staircase that led to two separate wings.

"You and Diedre will be sharing a room." Yvonne opened the door to the large bedroom that included two queen-size beds. Yvonne pointed. "The bathroom is for both of you." Then she swung open the door to a large closet. "You can keep your things here."

Rachel was struck by the size. It was bigger than her entire bedroom when she shared an apartment before she joined The Haven.

"Dinner guests will be arriving in a few hours. I suggest you freshen up." Yvonne opened Rachel's luggage and began to put the items on the hangers and shelves. She spotted a metallic Dolce & Gabbana dress. "Wear this tonight. The sheikh likes to see the ladies shimmer."

Rachel was speechless. *Sheikh?* She finally got up her nerve to ask a question. "Was he one of the men on the patio?"

"No. Those are members of his entourage. The sheikh is on a day-trip with his host."

"Liam?" Rachel couldn't think who else the host could be. Yvonne let out a low laugh. "No, dear. Not Liam."

"But you said 'host,' and since I'm a spokesperson for The Haven, I naturally assumed it would be him. Or Noah."

"The Haven. Right." Then Yvonne explained carefully, "You are here to be a hostess. You will live a very comfortable life and will do whatever is asked of you." Yvonne was about to exit. "Now be a good girl and freshen up. Especially down there." Yvonne pointed to Rachel's lower abdomen. "They like it very clean, so if you didn't get waxed before you came, we'll send someone up."

Rachel was dumbfounded. "Waxed?"

Yvonne almost pitied the girl. "Yes, dear. Waxed. By the expression on your face, I am going to assume not." Yvonne turned toward the bathroom and fetched a robe. "Take a shower and put this on. Sonya will be up in half an hour to take care of those curly hairs." She turned and left.

Rachel sat on the bed. A sense of doom fell over her. She began to sob and rock back and forth.

Chapter Twenty

The War Room

By seven o'clock, everyone was in place, either in person or on video feed. Annie started. "Maggie was held prisoner for a couple of hours at The Haven this morning." Gasps came from everywhere. "Apparently she took it upon herself to leave her stakeout position with Jimmy and sneak around the perimeter of the property, which is where she was caught by security. Maggie, do you want to take it from there?"

"Sure thing. As Annie said, I strayed from the truck where Jimmy and I were parked, but for good reason. It was five thirty in the morning, and a black Escalade pulled into the driveway. I wanted to see who would be showing up at that early hour. I saw two women get out of the Escalade but only one get back in. Jimmy told me after we reconnected that the older woman was a Simone Jordan, who works for Daniel Ruffing. He saw her as the SUV came out of the driveway because she had lowered the rear window on the side closer to him.

"Unfortunately, even though I was on public land, I was

threatened with a gun and forced to spend about two hours in a barren room. A man I think was Noah Westlake finally came in to talk to me, and I gave him the excuse that I was looking for my dog. I guess he bought it because he let me go. As he was escorting me down the hallway, I heard a voice in the background answering the phone. I swear it was Gabby's voice. She was about twenty-five feet away, and the man was standing between us, so I couldn't get a good look at her. But I recognized her voice."

"Do you think she spotted you?" Myra asked.

"I don't think so. If she did, she didn't say anything. We have to get in there and get her out."

"Hold up on that for a minute. Although they did stop her from flying home to see her mother, it doesn't appear that any of them are being held against their will. After all, despite security, anyone who wanted to leave could simply walk away from the farmers' market. So why do you think she hasn't simply made a run for it?" Charles asked.

"Good question," Maggie replied. "But if you remember, in her last message she said, 'strange happenings.' Maybe she put her reporter hat back on and is trying to get more information."

There were mutters of agreement. "That could be true," Annie concurred. "But why hasn't she reached out since?"

"Perhaps she hasn't been able to," Myra suggested. "Also, consider this. People might be able to walk away from the farmers' market, given how public it is. But Gabby wasn't at the farmers' market, and it is possible she could not simply walk away from The Haven where she is."

"Then we need to send someone in," Nikki said. "And it certainly can't be Maggie."

"Which leaves Yoko and Alexis," Charles pointed out.

"I would suggest Yoko because she can use her martial-arts skills if necessary. Anyway, I have an idea percolating for Alexis." Myra gave Charles a quizzical look as he pulled up a photo of Simone Jordan. Charles continued, "Their height, weight, and shapes are similar. Simone works for Ruffing. Jimmy saw Simone leave The Haven. There is a direct connection between Ruffing and The Haven, but we don't know the what or the why. Now we learn that there is a direct connection between Jordan and The Haven, and we already knew that there was a similar connection between Jordan and Ruffing. Alexis could be a good decoy."

"It appears we have several puzzles." Annie started to make a new list on the wall:

1 GABBY IS STILL AT THE HAVEN. WHY?
2 WHY IS RUFFING INVOLVED WITH THE HAVEN?
3 WHY IS JORDAN INVOLVED WITH THE HAVEN?
4 WHO WAS THE OTHER WOMAN IN THE CAR?
5 WHERE DID SHE GO?

Fergus had information he began to share. "We received more information about Trident Enterprises. In addition to bankrolling The Haven, they also own a dry cleaner, a car wash, and a Laundromat."

Nikki went further. "We checked on the alleged founders of The Haven: Devin Marlow, Christopher Giamelli, and Isaac Greenstein. None of them exist. Or *ever* existed."

Fergus confirmed it as well. "Nothing from Interpol or Scotland Yard, either."

"So the founder story is a cover as well," Charles stated.

"Let's add this information to the list." Annie began to write.

1. GABBY IS STILL AT THE HAVEN. WHY?
2. WHY IS RUFFING INVOLVED WITH THE HAVEN?
3. WHO WAS THE OTHER WOMAN IN THE CAR?
   WHERE DID SHE GO?
4. WHY IS JORDAN INVOLVED WITH THE HAVEN?
5. TRIDENT ENTERPRISES—BANKROLLS THE HAVEN, OWNS CASH BUSINESSES.
6. FOUNDERS ARE FAKE.
7. WHAT DOES DIECINUEVE CAMINO DE LA LUNA AMARILLA REPRESENT?

Nikki projected her notes onto the big screen and reviewed them. "According to statistics, Florida is the third largest state in human trafficking. Drugs and gun smuggling is also a serious problem. After a number of hurricanes and tropical storms, the Flamingo area of the Everglades lost most of its navigation aids."

"Therefore, the site where The Haven is located could very well be a portal for both drug and human trafficking." Charles pointed to the area Nikki was referring to.

Silence fell over the room. "Money laundering would also be part of this grand scheme."

"So how do we prove it?" Myra asked casually.

Annie jumped in. "Yoko, when you were at the market, you said you saw men who looked like security guards. That would fit well if they are doing something illegal."

"Indeed," Charles observed.

"We have to get in there," Myra said.

"Okay. I'll go there tomorrow. I'll take the flyer they gave to Maggie. It says they have an open house every Monday evening. I'll tell them I saw them at the market and wanted to know more. Maybe I'll be able to connect with Gabby, and we can get answers to some of these questions."

"Be very careful," Maggie warned. "That guy who grilled me is probably on high alert."

"Gotcha," Yoko replied.

"For now, Nikki, Charles, and Fergus, see what other shell companies are tied to Trident. We need to follow the money, but first we need to find it."

"I'll work with Jimmy tomorrow and see what else we can unearth. Check a little deeper on Simone Jordan."

"I'll also look into what or where *Diecinueve camino de la luna amarilla* is," Fergus offered.

"All in?" Myra asked.

"Whatever it takes!" came the battle cry, with fist pumps and high fives.

Chapter Twenty·one

Diecinueve camino de la luna amarilla

The bikini wax was excruciating. Rachel worked her way through her thoughts over the past several days. This day in particular. She may not have had an education, but she had enough experience with lowlifes, creeps, and grifters to know something was terribly wrong with the situation in which she found herself. But before she could figure out how to escape, she had to figure out where she was. She was confused about who was in charge of this alarming situation, but she bet it was someone extremely powerful. One normally doesn't have dinner with a sheikh.

Rachel retraced her journey in her head. During the airboat ride, the sun was behind her, so they had been heading west. The helicopter pad had to be somewhere on the fringe of the Everglades because as soon as they were airborne, she could spot the area where the water changed colors. That was where the Gulf of Mexico and the Caribbean met. From there the chopper headed south. It was an hour flight. Geography. Another class where she had paid little attention. But everyone living in South Florida knew how close

Cuba was to the United States. *But why would I be in Cuba?*

Rachel had a lot more thinking to do, but for the moment she needed to find out more about what her real purpose was. "Spokesperson" just didn't seem to fit.

About an hour after Rachel's wax job, the door to her room opened. "Hi, I'm Diedre. You must be my new roomie." The slim twentysomething blonde sat on the bed opposite Rachel.

"Hi, Diedre," Rachel responded dejectedly.

"Hey, perk up, girl. It's not so bad here."

"Where is here?" Rachel asked with pleading eyes.

"Welcome to Cuba!" Diedre pronounced it "koo-bah." She pulled out a pack of cigarettes and offered one to Rachel. "Don't tell anyone. After the dental job, I was told I had to quit smoking, as well as drinking coffee and red wine."

"Wait! Cuba?" Though she had already figured out where she was, Rachel pretended to be in shock. "How in the . . . ?"

"Yes indeedy." Diedre took another inhale of her cigarette.

"I don't understand. What's going on?" Rachel got up and started to pace.

"Honey, welcome to the twisted arcade of some of the world's most powerful and wealthy men."

"But what are we doing here?" Rachel had a sinking feeling that she already knew the answer.

"In the olden days, we used to be called 'concubines' or 'courtesans.' Now we're referred to as 'hostesses.'"

Rachel was wringing her hands. "But this is not what I want. This is not what I signed up for." Rachel was trying not to freak out.

"Easy, girl. There's no way outta here." Diedre reached for a big clamshell and put out her cigarette. Then she flushed the stub and ashes down the toilet. Gesturing to the bowl, she said, "I think Yvonne knows, but she's never said anything."

Rachel stared at Diedre. "How can you be so calm about this?"

"You get used to it. You really don't have much of a choice. Even if you escape the property, you'll never get off this island. At least not alive." Diedre checked her makeup in the mirror and put on more lip gloss. "I've been here almost a year."

For a moment, Rachel thought she recognized Diedre. "Were you ever at The Haven?"

"Yeah. A year ago. I was still a Tyro when they offered me this gig. Although they made it sound like something completely different. If you get my drift."

Rachel leaned closer and looked for the opal ring like the one she wore. She did not see one. "Were you a Pledge?"

"No. I was only there for about a week. They told me that I had much more promise and they wanted me to work at recruiting followers and getting donations." Diedre got up and retrieved a can of room deodorizer. "One of the maids and I have a pact. I give her food; she brings me smokes. Some of the other girls have different deals with the help. It's like we're all prisoners here. You learn how to survive without too much pain."

"Others?" Rachel thought she had found her way to hell. She slumped down on the bed.

"Yep. There are seven of us, including you and me. Three others are from The Haven—all of them were Pledges—and the other two were music groupies." Diedre reached over and patted Rachel's hand. "Like I said, you'll get used to it. It's not so bad really. It's not like we're working twenty-four/seven. It's usually just weekends." Diedre continued to fuss with her hair. "Most of the men are high-powered dignitaries. And I mean high, as in leaders of countries or related to leaders of countries."

Rachel was stunned by Diedre's matter-of-fact attitude.

"How do you know all of this? I mean, do they tell you who they are and what they do?"

"Sweetie, you've seen most of their faces in magazines and on the news," Diedre continued. "This is like their little playground hideaway."

Rachel was deflated. "You mean this is how I am going to spend the rest of my life?"

"Who knows how long they'll keep us here." All of a sudden, Diedre's own words sank in. She shuddered, realizing that they might never be allowed to leave. They knew too much. A prickly sensation crawled up the back of her neck.

Rachel noticed the instant change in Diedre's demeanor. "You okay?"

Diedre shook herself back to being nonchalant. "Yeah. Must be the buzz I got off the smokes." Rachel knew right then and there that she had to figure out how to get off the island alive.

Rachel's mind went to the unthinkable. She just didn't let on.

"Okay, girl. Let's put on our costumes and slap on a smile."

Diedre reached down and pulled Rachel off the bed.

They got dressed in silence, each wondering what the other was thinking.

Rachel donned the one-shoulder gold lamé D&G gown Yvonne had picked out, gold sandals, and hoop earrings.

Diedre was equally glamorous in her Versace metallic animal-print cocktail dress.

"Ready to roll?" Diedre asked wryly.

"Do I have a choice?" Rachel replied.

"Now you're getting it."

Diedre gave Rachel a quick lesson in the garb the men would be wearing. She also instructed her to say very little, smile, nod, and touch her guest's arm from time to time, pretending to be interested.

Diedre led the way to the main hall and elaborate stair-case. As they descended, Rachel spotted several men wearing the same type of clothing she had seen earlier. It was a caftan-type robe called a *thawb*, and a turban-like headdress called a kaffiyeh, wrapped with an agal leather band.

Rachel thought she recognized three of the other women. But, like her, they had gone through a metamorphosis from plain and frumpy to gorgeous and glamorous. Two things stood out to her—their teeth and their rings. The Pledge rings. Diedre didn't have one because she had never moved from Tyro to Pledge. Rachel politely introduced herself to the group, and the men simply bowed their heads. Then she rec-ognized a person from all the newspapers and the society pages, Daniel J. Ruffing. *This must be the playground people whispered about.* It hit her like a ton of bricks. *I'm in way over my head.*

The dinner lasted for almost three hours as the men dis-cussed their latest acquisitions, including boats, planes, chateaus, and small islands. One of them implied he had just bought a US senator, which caused a roar of laughter among the powerful men.

As Diedre had instructed, the women barely spoke to the men. They simply pretended to hang on every word, smiling, nodding, tossing their hair, and giggling when one of them made a joke. It was purely theater.

After dinner, drinks were served on the veranda, where the men enjoyed their Cuban cigars and sipped Rémy Martin Louis XIII Cognac costing over four thousand dollars per bottle.

The moment that Rachel was dreading had finally arrived. The women lined up, side by side, each man choosing one. They were escorted to the area behind the grand staircase, where several rooms awaited. The rooms looked like some-thing out of a porn movie from the 1970s, with mirrored ceilings, red shag carpeting, and black satin sheets. Rachel started to tremble. She didn't think she could go through with whatever lay ahead. Earlier, when she was offered wine and cognac, she politely declined, thinking she wanted to keep her wits about her. Now she wished she had drunk more than enough to withstand what was next.

The man guided her to the bed, pushed her down, and proceeded to undress her. He wasn't rough in the beginning, but when she was down to her bra and panties, he tore them off. She was about to cry out when he put his hand over her mouth and shoved himself inside her. He hadn't even taken the time to disrobe. The man grunted and groaned and finished his business in less than three minutes. Rachel was relieved that he was not a man of huge girth. Maybe that's why he needed to come to this place. He could have sex without being concerned about ridicule over his size or lack of endurance.

He rolled over and got tangled in his garb and clumsily fell off the bed. Rachel thought it was almost comical, except for the rape part. He straightened himself, nodded at her, turned, and left.

Now what? Rachel thought to herself. *Would there be another horny man waiting in the wings?* A few minutes later, there was a soft knock on the door. It was Yvonne. "You may go back to your room now." She sounded like a receptionist talking to a client. Or a nurse to a patient. Rachel's mind was in total chaos over what had just happened. She was back to pinching herself; but this time, it wasn't from anticipation about the glorious future she hoped for. Her grand dream had turned into a nightmare.

Chapter Twenty-two

Noah knew he had gotten himself, and his brother, into an extremely unpleasant situation. It wasn't so much what was being said, but it was about what wasn't being said. Lots of conversations between Ruffing and his flunkies, or pals, were in some kind of code. And Ruffing seemed to be getting richer by the day. Ruffing was also busier with offshore deliveries, calling Noah at all hours of the night.

During his latest midnight run to a charter fishing boat, Noah had noticed lights from other nearby boats. Most of them were white, indicating they were anchored, but he thought he saw one flash several times before going out. As he approached the fishing charter, one of the crew tossed a rope to Noah so he could tie up next to it. They would exchange the packages, using a boat hook or a pulley. That night, as one of the coolers was coming off the fishing boat, it hit the side of Noah's cigarette boat and nearly went into the drink. Noah was able to grab it and pull it onto his deck. They signaled each other that the exchange was complete, and Noah untied the rope and headed back to Miami.

When he reached the dock, he noticed a big gash in the cooler. As he inspected the container for damage, he realized that the crack was a split in one of the seams. Hoping none of the contents were waterlogged, he tried to pry it open since he didn't have a key to the lock. He didn't think anything of it. He had been running delivery errands for several years and had never questioned the contents. Until that run, when he saw bags of white powder. Lots of them. He started to sweat, even more than from the Florida heat. Daniel's other cronies would be picking up the coolers shortly. He needed to think. *Try to glue the container back together? Toss it overboard?* He was in a panic.

In the distance, he spotted Rico heading in his direction. Rico was one of Ruffing's top men. Would Rico believe him if he told him the truth? Or would Rico think Noah was trying to steal from Ruffing? The fishing-boat captain could corroborate his story. Noah could also pretend he didn't see anything as he clumsily tried to push the two sides of the cooler together. He decided to go with the truth.

"Rico. Hey." Noah put concern into his voice. "I had a little problem tonight."

"What kind of problem?" Rico's dark black beard encircled his gold-capped teeth.

"While I was exchanging coolers, one from the fishing boat hit the side of my boat, and it cracked." Noah pointed to the cooler without getting too close. "You can see where it dinged the boat."

Rico bent over to take a closer look. He cocked his head and eyed Noah. "I'll take care of it." Rico stood and hoisted the cooler onto a small dolly, keeping the cracked side facing him. He looked at Noah again. "I'll be back for the other two in a few minutes." Rico ambled toward the end of the dock, where he placed the cracked cooler on the deck of another boat. Noah looked away. He was worried that Rico would think Noah was learning too much about Ruffing's business.

Noah stuck to the ritual of tying up the boat and cleaning the deck, acting as if nothing had gone awry. Rico retrieved the other two coolers, saying nothing to Noah. Noah didn't know if that was good or bad. He was hoping for the former.

Noah knew that Ruffing was a wheeler-dealer. Many of his assets and business dealings were public knowledge. Noah was willing to bet this particular venture was not one of them. Drug running and money laundering. Several times in the past, Ruffing had demanded that The Haven provide female entertainment for his buddies, but Noah was never given details. He was under the assumption that once the girls served their purpose, they would return to some other life. Yet, so far, none of the women who were told they would be "spokespersons" had ever returned. At least not to The Haven. Until that night's incident with the cracked cooler, he hadn't given the matter any thought. But now his suspicions skyrocketed after the revelation as to what was in the coolers. Ruffing was clearly involved in drug running and human trafficking. But to what extent?

For the moment, Noah was going to keep his eyes and ears open and his mouth shut. He was regretting ever having gotten involved with Ruffing. For the first time since his father's arrest, Noah was embarrassed and ashamed. How could he have been so easily fooled into thinking everything was aboveboard? He had enough self-awareness to realize that he was a victim of his own making. He had been willing to turn a blind eye, and now he found himself deep in a world populated by unsavory people, criminals, to put it plainly. People who could destroy him and Liam.

Unlike Noah, Liam had no idea about the depth of Ruffing's involvement with The Haven. As long as Noah kept the books balanced, Liam assumed his mission was successful on its own. *Poor bastard,* Noah thought. *But what can we do about it now?* He surely couldn't go to the police. For one thing, he would incriminate himself, and second, he would probably be putting a bull's-eye on his back, and perhaps Liam's as well. Ruffing was too powerful to be taken down; and if he ever was, Noah knew he'd be going down with him.

Liam was on his fifth speaking tour and retreat. This time he was in Tibet. While he enjoyed meeting like-minded people, he felt he should be spending more time at The Haven. Even though the Luminaries were well versed in modern spirituality, Liam knew most of the people were there because of him, because he had empathy, something that had been forbidden and discouraged in his formative years. His mother was cold and emotionally detached. His father little better. It took Liam years to forgive her for making him feel unloved and undeserving. Now he was free from guilt, shame, and fear. He was in a good place mentally and spiritually, but there was still something missing emotionally. Something big. It was love. Romantic love, the kind you share with a partner—someone who knows your essence; someone with whom you can share your deepest secrets. There were a few women over the years who had sparked Liam's interest, but none of them were spiritually enlightened. Watching the latest episode of *The Bachelor* was not his idea of anything worthwhile, which was what most women his age seemed focused on. It was all too superficial for him.

But then he met Gabby. Gabby Richardson, a bright, beautiful woman who was truly on a quest for enlightenment. She was kind and engaging. He could not understand why Noah had come to dislike her. Perhaps it was jealousy, or even fear.

Liam thought about it. He and his brother had done almost everything together since they were born until the time Liam had gone on with his education and then his vision quest and Noah had chosen to go to work for Daniel Ruffing. When Liam returned, he had noticed a change in Noah. Nothing terribly drastic, but Noah had become a bit more cynical. He certainly was adept at making good money, especially in getting the funding for The Haven. Liam could not quite put his finger on it. His thoughts returned to Gabby.

He mulled over the incident at the airport. Why had Noah sent Guardians to bring her back? She could have refused to return. But she hadn't. Liam thought she might quit The Haven after they thwarted her plans to see her mother. But again, she didn't. She could have complained. But she didn't. If his sixth sense was correct, there was a connection. But then again, it could just be his male hormones reminding him that it had been a long time since he had been intimate with a woman. How to broach the subject with Gabby would be challenging. He did not want to be viewed as a predator, seeking out the companionship of a woman who had not indicated any interest. If he could just go for a walk with her. Maybe hold her hand? It was a conundrum he was going to meditate on. He hoped he would find an answer.

When Noah returned to The Haven, there were several messages from Ruffing. His palms began to sweat. What if Rico had said something? He reached for the desk phone and dialed Ruffing's number.

"Hey, dude. Nice property you sent." Ruffing sounded congenial. Noah had to think about what Ruffing was referring to. Then it hit him. Rachel.

"Oh good. Glad it worked out." Noah was waiting for the other shoe to drop.

"Do you think you can send another one for next weekend?" Ruffing asked, knowing full well that it was more of a demand than a request.

"That's not a lot of time." Noah didn't want to piss him off.

"I realize that, but there is a small group of industrialists and politicians visiting, and I'd like to have some entertainment for them. We could use two more."

"I'll see what I can do," Noah replied, his palms even more sweaty than before.

"Attaboy." With that, Ruffing ended the call.

Noah sat in his office, trying to remember to breathe. He flipped through the pages of the binder that contained all the personal information on the members. He had to find someone who had no family connections; someone who wouldn't be missed, at least for a while. Gabby was out of the question. He needed her at The Haven until her trust fund became available. And she had family. The more he thought about the situation, the more he just wanted to disappear.

Chapter Twenty-three

The Haven

Yoko dressed very casually for her visit to the open house at The Haven. She pulled out her road atlas and traced her way through the thick, overgrown roads. When she arrived, a young man dressed in the same outfit she had seen on those at the market greeted her at the gate. "Welcome to The Haven. How can I assist you?" Yoko thought that he was just a teenager.

"Hello. I'm here for the open house." Yoko waved the flyer at him.

"Oh yes. Please park your car over there." He pointed to a small gravel area with signs that said VISITOR PARKING. "Someone will be with you shortly."

"Thank you." Yoko proceeded to the indicated area and parked the car. As soon as she got out, several white-clad people greeted her. "Welcome to The Haven." They nodded but didn't introduce themselves. "Hi, I'm Tina."

"Hello, Tina," they said in unison. Yoko controlled the urge to smirk, thinking that very often the sisters would also respond in unison, but this crew was on a totally different wavelength. Just what this place was all about was what she was there to find out.

"Please follow us." They surrounded her as if they thought she might run away. They led her to an open area of the compound. It was covered with St. Augustine grass, a favorite in Florida because of its heat tolerance. Benches and planters encircled the quarter acre of greenery. Several buildings surrounded the green area. They were all relatively new, prefabricated buildings. Some resembled barracks. Another was a cottage with dream catchers and wind chimes hanging near the door. There was also a large main building and smaller bungalow structures. A five-car garage was near the main house, and on the far end, she could see a large vegetable garden. All in all, it looked like a mini campus of sorts. She took copious mental notes.

Yoko was led to one of the benches. It appeared she was the only one dressed in civilian clothes. There were approximately twenty or so identically clad people in white, some wearing green scarves, others wearing blue. There was one man wearing purple.

A light-sounding bell rang three times. Yoko knew that was usually the signal before a meditation practice would begin. "Good evening," said the purple-and-white-clad man. "Let us begin with a short meditation." Yoko looked around and saw that everyone had placed their hands in what is called a mudra position. The index finger touches the thumb forming a circle. They did it with both hands. It was like making the "Okay" sign with your hands resting on your lap. Yoko followed suit, except for closing her eyes completely. She opened her lids slightly. It was just enough to be able to check out what was going on around her. The bell rang three more times, and everyone chanted "Om." Then there was silence. Yoko kept squinting and rolled her eyes back and forth as best she could. Time seemed to have come to an abrupt halt. *How much longer is this going to last?* she wondered. Finally, the welcome sound of the bell ringing was heard again. And again, and again.

The Luminary, the man with the purple scarf, began his speech about world peace, oneness, wholeness; the spiritual laws of attraction, reflection, and divine oneness. All of it sounded quite profound and enlightening. Yoko was waiting for the catch. And she waited. Almost an hour had passed, and she still hadn't heard a sales pitch. The Luminary finished up with a kind blessing: "May you be happy, may you be safe, may you be filled with peace."

So far, nothing untoward. At least nothing obvious. The bell rang again, one more "Om," and everyone broke into applause and hugged each other. The applause part struck her as a bit strange. Even the hugging to a certain extent although she could certainly relate. The sisters hugged all the time.

The Luminary approached Yoko. "Hello. Nice of you to join us this evening."

"Thank you. It was very inspiring." Yoko smiled, waiting for the sales pitch. Again, nothing.

"Please, take this with you." He handed her what looked like a brochure. It had Liam's photo on the front. "He's the master teacher here. Unfortunately, he is out of town this week. Perhaps you can come back another time?"

Yoko froze. She thought she would get a tour and spot Gabby. "Oh, I thought your words were most enlightening. Can you tell me more? Or am I taking up too much of your time? I would love to see the rest of this peaceful and serene place." Yoko gave him the biggest puppy-dog eyes she could muster.

"I don't usually do that myself," he said nervously. "None of the higher masters are here this evening."

"But I am quite interested, and I may have to leave town at the end of the week." Yoko knew she was pushing it, but she had to do something before she was expected to leave. They were in a tight squeeze because they still hadn't heard back from Gabby, and Gabby hadn't been seen at the market. Nor was she at the open house. Until they could locate her or find more clues, they had to move fast.

"Please? Just a walk around this lovely garden space, and share a little more insight?" Yoko knew she was borderline flirting with the guy, but as the Sisterhood slogan goes, "Whatever it takes!"

Yoko brazenly linked her arm through his. "You didn't tell me your name."

The man cleared his throat. "I'm Becker."

"Hello, Becker. I'm Tina. So tell me. How long have you been here?"

"Almost three years." He was starting to relax. He thought perhaps that if he could recruit someone, he'd gain a lot of points with Noah and maybe put a dent in his debt to the organization.

As they approached the arts and crafts cottage, the door swung open. Two women exited. One walked toward the dining hall, the other walked in their direction. The second one was Gabby. She gave Yoko a strange look. Yoko wasn't sure if Gabby recognized her.

Gabby was stunned to see a familiar face, but she didn't want anyone to know that she knew this visitor. Gabby smiled at Becker. "Will I see you at the market this weekend?" she asked. "They added Friday to the schedule, and it starts at noon."

Becker clumsily disengaged his arm from Yoko's and started to stammer. "Uh, no, I mean, yes. This is Tina. She was here to attend the open house. I . . . I . . . I was showing her the garden. I didn't want her to trip on any of the stones on the path." Becker was overdoing it. Both Yoko and Gabby stifled their giggles. Yoko started to cough.

"Water? Could you get me some, please?" Yoko pleaded with Becker.

"Yes, of course. Please sit. Wait here. Gabby, you stay with her."

That was music to their ears.

"Are you okay?" Yoko asked.

"Yes. But there are odd things happening here. Lots of closed doors, and secrecy is the norm. Technology is conspicuously absent."

Becker was almost running with a cup and a bottle of water.

"Here. Here." He practically shoved the cup into her hand.

"Are you okay?"

"Much better. Thank you. Must be all the tropical plants," Yoko lied. "I suppose I should be going. I've taken up much too much of your time." Yoko was still trying to figure out how to contact Gabby again. "Did you say you would be at the market?"

"I hope to be. I'm working on some decoupage boxes I hope to sell," Gabby replied.

"Me as well," Becker added. He hadn't been that attracted to a woman since . . . he couldn't remember when. *That Tina woman is quite a looker,* he thought. *And I always had a thing for older women.* Then he started to blush.

"Great. I'll see both of you at the market. Thanks again." Yoko tried not to rush to her car. She could hardly wait until she could let everyone know that Gabby was all right.

Yoko sent a group text to everyone:

Found GR. She is OK. Meeting at mrkt Sat. Will call ASAP.

She hit the gas pedal as if she were stomping out a fire, navigating the turns in the road as fast as safety would allow. She wound her way through the town of Homestead and reached the Ronald Reagan Turnpike. If traffic was light, it would take her only another thirty-five minutes to get back to the hotel. When she arrived, Maggie and Alexis were anxiously waiting and bombarded her with questions. "Where is she? How is she? How did you contact her?"

Yoko could barely catch her breath. "She's okay. I ran into her after the open house. A huge stroke of luck. When I first arrived, there was no sign of her. I sat with a small group, meditated, listened to someone named Becker speak. No sign of Liam. Becker was about to lead me to my car when I asked him for a little tour. I have to admit, I used some of my feminine wiles because he was clearly uncomfortable showing me around without the permission of whoever really runs that place."

Maggie's eyes welled up again. "I cannot thank you enough, Yoko."

Alexis hugged both of them. "We should call in."

Maggie punched in Annie's speed dial number. "Hey! We need to schedule a call."

"Yes, we do!" Annie's voice was filled with delight. "Give us an hour."

"Will do." Maggie hung up and flung herself on the bed. "Now I can eat!" She picked up the room service menu and ordered enough food for ten people.

"Are you expecting guests?" Alexis teased.

"Nope. So what are you both going to order?" The women cackled with delight. The Maggie they knew and loved was back.

Chapter Twenty-four

Diecinueve camino de la luna amarilla

When Rachel returned to her room, she stripped off her clothes, including the shredded underwear. She got into the shower and scrubbed her body until it was raw, sobbing uncontrollably the entire time.

Diedre heard Rachel's wails and rushed into the bathroom. She pulled out a soft terry cloth robe and towel, opened the shower door, and wrapped Rachel in them, hugging her tightly. "I know, sweetie, I know." She walked Rachel to her bed and used a hair dryer to help dry her hair. Then she just sat with her, lending what comfort she could.

Once Rachel regained her composure, Diedre spoke to her softly. "Honey, the first time is usually the worst. Things should get better from here on out." She dug the cigarettes out from under her pillow and lit one up. "I don't know if it's the shock at what we're doing that finally sinks in or the fear of what's to come." She took a drag of her cigarette. "But I will tell you this, I've never been assaulted physically, if you don't count the rape part of it. I mean, they won't let anyone hit you or abuse you in *that* way." Diedre let out a long exhale. "Most of the time the men are too drunk. I think they get off on the *idea*, not so much the act itself."

"The power thing?" Rachel was finally able to speak without hiccupping.

"Yep. They are powerful men, and their penises are their divining rods." Diedre stomped out her cigarette, and Rachel giggled for the first time since arriving at this terrible place.

"How often does this happen?" Rachel wanted to know what was to come next.

"Usually once a week, for the two days of the weekend. These guys can't be absent from the public for too long without arousing suspicion. They come here to say they've been here, eaten, drunk, smoked, and had their way with beautiful women. It's a revolving door of narcissists, sociopaths, and dirtbags."

"So when will we be on call next, do you suppose?" Rachel was steadying herself for the answer.

"I hear there is going to be a few of them here in a few days. Politicians and industrialists."

"Here's an important question. What about STDs? Sexually transmitted diseases?"

"That's what this is for." Diedre went into the linen closet and produced a new package that contained a red bottle with a small hose.

"You've got to be kidding." Rachel recognized the contraption.

"Better to be safe." Diedre handed her a bottle of Betadine solution. "Go," she said, pointing to the bathroom.

Rachel complied. Diedre was becoming her coach and confidante. She called out from the bathroom, "Do we have to have breakfast with them tomorrow?"

"Nope. They get room service, so they can nurse their hangovers in private. Then they get out of here."

"Do they take the helicopter?"

"Not all of them. Just the Americans. Most of the other men come from countries that have diplomatic relations with Cuba, so the country is not officially off-limits to them. They usually fly their private jets here. There is a landing strip about a mile away, and the club provides a shuttle service."

"How do you know all this?" Rachel reappeared from the bathroom.

"Months of observing, eavesdropping. Many of these guys are so impressed with themselves, they can't help but brag about something."

"Wow. You hear crazy stories, but you would never think you were part of a story like this one." Rachel sat back down on her bed.

"Kind of a horror story, set in Disneyland." Diedre chuckled. "Ironic, eh?"

"Messed up is more like it."

Diedre got up and went over to the credenza and poured two fingers' worth of Glenlivet XXV single-malt scotch into two tumblers. "Here. Drink this."

Rachel was about to protest that she didn't drink scotch but decided she could probably use a slug of something to calm her down. "I don't usually drink scotch, but this is no time to be picky. What the heck."

"Bottoms up!" Diedre clinked glasses with her, and they both chugged the expensive elixir.

"Whoa!" Rachel exclaimed. "Smooth and yet not so smooth."

"Just like this place." Diedre paused. "You get used to it."

Chapter Twenty-five

Pinewood

In her usual race-car-driver fashion, Annie zoomed across the farm to get to Myra's lickety-split. Fergus decided to drive the other golf cart at a more reasonable speed of thirty-five miles per hour. The last jaunt to Myra and Charles's had almost sent him flying. This time, he was going to take matters into his own hands. He would be only a few minutes behind Annie, but at least he wouldn't be holding on for dear life.

Annie's cart arrived in the usual cloud of dirt, dust, and stones, setting off Lady and her pups to yowling and yapping.

She jogged to the door and flung it open.

Myra and the pooches were waiting for her to make her entrance. "This is great news about Gabby!" She gave Annie a big squeeze.

Annie began to recount the phone call. "According to Yoko, Gabby indicated that there were some very odd things going on at The Haven. We need to get to the bottom of this. And we can figure out a plan to move forward once Gabby and Yoko hook up again at the market. We can't let Maggie go because someone might recognize her regardless of what disguise Alexis can put together."

"I agree. Come sit. The others should be here shortly."

"Who's joining us tonight?" Annie asked.

"Kathryn is back from her haul, Nikki and Jack are on their way, and Isabelle will call in with the others."

"Jack?" Annie looked surprised.

"Nikki asked him what he knew about Daniel Ruffing. Jack called Bert Navarro to see if Bert had any intel on Ruffing. Bert contacted his people at the FBI and got an earful. Jack is going to catch us up."

"So we're finally starting to get more pieces of the puzzle." Annie's wheels were turning.

Charles walked into the room from the pantry, and said, "It indeed looks that way. Fergus also has more info. Where is he, by the way?"

"That chicken wouldn't ride with me. I have no idea why." Annie shook her head and started to giggle. "He should be here shortly." And at that moment, the dogs announced Fergus's arrival. Before he could get a foot in the door, they were jumping and nuzzling him. Fergus happily handed out treats as he entered the kitchen.

Annie started to make clucking sounds like a chicken. "Aren't you the funny one?" Fergus gave her a smirk.

"If the feathers fit, then you're a chicken." She folded her arms to punctuate her sentence.

"With such short notice, I was only able to prepare some grilled salmon with a salad," Charles announced.

"Let's get out of here," Fergus joked. "No worries, mate. You always provide." He slapped Charles on the back.

Within a few minutes, the dogs announced the next arrival. This time it was Nikki and Jack. Each took their turn with hugs and kisses.

"Jack, it's so nice to see you." Annie beamed.

"Ditto. Everyone always seems to be in different places," Jack remarked.

"And doing different things," Nikki added. "It's rare we're on the same team these days."

"I'm just a messenger today," Jack replied.

"For now," Annie kidded.

Another round of yapping heralded Kathryn's entrance. "Well, lookie who's here! Jack Emery! Nikki, how did you pull this one off?"

Nikki gave Kathryn a hug. "He claims he's only a messenger. And since he was actually home tonight, I thought I'd drag him along."

"Good to see you." Jack gave Kathryn a bear hug.

"We have to get on the call in less than an hour. Cold fish is not very appetizing unless it's caviar." Charles motioned toward the buffet he had set up on the counter. Everyone fixed a plate and sat at the long kitchen table. It wasn't often that Jack was at the same table, so the conversation revolved around the latest tales of the Men of the Sisterhood.

With less than ten minutes to spare, everyone climbed out of their seats. Fergus scraped the plates, Annie washed, Myra dried, Nikki put them back into place, while Charles wiped down the stove. "I believe that is a record for us!" he said gleefully as he checked his watch. "One minute to spare. Let's hustle!"

The group marched down the steps, saluted Lady Justice, and took their seats. The screens had been fired up earlier, and the women who weren't physically present began to dial in, their faces popping up on the screens.

"Hellos," "How's it goings?" and a few "Hey theres" were exchanged.

"Jack!" Isabelle exclaimed. "Nice to see your face!"

Yoko, Maggie, and Alexis concurred.

"What about mine?" Kathryn pretended to pout. "I've been on the road for days!"

"Hello, Kathryn!" Maggie bellowed. "And you don't look any the worse for wear either!"

"Thank goodness for small favors." Kathryn chuckled.

"Let's get down to it, shall we?" Charles urged.

"Yoko. Tell us about your exchange with Gabby."

Yoko recounted her trip to the open house and how she had fortuitously run into Gabby. "Tell them about your feminine wiles," Maggie teased.

"Oh jeez. So I flirted with the guy. It was the only way I could get a few more minutes at the site."

"Whatever it takes!" the sisters chorused.

Yoko continued, "Gabby mentioned the farmers' market and that she planned to be there this weekend. Evidently, the market will start opening on Fridays at noon."

"You said there were men who looked like security guards. How will you be able to have a conversation without drawing suspicion?" Myra inquired.

"I'm not sure about that. I assume she's going to share some information with me. How she plans to do it, I have no idea. I'm going to have to leave that in her hands."

"Okay. Gabby had been a top-notch journalist who just burned out. She's smart and resourceful. I'm sure she'll figure something out," Annie assured them.

Yoko continued, "She made a point to mention making decoupage boxes that she was hoping to sell. It sounded like a big hint to me."

Maggie burst out laughing. "Gabby is a lot of things but a crafter isn't one of them, so it must be some kind of ruse."

"Then it surely sounds like it was a hint," Jack agreed.

"So what can we do in the meantime?" Maggie asked.

Jack pulled out his tablet and began to relay the information he had obtained from Bert. "As Nikki mentioned, Ruffing is tied to a number of shell companies that have offshore bank accounts. Like all of you, the fact that Ruffing would obtain a piece of property that has no serious value and invest in a spiritual group was a big red flag. At least it was to the FBI. It's common knowledge about the lease in Cuba, because its location prevents any government agency from inspecting or surveilling the estate. The source of his income is also sketchy. In spite of all of his holdings, the math doesn't add up. Obviously, he wouldn't be the first billionaire hiding money in offshore accounts, but it's the origin of the money that's led to speculation."

Nikki broke in. "At our last meeting, I mentioned the lack of security in parts of the Everglades."

Jack continued, "The FBI thinks he may be running drugs up the coast of Florida into Alabama."

"Do they know where the drugs are coming from?" Myra asked.

"They have some intel, but again, nothing concrete. Yet," Jack answered. "As I mentioned earlier, there seem to be some questions surrounding one Mr. Daniel Josephson Ruffing and his source of income. They have a very good lead that he's running the drugs through his marina. They could bust him now, but they're looking at the bigger picture. Ideally, they'd want to round up his entire ring rather than just one dirtbag. And because he has so much money at his disposal, they want to be sure there isn't a mole. For now, they're just observing."

"Okay, but what does that have to do with Cuba?" Isabelle asked over the video screen.

"That's part of the puzzle. Ruffing has his hands in a lot of things. With the connection of The Haven to Trident Enterprises, the Laundromat, the car wash, and dry-cleaning operation, they believe they're all part of a money-laundering operation. Literally. That's where he launders the drug money."

An eerie silence fell over the room. "So Cuba is something entirely different?" Alexis asked.

"It seems so. It's probably another offshoot of his global enterprises," Jack answered.

Myra stroked her pearls. "But the FBI is looking into the drug running?"

"Yes, and Ruffing is slick."

"So what should we be doing now?" Myra asked.

"My suggestion is to wait until Yoko connects with Gabby again. Maybe Gabby can lead us to something drug enforcement can follow."

Maggie started to growl. "I don't like waiting around."

"None of us do, dear," Myra offered. "But it's only for a few more days."

"True." Maggie sighed with resignation. "But we do have some intel on Simone Jordan." Maggie proceeded to explain Simone's tough journey from abject poverty in the Caribbean to her arrival in the US, where she put herself through school and eventually went to work for DJ Ruffing. "From what we could glean, she is basically a concierge for him. Helps him plan parties, makes arrangements for guests, et cetera. On the surface, what she does doesn't seem nefarious. Just a loyal employee doing what's asked of her. She does, however, have carte blanche at most of the high-end stores in Bal Harbour. She was seen recently with a young woman on a shopping spree. She signed for all the purchases."

"We don't know if they are her accounts just yet. But we have some intel on an apartment in Miami Beach that is also connected to Ruffing," Jack added. "On the surface, it appears that it's one of those corporate write-offs he uses for guests for business meetings. That multimillion-dollar condominium, Faena House, is owned by a different shell company, Golden Shores LLC. It's the same one that owns the Golden Shores Marina. And Golden Shores LLC also holds

the lease for several of Ruffing's vehicles. Mostly SUVs—
Cadillac Escalades.

"The feds have someone watching the building. Recently,
Simone was seen with a young woman in her twenties entering the building. They stayed two nights and left early the
next morning. No one has been seen coming or going over
the past couple of days."

"Do we know who that other woman was, and was she
the same woman on the shopping spree?" Myra asked.

"No, we haven't been able to identify her, but we have a
partial photo. It's a bit grainy. Hard to see her face." Jack uploaded the photo.

Maggie jumped in. "How early in the morning did they
leave? Do you know, Jack?"

"I believe I was told that it was about five o'clock. Why do
you ask?"

"Because I was staking out The Haven one morning and
Simone Jordan and another woman drove up at five thirty in
a Cadillac Escalade. When the car left, only Simone Jordan
was in the car."

"So, what do we think all of this means?" Myra asked.

"We're not sure. Assuming Ruffing is in the drug trade, we
don't know what the Simone Jordan connection to that, if
any, is. But maybe she has something to do with what goes
on at his Cuban property."

Annie looked into the monitor at Maggie's face. "Since we
have a few days, I think you and Jimmy should put a tail on
Simone. I'll clear it with his boss."

"Can do. Jimmy has a good handle on her. Shouldn't be
too hard." Maggie nodded.

"This time, please try not to get caught." Myra shook her
finger at the screen.

"This has been very helpful, if a bit confounding," Charles
added his opinion. "We have a few days before Yoko can

meet with Gabby again. Can we recon as soon as we have more? Or can you get in touch if you find out anything else?"

"Absolutely." Jack was more than happy to help. He knew that government agencies were prohibited from doing certain things, but the Sisterhood was not bound by any such restrictions. None at all.

"I need to get going," Jack said. "I hope this was helpful."

"Very much so." Myra patted him on the cheek. "You are a darling to have come out tonight."

"Anything for my girls." Jack nodded to the women in the room and saluted Lady Justice. Regardless of their methods, every one of the people in the room wanted only one thing: justice.

Chapter Twenty-six

Miami

Jimmy and Maggie sat in a silver Kia SUV on a side street from Simone Jordan's current residence. It was a modest ranch-style home in Coconut Grove, but the landscaping was stunning. Fuchsia-colored bougainvillea climbed the side of the house. Several gardens, filled with blue daze, purple Persian shield, lantana, and black and blue salvia were surrounded by large hammock and palm trees. Hot pink pentas dotted the grounds. It was a sea of shades of blue and green. "Wow. Yoko would really appreciate this," Maggie gasped in wonder.

"Quick, get down," Jimmy warned in a loud whisper. "There she is." Simone exited through the front door and strolled around her flower beds.

"Is she smiling at the flowers?" Maggie muttered.

"Kinda seems that way." He shrugged.

Simone was carrying a basket in one hand and pruning shears in the other. She proceeded to cut some of the flowers and put them in the basket as Jimmy and Maggie looked on from a distance. After carefully cutting off the blooms, Simone went back into the house. A few minutes later, she came back out with the flowers wrapped in paper, the kind you'd get from a florist.

Simone opened the side door of her car, placed the flowers on the passenger seat, and climbed into her red Porsche 911. Simone enjoyed driving her car. Too often she was being transported in one of Ruffing's vehicles. But behind the wheel of her own car, she felt a sense of freedom. She started the car, pulled out of her driveway, and headed north. Jimmy and Maggie followed her at a safe distance.

"I hope she's not in the mood to blow out her engine today." Jimmy smirked. "I don't think we could keep up with that beauty."

They followed Simone for several miles, proceeding north on South Dixie Highway. So far the traffic did not present a problem, and they remained close enough to her car to keep it in sight.

Simone turned off the highway and proceeded west for about a mile until she came to Victoria Nursing and Rehabilitation Center. She parked her car in a visitor's spot and brought the flowers inside.

Maggie was almost out of the car before Jimmy could put it in park. "Jeez, you are a maniac," he growled. "Where do you think you're going?"

"To see who she's visiting." Maggie jogged off toward the front entrance. She got there just in time to hear Simone greet the receptionist. "How is she doing today?" Simone asked.

"Your mama had a good breakfast today," the pink-haired receptionist replied. She looked up in Maggie's direction. "I'll be with you in a moment."

Maggie nodded, pretending to be reading some of the notices on the bulletin board: FAMILY BINGO WEDNESDAY; BAR-B-QUE THURSDAY; AFTERNOON TEA SUNDAY. She continued to eavesdrop.

"Do you think she's up for a walk around the atrium?" Simone asked in her deep, sultry voice.

"Only if you tell her you're taking her shopping," Pinky joked.

Simone laughed. "I'll take that advice. See you later." Simone signed the clipboard and proceeded down a hallway.

Maggie approached the desk, eyeing Simone's signature to see her mother's name: Mabel Jordan.

"Now what can I do for you?" Pinky asked.

"I'm looking for a place for my great-auntie. Do you have a brochure?" Maggie asked politely.

"Certainly." Pinky smiled and handed her a packet of information. "We have rehabilitation services and long-term care. What are your aunt's needs?"

"She's in the hospital now. They think it's her liver." Maggie moved in closer to the receptionist. "Auntie sure enjoyed a cocktail or six every day, if you know what I mean."

Pinky giggled. "Oh, I have an uncle like that."

"I couldn't help but notice the woman who was just here. Is she a famous model or something? I thought she looked familiar."

"Oh, that's Simone Jordan. Her mother has been here for almost a year. Poor dear." Pinky fidgeted with her collar. "I mean for both of them. Simone comes by almost every day with fresh flowers from her garden." She pointed to a vase on the counter. "Those were from yesterday."

"Mmmm . . . lovely," Maggie muttered, hoping Pinky would continue to be forthcoming and give out some privileged information.

"Caring for an aging parent can be very stressful," Maggie added, hoping for a response.

"Yes, especially when they no longer recognize you. So sad. Simone has no other family."

"That is *very* sad," Maggie concurred. "I better get going.

I need to get back to the hospital. Thank you for this." Maggie patted the large envelope. "Enjoy your day."

She walked quickly to the car and told Jimmy what she had found out about Simone's mother. "And she comes here almost every day with fresh-cut flowers."

"That's dedication," Jimmy offered. "I wonder how long she's going to be here?"

"I suspect maybe less than an hour. She said something about taking her mother for a walk, but I cannot imagine that would take very long."

About forty-five minutes had passed when Simone walked out of the building. She got in her car and headed home, where she would rendezvous with someone from The Haven for a trip to Fort Lauderdale, where she was going to meet Jennifer, the next "spokesperson" for The Haven. She was beginning to hate her job.

Jimmy and Maggie were able to tail her all the way back to her house, where a black Escalade was waiting in front.

Simone got out of her own car, waved to the driver of the SUV, and got in.

"That's interesting," Maggie observed. "Another job for Ruffing, you suppose?"

"Probably. That license plate we ran from the other day is registered to one of Ruffing's shell companies. Text this plate to Charles and see if it's another one of Ruffing's."

Jimmy read the letters out loud as Maggie punched them into her phone. A few minutes later she got a reply:

Golden Shores

"It's Ruffing's all right. I wonder how many of these he has."

"A fleet of them, I would imagine." Jimmy pulled away from the curb and followed the SUV onto Interstate 95 for the drive north. The SUV turned off at the Fort Lauderdale exit and proceeded to a large professional building.

"Well, you can't jump out of the car again. She'll recognize you. My turn." Jimmy looked both ways as he hurried across the street, hoping to enter the building before Simone could disappear into an elevator, but he was seconds too late. He watched the light above the elevator doors and noticed it stopped at the fifth floor. He immediately went to the roster to see who occupied that space. It was a dentist's office. In fact, according to the registry, the dentist occupied several floors. It was a huge and well-known practice. Especially for the rich and famous. "Get a Celebrity Smile" was their popular slogan.

About two hours passed before they spotted Simone exiting with another, younger woman. The second woman looked a bit wobbly as Simone helped her into the SUV. Jimmy and Maggie followed the SUV all the way to the shops at Bal Harbour and watched as the driver dropped the two women off at the Neiman Marcus entrance.

"Now what?" Maggie frowned at Jimmy.

"I guess I get to go into the shopping area, and you get to sit in the car," Jimmy said, a big smirk on his face.

Maggie pouted.

"Well, if you hadn't been in such a hurry to jump out of the car earlier, you wouldn't have been seen."

"Yeah, and you're just lucky she didn't see you at the dentist's building. But I guess it's all for the best. I might get sidetracked with all that glitz and glamour." Both broke out laughing. Maggie was *not* a glitz-and-glamour type of gal.

She slapped Jimmy in the arm. "Get moving."

"I'll keep you posted." Jimmy scurried to the entrance, where a wave of perfume hit his nostrils. Several women were handing out samples. Jimmy said, "Thanks," and slipped the sample into his pocket.

He followed the women to Le Zoo, where they sat at a table. He noticed the familiarity between the maître d' and

Simone. It looked like she ordered for both the women. A short time later, a waiter appeared with a tray of salads. After they ate, they headed to several shops. Jimmy texted the names to Maggie as the two women entered. Over the next two and a half hours, the women visited Chanel, Fendi, Gucci, Prada, Aquazzura, Versace, ending with Neiman Marcus. Maggie forwarded the information to Annie and Myra with each update from Jimmy.

Within two minutes, the black Escalade appeared, and the women climbed in.

Jimmy was only a few feet behind them.

"After all that time, no shopping bags?" Maggie was aghast.

"They're having them delivered."

"And you know that how?" Maggie peered closer to Jimmy as he started the engine.

"I strolled into Fendi while they were in there."

"And you didn't buy me anything?" Maggie slapped his arm.

"Cut it out, will ya?" he moaned. "That's the second time you've done that today."

"Get moving. Rush-hour traffic is getting heavy."

"Yes, ma'am!" Jimmy turned the wheel and skidded slightly onto the main road.

"Jeez, you drive like Annie!" Maggie shouted at him.

Once he got a car's length behind the SUV, he reached into his pocket. "See, I did get you something." He handed her the perfume sample. It was Miss Dior.

Maggie was stunned. "Where did you get this?"

"They were giving them out at Neiman Marcus when I first went in," Jimmy calmly replied. "Why?"

"Long story. But it's kinda eerie." Maggie opened the small sample bottle. "Yep. Miss Dior, all right."

"Eerie, how?" Jimmy prodded.

"You know the story about Myra's daughter, Barbara?" Maggie said pensively.

"Yeah. Terrible. What about her?"

"Miss Dior was Barbara's favorite perfume."

"Well, it is a popular scent, no?"

"Yes, but the other evening when we were at Myra's, she had taken a nap and had a dream about Barbara. And a few minutes later, Yoko walked in wearing Miss Dior."

"So?"

"Yoko had never worn that perfume before, and she had no idea it had been Barbara's favorite. And now this." She inspected the vial again.

"That is kinda crazy," Jimmy declared.

"I'm hoping it's some kind of divine sign that we're on the right track. Even if we're not sure what track it is yet." Maggie sighed.

The SUV made its way down Collins Avenue, where it came to a stop at Faena House. Both women exited the vehicle and entered the posh condominium building. Maggie sent Annie another text:

Faena House

"I guess this is where we wait," Jimmy said.

"But for how long?" Maggie didn't want to hear the answer. "I'm getting a little buggy having to sit in this thing all day." Maggie sent Annie a text.

OK to talk now?

Annie dialed Maggie immediately. Before Maggie could get a word in, Annie announced, "Avery is sending one of his people down. She should be arriving within the hour."

"Oh, thank goodness," Maggie said with relief. "This shopping thing is tiring." She chuckled.

Annie had put her phone on speaker so Myra, Charles, and Fergus could hear the conversation.

"I take it the two women have not left the building?" Charles inquired.

"Correct." Maggie noticed a DHL truck driving up to the front of the building, and when the driver got out, his arms were full of shopping bags. "And a van just pulled up with shopping bags from all of the stores they hit this afternoon."

"Still no word on who the other woman is."

"Well, she's surely going to be well-dressed, whoever she is," Jimmy tossed in his two cents. "I could barely afford to breathe the air in the mall."

"Speaking of breathing." Maggie began to tell the story of the perfume sample to Annie. When she finished, there was silence on the other end. "Hello? Are you still with me?"

Myra was the first to speak. "I know this is clearly a sign. I feel like we're getting much closer to this whole Ruffing thing."

Charles agreed. "It seems as if The Haven isn't the problem. It's Ruffing's involvement with them. He's clearly using them as a front for his criminal enterprises. We believe he's laundering money for his illegal drug partners."

"But what's with Simone and the two young women?" Maggie asked.

"Maybe Simone likes to treat women to nice things," Annie offered in jest.

"But this is the *second* woman in less than a week," Maggie emphasized.

"While you were sending us the updates earlier, Jack looked into Ruffing's house accounts," Charles told her.

Jimmy's mouth gaped open. He knew Annie was rich and powerful, but prying into personal accounts?

"How was he able to get the information?" Maggie inquired. "Aren't his accounts hidden through those shell companies?"

"Most of them are," Charles informed them. "But he is a

show-off and a braggart and likes to boast about all the house accounts around town that he has. So when you sent us the names of each store, we called them to confirm that Mr. Ruffing's guests were completely satisfied with their shopping experience. 'Most assuredly' was the standard answer."

"So how does this fit into the drug thing?" Maggie asked.

"We. Don't. Know." Annie pronounced each word individually. Rarely was this group of women stumped.

"It's the same thing regarding Cuba," Annie added. "We don't think Cuba has anything to do with the drugs."

"As Jack surmised, Ruffing is probably involved in a lot of shady dealings. We just have to peel them off one at a time," Myra chimed in. "Now that we have a slight edge and know where Gabby is, we're making progress. I just know it." Myra smiled. "It's the Miss Dior."

Once again the conversation went silent, then Lady let out a light bark in the background. "See? Lady agrees!" Myra felt a surge of excitement.

"So when does our relief arrive? I'm hungry!" Maggie yelped.

Jimmy couldn't help but reply. "You ate four sandwiches, two bags of chips, a muffin, and a power bar! You left me nothing!" Jimmy crinkled one of the empty bags of chips. "You hear this, folks?" He crumpled the bag again, this time closer to Maggie's phone. "It's the sound of Maggie eating her way through the entire day!"

Howls of laughter came through the phone. "Glad to hear the heat hasn't stifled your appetite," Annie kidded. "Sorry, Jimmy. You should have known to pack for four people."

"That still wouldn't have been enough." Jimmy pretended to sulk.

Fergus broke in. "Avery's agent, Sasha, is going to cover for you. She just arrived at the car rental at the airport. She should be there within the half hour."

Jimmy fished for crumbs. "Don't bother," Maggie warned him. "I licked the inside of the bags."

Jimmy shook his head. "Some people never change."

"Dinner is on me, you guys," Annie chirped. "I'll tell Yoko and Alexis to meet you at Joe's Stone Crab. And I'll make the reservation for you."

"That's great! Thanks, Annie!" Jimmy gushed.

"Oh, man, I'm a mess," Maggie whined.

"Yeah, too bad you couldn't have swiped one of those shopping bags from the delivery guy," Jimmy joked.

"Well, I do have some wipes. I'll try to clean up as best I can."

"I'll ask Alexis to grab a fresh outfit for you. You can change in the ladies' room at Joe's. I don't want them to think one of my employees is a bag lady."

A few more chuckles came through the phone. "Thanks, Annie. You're the best."

"What about me?" Fergus moaned.

"And me?" Charles kidded.

"Let's not forget Myra," Myra said about herself.

"You are *all* the best. Honest!" Maggie wasn't lying.

"Sasha should be arriving momentarily," Fergus called out.

"Okay, kids. Enjoy the rest of the night," Annie signed off, with Myra adding, "Good job! Have fun."

Chapter Twenty-seven

The Haven

During phone duty the day before, Gabby had taken another message from the sultry-voiced woman. "Package is being wrapped. Will be ready for delivery on Saturday." Just as before, no cordial "hellos" or "good-byes." Of course. Gabby had no idea what the message meant, but it didn't sound like it was about a birthday present. After her shift, she had made her way to the crafts cottage. She had to make a decoupage box, with the hope that she could pretend to sell it to Yoko on Friday at the market.

She flipped through a pile of old magazines and began to tear out pages. She had gathered quite a pile when Becker entered the cottage.

"About last night," Becker began. "I was a bit befuddled having someone interested in The Haven when no one else was here to give her the tour."

"No problem. I think you did a superb job." Gabby stuffed the pages into a large envelope.

"What do you have there?" Becker eyed the pages.

"Something for my decoupage project."

"I don't recall you ever doing anything like that before," Becker said.

"I thought I'd try to bring out my creativity and make some things for the market." Gabby hoped Becker would renege on his intention to go on Friday. "Will you be joining everyone?"

"I'm not sure. Liam may be back, and I want to be here for his debriefing." Becker hesitated. "But do tell Tina that I hope she will come by again."

Gabby caught herself just in time before she asked who Tina was. "You mean . . . oh the woman who was here the other night?"

"Yes. Please." Becker was starting to blush.

"Certainly." Gabby put a large elastic band around the envelope and set it on a shelf. She didn't want Becker to see what she was cutting out of the pages, especially since she had little idea of where to start.

"Thank you, Gabby." Becker turned and headed out the door.

Gabby felt as if she had been holding her breath the entire time. She checked her watch. Everyone should be either in class or in the garden. First things first. She had to decide how much information she could share since she only had obscure clues. She found an unfinished wooden box that was about the size of a shoe box. It had hinges and a clasp. A tube of glue and brushes were in the supply cabinet.

She cut out the letters individually: M E N E A S T E R N E U R O A C C E N T S. D E L I V E R Y S A T. She would then place the letters in various random spots of the box, on top of the colorful flowers and landmarks. Gabby made it look like one of those old steamer trunks that had been all over the world with stickers of where it had been. She knew, with enough time, Maggie would figure it out. She was always good at puzzles. Maybe that's why she was such a good journalist.

She gave the box a coat of polyurethane and set it on a table to dry. She would put a second coat on it later.

Miami Beach

Sasha had perched herself in a good spot to view the comings and goings at Faena House. She had a very clear photo of Simone and a blurry one of the second woman. Jimmy tried to snap a quick photo of them while they had been shopping. A large black SUV pulled up to the front entrance and two women got in. Sasha identified Simone immediately. She started her car and began to follow the Escalade, staying far enough behind so she wouldn't be noticed. The driver looked a bit like a thug, so he could probably sniff out a tail right away.

They drove over the Julia Tuttle Causeway and headed downtown. The black SUV stopped in front of Salon Ethos, where the women got out. Sasha adjusted her specially equipped sunglasses and snapped a photo, and immediately sent it off to Avery, who forwarded to Charles.

Sasha waited for almost three hours before the pair exited the salon, but except for her clothes, the other woman looked completely different. She snapped another photo and sent it with the word *After*. The SUV returned, and the women got in and proceeded to return to the Faena House. This time only the younger unidentified woman got out. Sasha quickly sent a text:

Target moving. Other at apt. Pls advise.

In just a few seconds she got her orders by text:

Follow original subject.

Once again, Sasha stayed a safe distance behind as the

SUV made its way to Coconut Grove. Simone exited the SUV, went into her house, and came back out a few minutes later. She cut some flowers, put them in a basket, and got in her Porsche. Sasha sent another update to Avery. The red sports car headed to South Dixie Highway, made a few turns, and parked at Victoria Nursing and Rehabilitation Center. More intel was sent to Avery. After about an hour, Sasha saw Simone leave the building. She looked in Sasha's direction. Sasha thought, *I'm going to have to ditch this car. Good idea anyway. This surveillance could take more than a few days.*

Sasha quickly informed Avery she needed to switch vehicles. Avery sent the message to Charles, who arranged for Alexis to meet up with Sasha. Rather than wait for the elevator, Alexis took the stairs and ran to her car. Charles was sending Sasha's coordinates to Alexis. It appeared that Simone was heading back to Coconut Grove. Alexis followed the route that Charles provided, which pinged the location of Sasha's car. Once Simone was ensconced at her final destination, Sasha and Alexis would switch vehicles. Since neither Sasha nor Alexis had any idea what Simone's final destination was, their tailing her could very well become a wild-goose chase.

Simone pulled her car into her driveway while Sasha waited on a side street. Alexis sent a voice-to-text to Sasha:

Ten minutes out.

Sasha was about to send a reply when she noticed another black SUV approaching. Several minutes later, Simone exited her front door, wearing a different outfit. The driver opened the passenger door and Simone got in. Sasha strained to see if there was anyone else in the vehicle. A large tree obscured her view.

She sent Alexis a quick text:

On the move.

Sasha was certain the driver would notice her this time. She didn't dare let them out of her sight, but she had to be extremely careful. It appeared they were heading to Miami Beach again, so Sasha hung back as far as she could without losing them. She got another voice-to-text:

Two cars back.

Fortunately, the Biltmore wasn't too far from Coconut Grove, and Alexis had been able to catch up to them. Sasha sent a reply:

Black SUV Escalade. Stay on them.

Alexis pinged back:

Roger that.

Sasha felt a sense of relief as she watched Alexis move closer to the SUV. That enabled her to lie farther behind. They would catch up eventually.

Once Gabby's afternoon phone duty was over, she went back to the crafts cottage to inspect her creation. The Eiffel Tower, Leaning Tower of Pisa, Colosseum, and Taj Mahal were a nice touch. The letters she placed were large enough to read but not large enough to draw anyone's attention. She gave the box another coat, happy with her clever bit of spycraft.

Noah was relieved that Simone had been able to get Jennie ready with two days to spare. He felt like such a creep when he approached Jennie with the opportunity to be a "spokesperson" for The Haven. He didn't know how much longer he could continue to supply Ruffing with "hostesses." He knew the drug running and money laundering could blow up in everyone's face at any time, leading to maximum jail sentences if caught. But with all the "hostesses" Ruffing was demanding, things had gone to a new level. Not that running drugs was acceptable, but this? What started out as picking young women for an innocent job—at least he thought it was innocent at the time—had morphed into recruiting them for very unsavory work. It seemed that, as things had escalated, he had become involved in human trafficking. And now he was, to put it in plain English, a procurer. And the women he was procuring for Ruffing were people who had come to Liam and The Haven for spiritual enlightenment. He knew he should tell Liam when he returned from his trip. It would crush him, but maybe it would also save him. The "how" was going to be very tricky. Ruffing was very powerful and connected to many powerful and not very nice people.

Sasha wasn't too far behind Alexis and figured they had been heading back to the condo. Sasha and Alexis parked their vehicles a block away. Sasha looked for any traffic, but the street was empty. They swiftly swapped cars. Sasha would keep an eye on the condominium until her backup arrived. She needed to get some sleep. With Avery's people on another assignment, the sisters enlisted the aid of Jimmy again, who was happy to oblige. It would only be for several hours until Sasha could regroup, and he didn't have to worry about Maggie eating his Cuban sandwich.

With Simone in Miami Beach, it was a safe bet she wasn't going to be returning home anytime soon. If she were to leave, Alexis would get a heads-up from Sasha, as Alexis made a daring attempt to put a tracking device on Simone's car. When she approached the property, the red sports car sat in the driveway. Looking in all directions, she saw that the coast was clear for her to place the GPS bug under the car. She casually walked back to her vehicle and hightailed it out of the neighborhood.

*   *   *

Over the next two days, Sasha's surveillance yielded no additional information. Simone went back and forth to her house, to the nursing home, and the apartment. There was no sign of the other woman leaving the condominium.

Chapter Twenty-eight

Pinewood

Myra was stroking her pearls and pacing. Tomorrow would be the day when Yoko would reconnect with Gabby. The wait was driving her crazy. Charles knew that Myra didn't like to be idle when there was a mission, especially one with so many missing pieces.

The ringing of the phone made her jump. "Easy, old girl. It's Fergus."

"We have some more intel on the subject in Florida. Need to call a meeting."

"Will do." Charles looked at Myra. "Your magic pearls must be working. Fergus wants to have a meeting tonight."

"I do hope we can have enough information to finalize a plan. Dealing with someone like Ruffing is like handling a nest of hornets."

"Or a den of snakes." Charles kissed her on the back of the neck. It was something that always made Myra a little weak in the knees.

"Charles! Don't be naughty!" Myra enjoyed every bit of it.

"I'm simply trying to distract you, dear."

"You are doing a spectacular job." She leaned into him as he continued to nuzzle her.

Lady and her pups interrupted their canoodling with yapping and howling. It was their way of announcing Annie's arrival.

They had a special bark, yelp, or yap for everyone. Very smart pooches indeed.

"I heard Fergus has some intel for us?" Myra asked, trying to recover from her flushed neck and cheeks.

"Did I interrupt something?" Annie teased.

Both of them replied with different answers. Charles said, "Yes." Myra said, "No," which made the three of them burst out laughing.

"Hah. I get it." Annie winked. "Fergus should be here shortly. He still refuses to get in the cart with me."

When Fergus entered the kitchen, Charles called out, "Well, if it isn't the chinless wonder."

"Very funny, old mate." Fergus gave him a disapproving frown.

"If the shoe fits," Annie chided.

"Enough of the tomfoolery. Let's get down to business, shall we?" Fergus urged. "Who will be joining us?"

Myra answered. "Mostly everyone will be calling in except Kathryn. She should be here any minute." With that, the cab of an eighteen-wheeler rumbled into the driveway, and Kathryn hopped out.

"Let's fall to it." Charles led the way down the steps to the War Room, and each of them saluted Lady Justice as they passed by.

Charles powered up the screens. The map was lit with dots showing the locations where the subjects had been the previous few days plus some other locations.

One dot was The Haven, another Faena House, then Ruffing's marina, and the estate on Star Island. In a different color was the dentist's office and the Bal Harbour Shops. Two more dots indicated Simone's house and the nursing home. Then there was the dot on Cuba's coast.

The sisters were dialing in. Isabelle was still in San Francisco, Nikki was in her office; Alexis, Yoko, and Maggie were in Florida.

After the "hellos" and air kisses, Fergus began.

"Some of this is recap, some new. Jack informed us that the FBI and DEA have eyes on Ruffing's marina. Over the last several weeks, a cigarette boat has been spotted traveling to and from the marina between midnight and three A.M. An exchange of coolers, presumably carrying cash and drugs, is made. There is only one person who pilots the cigarette boat. He's been identified as Noah Westlake."

Gasps came from the others. "As in Liam Westlake's brother," Fergus confirmed.

"Is it just Noah or are there others?" Myra asked.

"From what Jack has discovered, it's only Noah who makes the deliveries. Once the exchange happens, Noah returns to the marina, where two men take the coolers and transfer them to other powerboats. Those boats go as far as they can through the Intracoastal and the canals. The coolers are once again transferred to airboats. The airboats navigate through parts of the Glades until they reach the Gulf. Once they get to the Gulf, they split up, and some go to Alabama and the rest to Louisiana."

"Do we know what the feds are going to do about it?"

"They were able to identify someone in the FBI who turned out to be Ruffing's mole. He has now been 'relocated.'" Fergus used air quotes to accentuate the word. "Now they can move forward with gathering more intel without its getting back to Ruffing."

"Do they have an undercover agent inside?" Myra asked.

"Not yet, but they've been able to use other means to trace

the distribution. An insider would certainly help, but Ruffing may be onto the interest being taken in him and his operation. He seems to be spending more time in Cuba lately."

"So in order for the authorities to catch him, he would have to be on US soil," Nikki mused.

"Correct."

"So do you think he's planning on skipping the country?"

Fergus continued, "There doesn't seem to be any evidence of that since he hasn't tried to move any money."

"It appears we are still in a state of suspended animation, then." Myra stroked her pearls.

"We should have more information from Gabby tomorrow," Yoko reminded them. "Hopefully, it will be a piece of the puzzle that allows us to move forward."

"The US government may not be able to take down Ruffing in Cuba, but that doesn't mean we can't," Annie said with gusto.

"Woo-hoo!" Kathryn bellowed. "Now yer talkin' my kind of language."

"Before you get too excited, let's wait until tomorrow when we have a bit more information." Myra could sense the enthusiasm among the women.

Kathryn sulked. "Oh, okay. If you insist."

"Now that's our good girl." Annie gave Kathryn's shoulder an affectionate squeeze.

"Anyone have anything else they can offer?" Myra asked.

"Nope." "Not yet." "Me either," came the responses.

"I have a good feeling about all of this," Myra said happily.

"Oh, by the way," Charles interjected. "I called all of the stores Simone and the unidentified woman visited and asked them to please duplicate everything, and to please bring the packages to the valet station at Neiman Marcus. Alexis, a black SUV will be picking you up in about an hour. He will drive you to the Bal Harbour Shops. The shopping bags should be awaiting your arrival. So please dress as closely as you can to Simone. We've sent you several photos. You don't have to get out of the car or speak to anyone. Just nod."

"Charles, why on earth would we do something like that?" Myra asked.

"To see exactly what the unidentified woman will be wearing when she eventually leaves the condominium. Once we're done, we'll donate the clothing to young women who are starting their own businesses. Sound all right with you?"

"Bloody brilliant!" Annie cheered. The rest of the women responded in kind.

"We'll send photos of the clothing as soon as I get back," Alexis added.

"Okay. Let's meet up again tomorrow," Annie said. "Until then, everyone behave."

Whoops and clapping ended the session, with a salute to Lady Justice.

An hour later, Alexis sauntered into the living room of the hotel suite, looking like a body double for Simone. "Wish me luck. Depending on what's in those bags, you may never see me again." That caused a burst of laughter. "As if," Maggie replied. Two hours later, Alexis needed two bellhops to bring up all of the beautifully packaged boxes from the high-end boutiques.

Chapter Twenty-nine

Friday
The Farmers' Market

Gabby had already been cleared to attend the market on Friday. The Pledge who covered for her before was going to be on phone duty that afternoon. She would have to be sure to only spend a short amount of time with Yoko. Otherwise, the Guardians would become suspicious.

She fiddled with the other two decoupage boxes she had made. She figured it would look like she really wanted to pursue this new endeavor. Naturally, she didn't put as much thought into the others, but they looked good. If someone wanted to purchase her covert operations box, she would tell them she was holding it for another shopper, and she would offer to make one just like it. She tried to calm her nerves. She knew that the Guardians were keeping a special eye on her since the episode at the airport. The fact that they were able to find her at the florist's was disconcerting. How that was possible kept haunting her.

Maggie was anxious to get to her friend, but she knew she had to steer clear of anyone who might recognize her from the morning she got plucked out of the foliage by security. For all she knew, they could have her on video. She paced the hotel room.

"You're going to rub tracks in the carpet," Alexis taunted her. "Help me finish with the photos of the clothes I picked up last night." Alexis jerked a finger at the beautiful designer outfits. "Then you can order room service."

Maggie clapped her hands gleefully. Food was always a good incentive.

Yoko was getting ready to leave for the market. She adjusted the broach, which served as a surveillance device. She would be able to record her conversations with audio and video feed, and it would be simultaneously sent to Charles.

She settled a straw hat on her head and did a little twirl. "Do I look like I want to join a cult?"

Maggie and Alexis couldn't help but laugh. "You look kinda normal," Maggie said with a straight face.

"Normal is good." Yoko took a slight bow.

They high-fived each other as Yoko headed out the door to go to the market, where she hoped and prayed she would get more insight and information from Gabby.

Yoko parked her vehicle away from the other cars and casually walked into the market area. She stopped at a few stalls on her way and looked at some merchandise. She didn't want to seem like she was on a mission. Which she was. *Mission.* The thought made her chuckle softly. After several minutes of browsing, she finally arrived at The Haven's stall where handmade items were being sold. She began studying some of the crafts, looking for signs of Gabby. For the first few minutes, she couldn't spot her. She didn't dare ask anyone for fear of casting doubts about the purpose of her visit. She breathed a sigh of relief when Gabby returned from one of the other stalls.

"Hello again," Yoko said to her. "Do you remember me? I was at the open house the other night."

"Oh yes. Nice to see you again." Gabby was in synch. "Anything in particular you're interested in?" Gabby motioned for Yoko to follow her to a table. "We have some new items this week. We make everything at The Haven." Gabby picked up one of the boxes. "Even the box itself is crafted in the woodshop."

"I love doing crafts," Yoko said coyly. "I also like gardening."

Keeping the conversation in line with what one would expect of the members, Gabby proceeded, "We also grow our own vegetables. Right over there." Gabby pointed to the stand several feet away.

Yoko had already taken notice of the security men standing in the wings. She would have sworn one of them had an eagle eye on Gabby. Wanting to move the encounter forward, Yoko said, "These boxes are very interesting. Decoupage was all the rage quite a while ago. I'm glad to see it's making a comeback." She smiled at Gabby. "How much are they?"

"This one is thirty dollars." She handed one of the other boxes to Yoko letting her inspect it. "But this one is my personal favorite." She lifted her box of clues and handed it to Yoko, retrieving the first one.

"Oh, I like this one," Yoko said, beaming. "How much is it?"

"Thirty. Just like the others."

"It's a deal!" Yoko exclaimed, as she pulled three ten-dollar bills from her big straw tote bag. "I have to be getting back. My job at the Biltmore starts in an hour."

"I hope you enjoy looking at it as much as you enjoy stashing your secret keepsakes." Gabby wrapped tissue around the box and put it in a white paper shopping bag. She made sure she was seen placing a brochure for The Haven in the bag as well. It was protocol. No one leaves without getting a dose of hype.

"Thank you," Yoko said. "I'm going to check out the veggies now."

"Of course. Have a lovely day." Gabby nodded.

As much as Yoko was excited to get the box back to where it could be deciphered, she knew she could not do anything to bring any attention to herself. Like racing to her car, for one.

She made a few more quick stops at other stalls just in case the goons were keeping an eye on her. As soon as she got back to the car, she peeled out and raced as fast as she could back to the hotel. She didn't want to take a chance that someone would spot her taking photos of the box, but she sent off a text to everyone that she had it in hand.

After thirty minutes of keeping her speed at the legal limit, she zoomed into the circular drive of the hotel, scaring the bejesus out of the parking attendant. "Sorry . . . sorry . . ." Yoko could barely catch her breath. She dashed for the elevator, apologizing to other guests as she brushed past them. "Excuse me. So sorry. My apologies." She didn't notice the appalled stares from people in the lobby.

She fumbled with the key card and finally got into the suite. She leaned her back against the door and took several deep inhales and exhales, breathing as if someone had been chasing her.

"What in the?" Maggie looked at the box with surprise.

"There are clues here," Yoko replied.

"The Eiffel Tower?" Alexis questioned.

"The Colosseum?" Maggie queried. "Wait. What are these letters scattered about?" She pulled out a pad and pen and began to write them down dividing up the letters. "There are seven Es; three Ns; three As; three Ts; three Rs; three Ss; two

Cs; one O; one U; one D; one L; one I; one V; one M; one Y."
Maggie counted, "Thirty-two total."

"Do you think the photos mean anything?" Alexis asked.

"Beats me. But let's send this off to Charles and Fergus.
They can run the letters through some software that will
come up with all the various combinations." Maggie quickly
sent the letters and two dozen photos of the box in various
positions.

"Now what do we do?" Yoko asked.

"We wait," Alexis said, knowing that was not one of Maggie's favorite pastimes.

"Anyone for room service?" Maggie pulled out the menu.

Within the hour, Charles managed to decipher the hidden
message, but it still made no sense. M E N. E A S T E R N.
E U R O. A C C E N T S. D E L I V E R Y. S A T. He asked
for everyone to call in.

Yoko, Maggie, and Alexis huddled around Maggie's laptop while Charles, Myra, Fergus, and Annie were on the
other end.

"Aside from the obvious, men with Eastern European accents are either picking something up or dropping something
off," Charles informed them. "It's the where and what that's
missing."

Maggie shook her head. "I wonder why she didn't include
anything, unless we're just not seeing it."

"Unless she doesn't know," Myra added.

They fell silent. "Unfortunately, this isn't very helpful,"
Annie said somberly.

"We should contact Jack or Bert and let them know we
heard there was an impending delivery. They can pass that
intel along to the FBI and DEA. Perhaps it's a drug run."
Charles was trying to put a positive spin on the little information they had received.

"I'll get on it," Fergus offered.

"What should we do now?" Maggie was almost whining. "We can't just let Gabby stay there, especially if something bad is going down."

"But maybe it's not going down at The Haven. Maybe it's the boats the FBI has been watching," Charles suggested.

"This is quite befuddling." Myra touched her pearls. "We usually have a single target. Now we're not sure what kind of target we're dealing with."

"My money is on Ruffing," Annie said with assurance. She certainly wasn't about to lose her fortune on a bet.

"Do we know where Ruffing is now?" Myra asked.

"Let me check the airline manifests. Even if he flies on his personal jet, a flight plan has to be filed." Fergus busily clicked away at a keyboard. The silence from the others was almost audible. Rarely was there a time when someone wasn't talking.

"Got it." Fergus beamed. "He's heading to Cuba tonight."

"And so are a few members of the Senate and a dignitary from Southeast Asia," Charles observed. "All government personnel must register their travel itineraries if they plan on leaving the United States."

"But why Cuba?" Myra asked.

"Their applications for a visa state they are on a special committee to file recommendations for tourism."

"That sounds like a pile of manure to me," Annie said.

"I'm sure there is no place on the forms that says: *Need Cuban cigars and rum*!" Fergus was able to break the solemn mood.

"We'll have to wait this out until we can get more information, I'm sorry to say." Myra was disheartened.

"But what about Gabby?" Maggie's frustration was mounting.

"Should I go to the market again tomorrow?" Alexis offered. "I have another disguise I can use."

"That's probably a good idea." Myra's spirit was slightly elevated.

"Sasha is still on Simone's tail. Perhaps she'll be able to report something soon. There's been no action for two days," Charles noted. "And tomorrow is Saturday. So perhaps we can figure out what delivery is being made."

"We need to keep prodding until we come up with something and get Gabby out of there," Myra said, coming out of her reverie.

"Whatever it takes!" was the chant.

Chapter Thirty

Saturday Morning

Noah was awakened by the ringing of his cell phone. He looked at the time. It was almost one in the morning. It was Ruffing, instructing him to make another delivery. Noah knew he had to make a decision, but getting out from under Ruffing would be no easy task. He also knew he had to tell Liam.

Noah pulled into the marina around 1:30 A.M. The coolers were in their usual spot on the dock, waiting for him to load them onto the boat. The sound of the ropes rubbing against the pilings made him jump. *Yes. It was definitely time to ditch this gig.*

He proceeded to the area where his craft would be in international waters, approximately twenty-four miles away from the coast. The exchange was the same as always, swapping several of his coolers for those from the fishing boat.

On his way back, he kept examining various scenarios in his head. He was in a state of flux. Just as he was about to pull into the marina, he was surrounded by Coast Guard patrol boats. A bright light almost blinded him. Someone on a bullhorn announced, "Do not attempt to destroy any property. We are coming aboard." It seemed instantaneous, as half a dozen DEA agents jumped onto the cigarette boat and started cracking open the coolers.

"Looks like several kilos here, boss," one of the men reported to his superior.

"Noah Westlake, you are under arrest for possession of a controlled substance with the intention to distribute." He spun Noah around and placed his hands behind his back as he proceeded to cuff him and read him his Miranda warning.

Noah thought better than to say anything. Once they processed him, he'd be able to get in touch with Ruffing.

Charles spun out of bed when his phone rang at four in the morning. It was Jack, informing him that Noah had been arrested.

"But I thought they were waiting for a bigger fish. No pun intended, old chap."

"They think they have enough on Ruffing but need corroboration, and Noah might be the best fall guy," Jack explained. "They also think it's Russian-mafia related."

"Thanks, mate. Sounds like things are moving fast. Keep me posted." Charles hung up as Myra was putting on her slippers and a robe.

"We should let Annie and Fergus know. I'll put on some coffee."

Charles gave her an affectionate pat on the butt. "Will do, love."

Just before dawn, Sasha spotted Simone and a younger woman leaving the condominium. She knew it would be a bit challenging to follow them at such an early hour without being spotted, but Sasha was a pro, so she put her car in gear and notified Avery that the target was on the move. Avery, in turn, contacted Charles.

*　*　*

"It appears to be an early morning for several folks in Florida." Charles gave the others the info about Simone and the unknown woman leaving the condominium. "Sasha will check in as soon as she has more intel."

They phoned Maggie, Alexis, and Yoko, and informed them of Noah's arrest and that Simone was on the move with another woman.

"Do you think they're going to try to flee the country?" Maggie asked.

"Ruffing's plane has already left, so if they plan on flying a commercial flight, they may have some difficulty boarding. According to Jack, all eyes are on Ruffing's employees right now. They don't know how many people in his circle know what he's been up to, or with whom, but they're closing in."

"Well, it's gone from a state of suspended animation to a boatload of excitement." Annie giggled.

The sound of a text caused a hush in the kitchen. It was Sasha:

Subject entering The Haven.

Gabby had had a restless night. She didn't know if Maggie was able to make any sense of her clues, especially since they were so cryptic. She tossed and turned until a hint of light signaled the break of dawn. Gabby wished she could have shared more hints, but she truly didn't know *what* was going on; all she knew was that *something* was. She thought she heard a vehicle pull into the compound. It was too early for a delivery. She quietly sneaked out of her bunk and tiptoed to the window. Two women got out of a black SUV and began to walk toward the back of the property. Gabby squinted to get a closer look at the younger woman. It was Jennie, a new Tyro. But she looked dramatically different. It was as if she had had a total transformation of her hair, her makeup, and her clothing. She also noticed a man following them with several pieces of luggage.

Silently, she cracked the door open and slipped out, looking in both directions. They were within earshot when she heard the tall woman say, "*Diecinueve camino de la luna amarilla.*" The man with the luggage and Jennie disappeared behind the lush foliage at the back end of the property.

A few minutes later, the sound of an airboat engine started. Gabby plastered herself against the building as the honey-toned woman returned to the SUV alone. The SUV left the property, with Simone as the only passenger.

Gabby was baffled and confused. *Who was* that *woman and where were they taking Jennie?* And what or where was "*Diecinueve camino de la luna amarilla?*" Gabby knew she had to get word to Maggie and soon. Yoko had mentioned the Biltmore. Gabby surmised that was where they were staying. She thought for several minutes. She had no cash. She had no car. She had no access to a phone. Then it hit her: Rachel's bicycle. She quietly made her way to the garage, hoping there was still air in the tires. It was a good thirty miles to the Biltmore. If the old bike didn't fail her, it would take almost two hours to pedal to Coral Gables. But there was no other way to get word to the women. She tied up the bottom of her skirt and wheeled the bike to the road and pedaled as if her life depended on it. And it probably did.

Noah sat in the interrogation room, waiting for someone to speak to him. It had been hours since his arrest. He was tired, dirty, and hungry. He had hoped they would let him make his one phone call right away, but that only happens on TV. His emotions were running wild. He sat with his head resting on his forearms on the table. He kept drifting in and out, not sure if he was awake or asleep. Either way, he was living in a nightmare. He couldn't take the fall for Ruffing, but he couldn't implicate him either. Ruffing would have him killed if he fingered him. Even if he were in jail, Ruffing would find a way to silence him. The longer he had worked for the guy, the more he knew that there were sleazy, immoral, and illegal transactions taking place. He had also learned that no one ever quit working for Ruffing. No one. They simply disappeared. He kept drifting in and out. Finally, two men wearing suits entered the room, each carrying a pile of folders. They explained the charges to Noah, reminded him of his Miranda rights, and asked if he wanted a lawyer. Noah immediately said yes and called Ruffing to ask him to send one of his attorneys. But Ruffing ignored his calls. During the raid, one of Ruffing's dockhands had informed him of the arrest and confiscation of the drugs. Ruffing just shrugged and acted as if he had nothing to do with Noah's drug dealing.

Gabby's legs were burning, and she cursed herself for not grabbing a bottle of water before she left. With no money, she had no choice but to keep pushing forward until she made it to safety or collapsed. She decided to take a short break and pulled the bike under an overpass, where she could be in some shade. She was soaked in perspiration; her hair was dripping wet. She massaged her calves before climbing back onto the thread-worn seat. Another forty-five minutes should get her there. Somewhere near the university, she got her second wind and began to pump the bike harder. She knew she wasn't far now. She tried to imagine what she looked like to the early-morning commuters. Another homeless soul. But then it occurred to her, *What if they don't let me into the hotel? I look like a vagrant, or someone who escaped from a mental hospital.* Her messy white garb would certainly suggest the latter.

With only the driveway between her and the entrance, she decided to walk the rest of the way and give her fanny a break. She didn't know which hurt more, her thighs, her calves, her feet, or her tush. Her hands were also feeling a bit tense from gripping the handlebars. She did a mental scan of her body. Pretty much everything hurt. As she limped toward the doorman, she gave him her winning smile. "Took a bit of a tumble on my ride this morning," she lied.

The doorman looked at her sympathetically. "Done it myself. Can I help you with anything?" He opened one of the side doors instead of having her go through the revolving door.

"I'm fine. Really. But if you could put that hunk of junk somewhere, I'll fetch it in a bit. It's my baby sister's. Why she keeps it, I don't know, but she'd kill me if she knew I had mangled it." Gabby wasn't sure what she was most impressed with, her ability to make up another lie or her ability to remain vertical.

"No problem, miss. Name is Mike." He pointed to his name tag. That was a hint as to whom she should tip later.

"Thank you so very much." Gabby turned to enter the second door as another doorman on the inside pulled it open. "Hi. A little argument with a bicycle." Gabby snickered.

Gabby glanced around the lobby to see where the house phones were kept and spotted one at a table near the concierge's desk.

Her hands were shaking as the hotel operator answered. "How can I help you?"

"Maggie Spritzer, please." Gabby's voice was also shaking.

When the hotel room phone rang, everyone jumped. They were not expecting to hear from anyone on the landline, although Maggie was becoming a popular favorite with room service.

"Hello?" Maggie asked cautiously.

"Maggie. It's Gabby. I'm in the lobby." Gabby was whispering.

"The lobby? Here?" Maggie was stunned.

"Yes. Here. The Biltmore." Gabby kept looking over her shoulder. Ever since that day at the airport, she had felt as if someone were either watching her or following her. And she was correct. About a hundred yards from the main entrance, a black SUV pulled in.

"I think I'm being followed. What room are you in?" Gabby was almost gasping for air.

"Room 1011," Maggie barked.

Gabby saw one of the men get out of the car, and she moved quickly toward the elevator bank. Worried that he might have spotted her, she pushed the eleventh and twelfth floor buttons. She would get off at eleven and hike down one flight of stairs. And she prayed her legs could do one last push.

When the elevator bell dinged, she wavered as she got off, looking in each direction for the stairwell. There was one only a few feet away. She kept repeating in her head, *You can do this, you can do this.* She was so weary that she used both hands as she took each step one at a time. She yanked on the door, not caring if it set off an alarm. She had to get to Maggie.

Maggie, Yoko, and Alexis stood ready at the door. They didn't know if Gabby was alone.

Maggie looked through the peephole in the door and saw Gabby stumbling down the hallway. Maggie and Alexis quickly scrambled to get her, while Yoko held the door open. They placed Gabby's arms around their necks and practically dragged her into the room.

Yoko went into the bathroom and brought back a couple of wet washcloths and a towel. Maggie opened a bottle of water and handed it to Gabby, while Alexis grabbed a robe for her. Gabby went into the bathroom and splashed water on her face, slipped off her rags, and enveloped her worn-out body in the plush hotel wrap.

"First things first." Maggie took Gabby's hands and looked her straight in the eye. "Are you okay? Do you need a doctor?"

Gabby wiped her face with one washcloth and placed the other on her forehead. "I'll be okay. No need for a doctor. I'm just a bit weary and dehydrated." She took a big swig of water. "Now *my* first question is, who are those men and why are they following me?"

"I think the bigger question is *how* did they find you?" Maggie was thinking like a reporter now. "This is the second time. I'm not trying to be funny, but did they ever give you some kind of tattoo, or piercing?"

Gabby sighed. "No. Nothing like that."

"Do you wear the same clothes? You know, clothes that are assigned specifically to you?" Maggie continued.

"Well, yes."

Yoko immediately started feeling through the hems of Gabby's clothes. She shook her head.

Gabby was twirling her ring and twisting her brain to come up with an answer. At that moment, everyone stopped in their tracks. The ring.

Maggie put out her hand and motioned for Gabby to take it off and give it to her. It was on tight. Yoko slathered Gabby's finger with lotion and gently slid it off.

The next questions that struck Maggie were: *How wired up is the ring? Is it simply a GPS device, or does it have broadcast capabilities such as audio or video? Is it a secret camera?*

Maggie put her fingers on her lips to indicate that everyone should remain silent. Maggie pulled out a pad of paper and began to write: *Need to tell Charles. I'll be in the other room.*

Maggie took a photo of the ring and disappeared into the bedroom. She quickly dialed Charles's number and explained that Gabby had found her way to the hotel, men had followed her, and it appears the ring was some kind of tracking device. She needed to know the extent of the technology before they could decide their next move.

Sasha didn't have a clear view of the SUV when it entered The Haven, so she couldn't see who got in or out of the vehicle. But once it pulled out, she followed it. It headed in the direction of Coconut Grove. Sasha kept at a safe distance as the SUV pulled up in front of Simone's house. Sasha strained to see if the other woman was with Simone. But only Simone exited the car. Sasha immediately texted:

Subject returned home. Alone. Other person unaccounted for.

Everything was breaking loose at the same time. Charles received the message that the second woman's whereabouts were unknown. Fergus checked the photo of the ring. It looked like a simple GPS device, but having the ring itself would be ideal. That way he could scan it and find the source.

At the same time, in Florida, Gabby was explaining what she knew to Maggie, Alexis, and Yoko.

"I don't know too much except early this morning a black SUV pulled in with two women." She took another gulp of her water. "One I did not recognize. Tall, slim, dark, honey-toned skin, with straight black hair. The other one was a new Tyro named Jennie. But she looked completely different from how she looked a few days ago. New hair, makeup, clothing. There was a man following them with luggage.

"The only thing I could hear was '*Diecinueve camino de la luna amarilla.*' And then, a few minutes later, I heard the sound of an airboat. And the taller woman got back in the SUV and was driven away."

"Do you think you can repeat all of that?" Maggie asked.

"Sure. But can I take a shower first?" Gabby looked at her with puppy-dog eyes.

"Of course! And some clean clothes."

"I'm kinda liking this robe." Gabby snuggled inside it. She was finally feeling calm and safe.

Maggie dialed into the secure network so that Myra, Annie, Charles, Fergus, Nikki, Kathryn, and Isabelle could hear the news. "Gabby is here. At the Biltmore," Maggie said with great relief. "She actually pedaled her way on an old bicycle. It took her two hours, but she's okay. A little shaky, but okay."

Annie and Myra squealed with delight.

"Now don't make fun, but I am going to order room service . . ." Her sentence was interrupted by the others in unison. "Of course you are!"

"It's not just for me, you know." Maggie pretended she was being defensive. "Anyway, I want you to hear the whole story from Gabby. She's taking a quick shower. Question: Do we know what 'Diecinueve camino de la luna amarilla' means yet? That seems to be a big part of this puzzle."

Fergus spoke first. "It's the address of Daniel Ruffing's Cuban estate."

The three women in Florida looked horrified. Maggie blurted out, "Then he may be trafficking women there!"

Lots of voices came through the speakerphone. Gasps, questions, expletives.

Several minutes later, Gabby came out of the shower with a towel wrapped around her head and wearing a fresh robe. She tossed the first robe onto the pile of funky clothes she had been wearing. "Someone should put a torch to that." She made a squeamish face and pointed.

Maggie motioned Gabby to sit on the sofa in front of the table that held the speakerphone. The other women surrounded the table, creating a circle.

Maggie started. "Hi, everyone. I have Gabby Richardson with us!" Loud cheers and hoots bounced through the speaker.

Annie was first. "Gabby, we cannot tell you how happy we are that you're all right." Myra echoed the sentiment, followed by everyone else with sighs and sounds of relief. "Did you really ride a bicycle?"

"It was more like I was pushing a bicycle with my legs. It was an old one-speed, with a basket, streamers, and a bell." She took another sip of water. "The only thing that was missing were the training wheels." Gabby chuckled nervously, still getting used to having both feet on the floor. A few soft laughs and giggles could be heard coming from the other end.

"Gabby, before you run out of steam, tell us everything you know. Even the smallest detail can be useful, even if you're not sure what it means," Myra encouraged her.

Gabby started from the beginning, recapping the incident from the airport to the florist and back to The Haven. "Noah gave me a tongue-lashing. I told him that Liam had given me permission, but he didn't seem to care. Liam gave me phone duty to cover for Maxwell, one of the Guardians, so I could contact my mother."

"Oh, you mean the one who called you a 'stupid bitch?' " Myra asked sourly.

"I can't believe you heard that, but yes. That's him," Gabby replied.

"Apparently you were fumbling with the phone but it made it to Maggie's voice mail before the call was disconnected," Myra said.

Gabby continued with as much information as she could remember. "One night I overheard Noah and Liam arguing. Liam was not happy about some people Noah had been dealing with. Then, one day when I was on phone duty, a couple of men who looked like gangsters came to The Haven. They looked out of place and had Eastern European accents." Gabby paused. "I could never hear what was going on behind closed doors."

Maggie asked, "So is that when you started to think there were 'strange happenings?'"

"Yes, partly. It was the phone messages I would take. 'Package ready for delivery.' That kind of stuff. There were no computers, except behind the locked doors of Liam's and Noah's offices. My orders were to take messages only. I was to tell anyone that whomever they wanted to speak to was not available. It was very odd."

Back at Pinewood, Annie was writing on the electronic wall that served as a type of blackboard.

Gabby continued, "Another strange thing is the laundry. It's always in bags with locks. The kind you'd put on luggage. The Tyros, the newbies, would do the heavy lifting, but no one ever saw the contents. Same thing with the dry cleaner. Bags in and bags out. All of it was under the supervision of the Guardians."

"Tell us about this morning," Myra urged.

Gabby recounted every detail of her observation with Simone and Jennie: the man with the luggage, the airboat, and "*Diecinueve camino de la luna amarilla.*" "There's one other thing: I befriended one of the other Pledges. Her name is Rachel. She told me in confidence that she was chosen to be a spokesperson for The Haven. She would get new clothes and travel to help raise money."

Charles cut in. "Anyone want to bet she's at *Diecinueve camino de la luna amarilla*? Also known as 19 Yellow Moon Road."

"Gabby, you mentioned every Pledge wears one of those rings, correct?" Alexis asked.

"Yes."

"So perhaps the other women are still wearing theirs?" Charles asked.

"It's possible." Gabby was starting to wane.

Annie jumped in. "Here is what we have:

1 Ruffing is funding The Haven through a shell company.
2 Laundry, dry cleaning, car wash—cash only equals money laundering.
3 Noah is in jail for drug dealing. Ruffing?
4 The ring is some kind of device.
5 Ruffing is currently in Cuba.
6 A woman was sent there this morning.
7 Dignitaries are going to Cuba. Are they going to Ruffing's?

"Gabby, where does Liam fit into this mess?"

"I really can't say. He hasn't been around very much lately. Noah has been sending him to conferences. It's almost as if he was trying to keep him away."

"I think we need to get down to Florida immediately," Annie broke in. "Fergus, Charles, get your 'travel bags.' "

The "travel bags" were a collection of very high-tech electronics capable of capturing information from the mainframe in the War Room. No big screens, or wallboards, but the ability to download almost anything they would need was neatly packed into several attaché cases. Airport security wouldn't be a problem. They would take Annie's Gulfstream jet.

"This may require several of us. Who's in?" Annie asked.

Shouts of "Count me in!" "Ditto!" and "When do we leave?" came through.

"We should leave tonight and get a fresh start in the morning. Can everyone be ready in say, three hours?"

"Yes!" and "Absolutely!" was the response.

"I'll call for the plane to be ready and have the Biltmore set aside some rooms for us. Maybe I can get them to clear part of a floor for us." Annie was confident she could convince the management to accommodate her. She would pay for any inconvenience should guests make a stink.

Charles spoke up. "First thing we need to do is have Gabby deactivate the ring until we get there." He looked at Annie.

"Tell her to put it in the freezer compartment of the mini-bar. We'll get rid of it entirely once we can physically inspect it. This should hold them off until we get there."

Myra went through the list: "Annie, Fergus, Charles, me, Kathryn, Nikki, Yoko, Maggie, Alexis."

Isabelle chimed in. "I'll meet you down there. I was scheduled to fly home but will go directly to Miami instead. I should be able to get there by midnight."

"Excellent!" Annie beamed. "I think we've got ourselves a mission in progress."

Hoots and hollers filled the room and came through the phone.

Chapter Thirty-one

South Florida

Annie's plane, carrying the sisters, Fergus, and Charles, took off and landed on schedule. Everyone had something to eat during the flight. Some of them napped. By the time the wheels touched down, the sisters were revitalized and raring to go. A small van met them at the private airport and took them to the hotel, where the bellman was waiting with several carts for their luggage. The hotel manager greeted them.

"So lovely to see you again, Annie. It's been a while." The older gentleman took her hand.

"Yes, Lester, it's been much too long. I need to get some golfing in soon!" Annie gave him a hug. She had known Lester from the years when he managed the Waldorf Astoria. After it was acquired by the Chinese, he felt it was time to move to warmer climes.

"Fortunately, we only had to move a few guests, and all of them got upgrades." Lester bowed.

"You've always been a miracle worker, my friend."

Greetings proceeded, with Annie introducing the group to Lester, with lots of handshaking and smiles.

"I asked room service to bring a platter of sandwiches and salads to your suite. Your Maggie Spritzer is a staff favorite." Lester beamed.

"That's our girl," Myra interjected.

Lester gave everyone their key cards and led them to the bank of elevators. "If you need anything, please call my private line."

"Thank you, Lester. We'll try not to bother you." Annie waved as the elevator doors closed.

When they arrived on the tenth floor, their luggage was coming off the service elevator. Fergus thought one of the men looked a bit dodgy but decided that finding out what properties the ring possessed and dismantling it came first.

There were two large suites at the end of the hall. Each had two bedrooms. The adjoining rooms had interior doors that allowed them to get from one room to the other without going into the hallway.

"Let's regroup in a half hour," Myra directed everyone.

A buffet of sandwiches, wine, water, salad, and cookies was arranged on one of the credenzas. "Don't tell Maggie," Charles joked..

"Tell me what?" Maggie was standing in one of the inner doorways.

"Just joking, kiddo." Charles smiled and gave her a hug.

Myra was next, then Annie, and Fergus.

"I suppose you want to see this, correct?" Maggie held out the ring.

"We do indeed. There was a rather unsavory character in the service elevator. He obviously found the floor from your ring," Charles commented.

Fergus had already started opening the cases of electronic equipment and begun to set their workstation up on the large mahogany desk. "Give it here," he directed Maggie.

Fergus scanned the ring. "Well, at least it's sterling silver."

He put a probe against the inside of the ring. Several small lights came up on a laptop screen. "Just as we suspected. GPS." He handed it back to Maggie. "No audio or visual recording devices."

Myra chimed in, "I suggest you wrap it in a laundry bag and put it down the chute. That should keep the trackers busy, especially after the truck picks it up in the morning."

"Perfect. Money laundering and laundering jewelry." Annie hooted. "They'll be on a wild-goose chase for a few hours."

Charles wanted to take every precaution. "They know she was on this floor. I'm going to set a few alarms outside."

"Brilliant!" Fergus expressed his approval. "We'll tell everyone to avoid the hallway and only move from inside. At least until the laundry truck is gone."

"I'll let them know," Myra said, and made her way to the other rooms through the connecting doors.

Fergus and Charles scrutinized the ring for any other properties, waiting for Isabelle to arrive to see if she could hack into the GPS system and try to track the other missing women.

Between the sisters' elaborate high-tech equipment, and Isabelle's expanded techniques she had learned from her husband, Abner Tookus, it was quite possible they could do a reverse trace to the source and clone the system. Myra checked her watch; her other hand was on her pearls. "Isabelle should be getting here in a couple of hours. Meanwhile, what else do we know?"

Nikki was standing next to Myra. "Jack said that Noah is to be arraigned on Monday. As of now, he has no lawyer."

Myra swiveled her head. "What? No lawyer? What about Ruffing's fleet of attorneys?"

"It seems that Ruffing hasn't returned any of Noah's calls,

so he's going to sit in jail for the duration. Besides, with the amount of heroin they recovered, I doubt he'd get bail."

"Do we know what the value of that haul was?" Fergus asked over his shoulder.

"They estimate about half a million dollars." Nikki looked down at her notes.

"And what about the brother, Liam?" Myra asked.

"He has been out of the country but is scheduled to return tomorrow. I have no idea whether he has access to any criminal attorneys, so Noah may have to settle on a court-appointed lawyer." Nikki continued, "Liam seems to be an unwitting participant. He lives very modestly and by all accounts is very sincere about The Haven and his work."

"How can he *not* know what's been going on?" Myra objected.

"Noah was the business guy. Liam was the front man. At least that's how it seems to be shaking out. After their father was arrested, Liam attended graduate school before going to Tibet. Noah went to work for Ruffing. Apparently, their father and Ruffing had some business dealings."

"Given the crimes Sidney Westlake was convicted of, I don't doubt they were involved in one or two questionable transactions," Myra added.

"Do you think Liam was hoodwinked?" Annie asked.

"I know it sounds unlikely, but it is possible. Gabby would know more based on whatever she witnessed," Nikki said.

"Why don't you go and sit with her and try to unravel more?" Myra suggested to Nikki. "Don't get too lawyerly on her. She's been through enough." Myra winked.

Nikki went into one of the other rooms, where a few of the sisters were having a bite to eat. "Gabby, I know you're probably exhausted from telling and retelling the story, but we're trying to figure out how deeply Liam is involved."

Gabby looked up in shock. "I can't imagine he would

agree to anything illegal or immoral. Noah, certainly, but not Liam."

"A lot of nefarious things were going on with The Haven as a cover. It seems unlikely that Liam wouldn't know anything at all."

"From working at the phone desk, I can tell you that almost all of the messages were for Noah. Like the one 'Package to be delivered Saturday.' The only messages for Liam were from colleges or organizations asking for him to speak at a conference or a workshop." Gabby thought carefully. "And Noah would have meetings with those men when Liam wasn't on the property. Except for one time. That was recently. But he was in Noah's office for less than ten minutes. When he left the meeting, which went on for a very long time, he mentioned that he was going to Tibet."

Gabby continued to describe the day-to-day goings-on at The Haven. By all accounts, it was very much like a commune. "Noah has been acting very irritable lately. I thought it might be money. We really haven't recruited many new members over the past six months. Or it could be something to do with these thuggish-looking guys. I just don't know."

Gabby told Nikki and the others about Rachel and how she was going to be a "spokesperson" for The Haven, to help raise money. "She wasn't supposed to tell me, but she was so excited that she had to confide in someone. Now I wish I could have talked her out of it." Gabby sounded somber.

Nikki patted her on the knee. "We'll get her back."

Gabby looked up at Nikki. "But how?"

The other women started to giggle. Gabby looked confused.

Maggie raised her eyebrows. "You'll see. We just need a few more details to put a plan in place."

"What kind of plan?" Gabby asked.

"As I said, you'll see. Why don't you go take a nap? We'll come and get you when Isabelle arrives."

Gabby gladly took the suggestion and lay down on one of the beds in an adjoining room. As soon as her head hit the pillow, she was out like a light.

Chapter Thirty-two

It was way past midnight when everyone regrouped, leaving Gabby alone to sleep.

Nikki started. "From what we could uncover, and from what Gabby told us, it appears that The Haven was a front for Ruffing's money laundering and drug smuggling. Jack said they are all over it but still need more corroboration. This may sound like a crazy idea, but how about I go to see Noah in jail?"

Gasps and *"what the?"* went around the room. "Hear me out. Noah needs a lawyer. The FBI and DEA need information. Maybe I can talk Noah into turning state's evidence? That would surely help wrap that big turd up in a bow."

"Yes, but I know I wouldn't be satisfied if they simply arrested Ruffing. He'd figure out a way to get out of it. Somehow. Maybe even going to a country that doesn't extradite people to the US." Myra paced.

"True, but not if all of his assets are seized," Annie added. "Some countries will not release funds when someone is under criminal indictment."

"Better still, the funds could be diverted. It's not like that hasn't happened to others we targeted," Charles broke in.

All heads turned in Charles and Fergus's direction. "We create another shell company." He looked at Nikki.

"But where will the money go?" Nikki asked.

"We put it in a fund to help the people who are going to be displaced once The Haven is shut down. We can donate to animal charities, women's charities. I am sure we'll have absolutely no problem sharing Ruffing's wealth with people who actually deserve it," Annie suggested.

"But won't that be evidence?" Myra asked Nikki.

"If the money has already been laundered, then it would be hard to trace it back to any of Ruffing's deals."

"That sounds good to me. All in favor?" Myra looked at everyone and pointed to the room where Gabby was sleeping. Ordinarily, the women would shout "All in!" but this time they whispered it and punctuated it with fist bumps.

"Next, we need to confirm the location of the women we believe may be at 19 Yellow Moon Road," Charles added.

"I am so glad we can say it in English now," Yoko joked. "My Spanish accent is nothing to be proud of."

Isabelle was busily tapping away on her laptop. "Got it!" She turned to look at everyone. "The home device for the GPS is at The Haven. I should be able to crack into that in a few minutes." Isabelle stretched and cracked her knuckles.

"Oh dear, I wish you wouldn't do that," Myra admonished her.

"It's how I work my magic." Isabelle winked and went back to pounding on the keyboard. "Here. Take a look." She turned her laptop so everyone could see the map. "Wherever there is a blinking dot, is where the rings are. You can see a cluster of them not far from here. That's The Haven." She pointed to the spot. "Over here is where we are right now."

"Can we ditch that one now? The laundry chute is beckoning," Charles observed.

"Now we can. I've cloned their system. But take a look at

this." She pointed to several blinking dots on the shore of Cuba. "Ruffing's personal amusement park, I would think."

"Can you tell how many there are?" Annie squinted to look.

"I count four. But that's only those wearing the ring. There could be others."

Annie jumped in. "Fergus, you have one of those drones in your bag of tricks, don't you?"

He gave her a sly look. "I never leave home without one."

Giggles and shushes went around the room. "We can't wake Gabby. Not yet," Myra whispered. "She needs her rest, and we will probably need her to work with us."

"I hope she can rise to the occasion because we're going to have to be quick. Ruffing knows that Noah was arrested. He may be making a lot of moves to make himself disappear," Annie said pensively.

"Right-o." Charles began to make another suggestion. "We should rent a yacht from Ruffing's marina and get as close to the shoreline outside of Ruffing's estate without drawing attention to ourselves."

"But why rent from him?" Yoko asked with a puzzled look.

"Because, if for any reason, he gets wind of a boat nearby and it's from his own company, he'll probably think little of it," Charles explained.

Annie immediately called Lester. "Sorry to bother you at such an ungodly hour, but can you arrange for a yacht and crew for tomorrow? From Golden Shores Marina? And another boat for Monday?" She listened for a reply. "There will be eight of us for tomorrow. I want everyone to be comfortable." Another pause. "About three days." Another pause. "Along the Gulf side of the Keys." She waited for another break. "Fabulous. Yes, as soon as you can confirm." She turned to the group. "He's pretty sure he can arrange it but will have to get back to us in the morning."

Annie looked at her watch. "Okay. It's almost two o'clock. Let's all get some shut-eye. We'll pack our usual incognito clothes and some casual wear."

Fergus added, "Charles and I will pack the equipment."

"Are we going to raid the estate?" Kathryn had a baffled look on her face.

"Since the US can't do it, we're going to have to!" Myra said in a loud whisper. "Kathryn, I want you and Alexis to wait here for Nikki to complete what she needs to do with Noah. Then the three of you can join up with us on the second boat."

Fergus explained, "We'll send a drone at night with heat sensors to detect people in the house. Once we know how many people we're dealing with, we'll make a plan." He was already setting up a program for the drone on his computer.

"Now everyone off to bed. We have some heavy lifting ahead of us!" Myra gave everyone a hug and shooed them off to their beds. "Nikki, wait up." Annie, Fergus, and Charles were still in the room. "I think you need to call Jack before you go off to talk to Noah. You can't offer him a deal if there isn't one on the table."

"You're absolutely right. I was getting caught up in the excitement of nailing that creep, Ruffing. I'll call Jack right now. He's used to me ringing him at all hours." She smiled.

When she called, a groggy voice answered, "Everything okay?" Jack tried to get his bearings.

"Yes. Quick question. What do you think about my going to talk to Noah? Maybe he'll turn state's evidence. And what about this Simone person? Do you think she might also be of help?"

Jack sat up quickly, listening to his wife's suggestions over the phone. "That is a very interesting idea, my love. Let me get in touch with Bert's contact at the FBI. Hang tight. I'll call you right back."

"What about Simone?" Myra asked.

"She will either be out on her arse or in danger. People leaving Ruffing's employ are terminated with prejudice," Charles noted.

"And she does have a mother in a nursing home. She'd want to protect her, too," Annie added.

Within minutes, Nikki's phone rang. It was Jack. "Okay. If you can get Noah to agree to talk, they'll put him in witness protection. They'll do the same for Simone and her mother. Probably send them back to Barbados under assumed names."

"And this is why I love you," Nikki cooed.

"All in the name of justice," Jack said warmly. "Now get some sleep. I certainly can use it. Good night, sweet dreams. Talk in the morning."

"It *is* the morning," Nikki teased.

"The other morning. You know, when people get some sleep, get up, and have coffee? That morning. Like in about six hours. Love you." Jack ended the call.

"Okay. This is what I suggest," Nikki began. "I'll stay here and go see Noah. Once I get more details, I'll find Simone. I'll wait for her at the nursing home and try to convince her to turn herself in. If she won't, then she's on her own. If she does, then the feds will have a lot more information to use against Ruffing. I assume that Noah will cooperate. He really doesn't have too many options at this point." Nikki took a breath, then continued, "Once I get him settled, I'll meet up with you. You can send me the coordinates and I can get a boat to take me to your location."

"It sounds like a good plan. While you're working with Noah, we'll have a good idea of how many people we're dealing with."

"One more thing," Nikki said. "Lizzie got hold of the politicians' itineraries while they're in Cuba. They will be meeting with some tourism and travel people the first day.

Then they will be attending a private party on Ruffing's estate on Tuesday."

"That's a tight schedule, but I'm sure we can manage it," Charles said, and Fergus nodded.

"Okay! We have a plan!" Myra was smiling from ear to ear. Annie wrapped her arm around her. "It's good we're all in shape for this!"

The women laughed. "I guess we're going to find out." Myra gave her friend a huge hug.

Chapter Thirty-three

Sunday

Nikki walked into the Federal Detention Center-Miami. She showed the guard her credentials. "I'm here to see Noah Westlake." She went through security screening, and a female guard patted her down and nodded for her to go through the gate. She made her way to the area where lawyers met with prisoners and sat in a glass booth waiting for Noah. Ten minutes later, a very bedraggled-looking man sat in front of her on the other side of the glass. He peered at her as he picked up the phone. Nikki did the same.

"Do I know you?" Noah asked curiously.

"Not yet. My name is Nikki Quinn. I'm an attorney."

"Did Ruffing send you?"

"No. I'm here because I'm your only way out of this mess."

"So if he didn't send you, then who did?" Noah rubbed his eyes.

"Let's just say I am part of an organization that helps people when the system does not work in their favor."

"I have no idea what you're talking about." Noah started to get annoyed. He needed answers. Clear answers.

"We both know that you will never get yourself out of this mess through normal channels. You will go to trial and be convicted. If you implicate Ruffing in any way, shape, or form, you will most certainly disappear. And not in a good way," Nikki continued. "I am here to offer you a way to disappear and still be safe." She paused. "The feds have a very good idea what he's been up to, and you can stop him from hurting other people. Getting him off the streets will not stop the flow of drugs, but it will make a dent." She paused again. "Besides, it will give you an opportunity to save Liam's reputation. They will have to close down The Haven given its ties to Ruffing. And from all the information we've gathered, it appears that Liam is innocent, that he had no part of the activity you and Ruffing were engaged in, including procuring 'spokespersons' for him." She let all of that sink in.

Nikki proceeded to explain in great detail how, if Noah turned state's evidence, the marshals would relocate him through witness protection.

"But what if he finds out? What if he finds *me*?" Noah was almost whining.

"I can assure you that once Ruffing is apprehended, he will never again have any contact with the outside world. Ever."

"How can you be so sure?" Noah asked.

"How do you think I turned up here today?" Nikki sat back with her arms folded, waiting for Noah to grasp the weight of what she was telling him.

Noah stared at her blankly. "I guess I don't have any choice, do I?"

"Well, you do have a choice. However, under the circumstances, my advice would be to take the deal." She pushed her chair back, hinting she was about to leave.

"Wait. Wait. Okay. Okay." Noah put his head in his hands. "Just tell me what to do next."

Nikki explained that she would be back later in the day

with the proper officials and that he should just sit tight and not speak to anyone else. She asked the guard to give Noah her business card should anything come up between now and later that day. She smiled at Noah. "You're doing the right thing. Not just for yourself."

Her words jarred him. He couldn't remember the last time he did anything for anyone else. His attempt at helping Liam was a debacle. Now he could make it up to him. Even if he never saw his brother again.

Nikki made her way back to her car and phoned Jack immediately. "Noah's in. I'm going to try to get to Simone now."

"I'll let the authorities know and will call you as soon as I know when they plan on meeting with Noah. Probably later this afternoon. Nice work!" Jack said warmly. "You be careful approaching Simone."

"Will do. I have Kathryn and Alexis. Either one of them can take her down if necessary." Nikki chuckled.

"That's my girl. Talk to you in a bit."

"Okay. Love you lots." Nikki was almost gushing.

She sent a text to Sasha:

Target?

Sasha replied:

Moving toward nurs hm.

Nikki quickly called Kathryn. "Simone is heading to the nursing home. Meet me there. Bring Alexis with you."

"Gotcha!" Kathryn replied.

A half hour later, the three women were parked next to each other in the parking lot of the nursing home. They spotted Sasha, who nodded that Simone was inside.

"How should we handle this?" Kathryn asked, rolling down her window.

"Let me approach her," Nikki said. "I'll show her my credentials so she knows it's legit."

"Do you think she knows about Noah?" Alexis, sitting next to Kathryn, asked.

"I guess we're about to find out." Nikki pointed toward the front door, where Simone had just appeared. She got out of her car and walked toward Simone.

"Excuse me. Simone Jordan?" Nikki asked politely.

"Yes, and you are?"

Nikki handed Simone one of her business cards. Simone scrutinized the information. "Why is a lawyer asking?"

"Noah Westlake was arrested."

"What does that have to do with me?" Simone was still being polite, trying to maintain her composure.

"Daniel J. Ruffing."

"Again, what does that have to do with me?" Simone was beginning to become irritated. She had had a bad session with her mother and was not in the mood for any nonsense.

"I have it on good authority that you are about to be arrested." Nikki waited for her response.

"Arrested? Me? But why?" Simone seemed puzzled.

"I don't think I have to spell it out for you," Nikki stated calmly. "You work for Daniel Ruffing, correct?"

"Yes, I offer him my concierge services." Simone was still not quite sure what to make of this stranger.

"Which includes procuring young women for him, human trafficking." Nikki looked her straight in the eye.

"I think I should call my lawyer." Simone was about to turn away.

"I am a lawyer, and I can help you with this." Nikki tapped the card Simone held in her hand.

"Why should I believe you?" Simone asked suspiciously.

"The latest 'hostess,' Jennie. *Diecinueve camino de la luna amarilla.*" Nikki watched Simone's face.

"But how? Who?" Simone was utterly flabbergasted.

"Can we go somewhere to talk?" Nikki urged. "My car is over there."

Simone was still leery, but if this woman had such specific information, perhaps it would behoove her to listen. Simone looked in both directions to see if anyone else was around. "Who are those two?" She nodded in the direction of Kathryn and Alexis.

"Let's just say they are colleagues. They're also aware of the situation. Come." Nikki ushered Simone to her car and explained as much as she could without violating laws and divulging privileged information. "Bottom line is, if you go to jail, there will be no one to look after your mother's care. She is in a lovely and safe place now because you're paying for it. Once the government seizes your assets, they will most likely transfer her to a not-so-lovely nursing home." Nikki watched as Simone processed the information in her head.

"So what do we do next?" Simone asked dryly.

"We meet with the FBI."

"When?"

"The sooner the better. I can probably arrange something for later today."

"This is all happening too quickly." Simone's accent was more prevalent now.

"Once you give your statement, they will arrange for you and your mother to go back to Barbados with new identities. They will find a suitable place for her and a place for you."

"Surely he'll be able to find me," Simone protested.

"No. No he won't," Nikki said confidently.

Simone stared straight ahead. "All right. Arrange it."

Nikki told Simone to go back home and pack her bags. Someone would be waiting for her to escort her to the meeting with the FBI.

Simone got out of the car without another word. She climbed into her Porsche for the last time and headed to the house she would vacate within hours. Sasha followed.

Nikki gave Alexis and Kathryn the thumbs-up and phoned Jack again. "Simone is in."

"You are something special, Nikki Quinn."

"And so are you, Jack Emery."

Nikki sent a text to Myra:

Bingo. Phase one complete.

In the meantime, while Nikki was on her mission to see Noah and Simone, the rest of the group arrived at Golden Shores Marina and were escorted to a 240-foot yacht, the *Bella Grande*. The dockmaster pointed to one tied to another piling, the *La Mancha*. "That one's for your second group tomorrow."

"Perfect! Thank you for accommodating us with such short notice." Annie smiled.

"It's a pleasure to serve," the man replied.

As soon as they were aboard and no longer within earshot, Myra shared the news about Noah and Simone turning state's evidence. Hoots and howls filled the deck of the luxury vessel.

"What about the crew?" Myra asked Annie.

"They are people who know people who know us. They are as discreet as anyone we've ever worked with before."

"I'm sure we wouldn't have it any other way, now would we?" Myra smiled.

The captain of the boat and the first mate welcomed them and gave them a tour of the boat, allowing each to pick out a stateroom.

The yacht could accommodate twelve quite comfortably. The second yacht would have the same amenities and space for the women once they were rescued from the estate. There were no ifs, ands, or buts. They weren't leaving the Bay of Cárdenas and the Straits of Florida without them.

Gabby was still unsure what she was involved with, but the accommodations sure beat the heck out of the barracks she had been living in. She threw herself on one of the beds. "Wow. This is scrumptious."

Maggie laughed. "That's one of my favorite words! Especially when Charles is cooking."

"He can cook?" Gabby asked with surprise.

"A man of many talents," Maggie assured her.

"I'm still trying to wrap my head around all of this," Gabby said softly.

"Yeah. It's a lot. And we ain't done yet!" Maggie gave Gabby a big hug. "I can assure you of this, you are in the best hands ever."

The yacht left the marina and headed south on Biscayne Bay. As they passed between Dodge Island and Star Island, Annie pointed in the distance. "I hear there's an estate that's about to be seized. It would make a great safe house for battered women." She linked her arm through Myra's as the boat set its course to Key West and beyond.

Both meetings went swimmingly. Simone gave up every ounce of information she had, including names, dates, and private cell numbers. Noah, too, shared all details he had: the names of the fishing boats, schedules, and the names of the men with the accents. He divulged evidence of the money laundering through the Laundromat, the car wash, the farmers' market, and the dry cleaner. They were moving over a hundred thousand dollars a week in and out.

The only thing that he didn't know was who was supplying Ruffing with the drugs. But finding that out would be up to the FBI and the DEA. Noah gave them enough information to put things into action, starting with a warrant for Ruffing's arrest and freezing all his assets. The agencies knew that capturing Ruffing might not be a possibility, especially if he chose to stay in Cuba. But cutting him off from his money would put him in a pickle.

Little did they know that the sisters had other plans for Ruffing. But before the wheels were set in motion, one of the things the sisters insisted on was that they be allowed to help relocate the members of The Haven, help them find gainful employment, and get them some street clothes. They shouldn't have to suffer because of Ruffing's criminal activities. A social worker would be assigned with the changeover, and Annie offered to help finance the transition.

Noah had only one request. He wanted to see Liam one last time. Nikki, Kathryn, and Alexis headed toward the airport to pick him up. Nikki recognized Liam from the photo on his books. After he cleared customs and went to claim his baggage, Nikki caught up with him and touched his arm. "Hi, my name is Nikki Quinn. I am a friend of Gabby Richardson."

Liam looked panicked. "Is she all right?"

"Yes, she is absolutely fine. But we need to talk. Get your bags, and we'll give you a ride." Kathryn waved from the far side of the carousel.

"Can you tell me what this is all about?" Liam asked as he heaved a suitcase from the revolving drum.

"As soon as we get in the car." Nikki followed him to the car.

Alexis was waiting behind the wheel as they approached. She pressed the button to release the liftgate of the SUV, and Liam placed his bag inside.

"Hello. I'm Alexis." She looked over the top rim of her sunglasses.

"I'm Kathryn." She shoved her big hand at him.

"So. What is this all about?" Liam asked casually.

"It's about your brother, and yes, he's okay. Physically, anyway," Nikki added, as Liam gave her a puzzled look.

"It also has to do with Daniel Ruffing," Nikki said plainly.

Liam almost flinched at the sound of his name.

Nikki began to explain everything to Liam. Almost everything. She told Liam about the arrest and that Noah was going to turn state's evidence against Ruffing and go into witness protection.

"Wait a second. You're telling me that my brother is going to testify against Ruffing in return for protection?"

"That is correct."

Liam was dumbfounded. "But how? I mean, how did this happen?"

Nikki went on to explain the money-laundering scheme, drug and human trafficking, and ultimately Noah's arrest. Liam sat in disbelief, especially when he learned that it was young women from The Haven who were being tricked into becoming courtesans.

"I never trusted Ruffing, but I kept giving him the benefit of the doubt." Liam ran his fingers through his hair. "I suppose I was in denial, too. Everything seemed to be working well, but deep down I had a feeling that something was amiss. It just didn't *feel* right." Liam sounded forlorn. "I guess that makes me a hypocrite, too."

Nikki looked at Liam. She could see why people would be drawn to him. His level of sincerity was palpable.

"No. It makes you a believer in all things positive." Nikki sighed. "Unfortunately, most of the time, the rest of the world doesn't work that way."

Liam chuckled softly. "Noah would always tell me that I had reality issues. I guess this is a *big* dose of reality, eh?"

"I can't imagine what is going through your mind right now," Nikki offered. "Just know that all your people at The Haven will be taken care of. Social workers will be helping them transition to jobs and housing."

"I'm relieved to hear that." Liam sighed. "I'd hate to think I was the cause of anyone's pain or suffering, especially if they believed in what I said about being a better person. Living an authentic life." Liam shook his head. "This is quite difficult for me to process."

"The other good news is that Gabby is okay and is working with us."

"You keep mentioning 'us.' Can I assume there are more of you?"

"Yes, you certainly can!" Kathryn bellowed, causing Liam to jump.

That, in turn, caused everyone to laugh. Nikki looked over at Liam again. Tears were welling in his eyes. Nikki squeezed his hand.

"It's going to be all right. In a few days, things are going to break wide open, but rest assured—you, Gabby, and your people will be safe. As will Noah and Simone. I know it's hard for you to accept me saying 'trust us,' but you're going to have to for now."

They were getting close to the detention center as Nikki explained what Liam could expect. He and his brother would be in a small interrogation room with a guard, and they would have a half hour together.

Alexis dropped Nikki and Liam at the front entrance. "Text me when you're ready to leave." She looked at Liam and gave him a warm smile. "Good luck. I know this isn't going to be easy. Places like this give me the creeps." She shuddered as she remembered the year she had spent behind bars, wrongly imprisoned for fraud.

Kathryn broke the mood. "We're not far from Bayfront Park. Let's go grab a coffee and sit by the fountain. It's only ten minutes from here."

"Sounds good to me." Alexis pulled out the road atlas she had brought and handed it to Kathryn.

It was late in the afternoon when Nikki finally notified Alexis that she was ready to go. Kathryn sighed. "It was kinda nice just to sit and zone out for a bit, eh?"

"Yes, it was. And to think we've barely started!" Alexis laughed as she retraced their steps to the car, and went to pick up Nikki and Liam.

Liam looked a bit shook but not a total hot mess. "That was rough," he said as he opened the door for Nikki.

"I can only imagine," Kathryn replied.

"Funny thing. Right now I feel a sense of relief," Liam mused. "I guess I was always wrestling with reality. Like waiting for the other shoe to drop, as they say."

"You have good instincts," Nikki said kindly.

"Acting on those instincts is obviously something I need to work on." Liam relaxed for the first time that day. Maybe that decade. Without warning, he started to sob. Nikki put her hand on his back and let him weep. She handed him a pack of tissues.

"I'm sorry," he blubbered. "I don't know what came over me."

"Reality!" Kathryn howled, followed by laughter from everyone, including Liam.

Alexis interrupted the chuckles. "Where to?"

"Good question." Liam looked at Nikki and shrugged. "I suppose I should stay away from The Haven, correct?"

Nikki thought of the empty rooms at the hotel. "You can stay with us until we can get that sorted out. Actually, we'll be leaving for a couple of days, so you'll have the suite to yourself."

"Suite?" Liam asked.

"We're staying at the Biltmore but have an errand to run tomorrow," Nikki said slyly. "We should be back in two or three days."

"What should I be doing while you're running your errand?" Liam asked.

"Play a round of golf? Go for a swim? Read a book?" Alexis suggested. "You could probably use a few days to unpack all of this, and I don't mean your luggage." Everyone chuckled.

"Speaking of luggage, what did you do when you were in Tibet?" Alexis asked.

"Mostly meetings with spiritual leaders trying to come up with plans to save the planet." Liam snickered. "I guess I should figure out a way to save myself!"

"You'll be fine," Nikki said reassuringly. "Have you considered teaching at a college?"

"That was my first idea when I got back from my first spiritual quest. I actually taught as an adjunct for a while. But then I got wrapped up in weekly meetings with local folks, then came The Haven. I should have stuck to my original plan." He sighed.

"Maybe we can help make that happen," Nikki offered. "We'll put it on our 'to-do' list. Find Liam gainful employment!" Cheers and hoots rang from the front of the vehicle.

Nikki elbowed Liam. "You'll get used to it."

Chapter Thirty-four

Sunday Evening
The Straits of Florida

After approximately fifteen hours of cruising from Miami, the *Bella Grande* docked within two miles of Varadero. From there it would be feasible to launch a drone for surveillance. If not, Charles and Fergus could take the dinghy, but they were confident their electronic devices would do the job.

It was past midnight. Time to do a run-through. The drone would broadcast live photos of the exterior of the estate as well as locate people, using thermal imaging. Even though they could identify the Pledges by their rings, it was imperative they know how many other people were on the premises. The first thing was to figure out what kind of security was there.

Nikki, Alexis, and Kathryn dialed in through their private server. Nikki spoke first. "We're heading out there at six o'clock in the morning. We should get to you guys by eight this evening at the latest."

"Super." Myra was stroking her pearls while the others logged in to see what Fergus was seeing.

Everyone watched as the first image appeared on Fergus's laptop. "Two armed guards—beachfront—one east and one west." Fergus manipulated the drone around the perimeter of the property. "Fence." He eased the drone down to enable him to read a sign. EL PELIGRO—ALTO VOLTAJE. "That's an electrified fence, mates."

"What can we do?" Yoko asked.

"We can do nothing if *you* can take out the guards on the beach."

"Talk to me," Yoko prodded.

"As soon as I get 'er back to the beach, I will *show* you."

The estate wasn't as large as some, but big enough to entertain a half dozen weekend guests. The building was U-shaped, with the middle opening to the pool area and a wing on each side. From the GPS signals they were getting from the rings, they could see that the women were in the east wing. The thermal imaging confirmed it; but it also confirmed there were four other people. Eight in all. Charles spoke first. "Who do you suppose those others are?"

"Maybe they came from somewhere else?" Myra suggested.

"Or they could be guards?" Kathryn added.

"I doubt he'd have guards staying in the same area of the house. Clearly there is no way out for them. Unless they can swim," Annie responded.

"We're going to have to assume they are also sex slaves. If not, we'll have to go to Plan B," Charles said.

Everyone looked at him and asked in unison, "What's Plan B?"

Charles gave a bit of a chuckle. "Not sure yet. But if we must come up with one, I'm certain we will." Nervous giggles filled the air.

Fergus moved the drone to the west wing. There was one image in the far-left corner on the second floor. They surmised that was where Ruffing slept. Below him, on the first floor, there appeared to be two more people. Fergus surmised they were in the staff quarters. No sign of others.

Fergus shifted the drone back to the beach area. There were mostly rocks, with a very small beach. The fence ended at the jagged shoreline. The only way one could enter the property from the beach would be to get past the two guards.

Fergus looked at Yoko. "This is what I suggest. We take both dinghies in. There will be one on the boat coming tonight. We'll tie one dinghy up on the beach by the fence, the other on the other side. Far enough so the guards won't see you or Kathryn sneak up on them. You will knock one guard out, then signal Kathryn to take on the other one. I know you can provide a good choke hold. Once they're both unconscious, we'll bind and gag them."

"And add a little chloroform so they can take a nice nappy," Annie suggested. "Or something of that nature." She winked at Myra.

Kathryn snorted. "I could take that little weasel with one hand."

Everyone laughed. They knew she was right.

"We also need to make sure we disable any communications capability they have with the main house or each other."

"Roger that," Kathryn replied.

"What's the rest of the plan?" Isabelle asked.

Charles began, "We're going to have to disable the entire security system in the house. Isabelle, do you think you can figure out a way to jam their system?"

"Shouldn't be too hard if we can pick up the radio waves."

Fergus grunted. "I'll see what I can do." He fiddled with his laptop. Seconds later, a screen with the radio frequency appeared.

"I don't know what you need *me* for, Fergus." Isabelle feigned a pout.

"Because there are still some things you're a tad better at than I." He gave her a bow.

"Aw shucks." Isabelle smiled. "Let's have a look." She studied the patterns and opened her laptop.

A hush fell over the group as they each studied the footage of the grounds and the location of the residents. Isabelle worked on a strategy to disarm the security system. She looked up. "It's a bit tricky. I'll be able to disarm it, but for only a short time. Twenty minutes tops. After that, it will recalibrate and reset itself."

"Okay, everyone. Let's put on our thinking caps and figure out a plan," Annie started. "Once we're in, we split up. Kathryn, you and Yoko should take Ruffing. The rest of us will round up the girls."

"What about the staff?" Alexis asked over the secure phone line.

"If the timing is right, we get everyone out who needs to be out, then trip the alarm," Charles stated.

"Why on earth would we want to trip the alarm?" Myra asked with a stunned look.

"So whoever is still in the house will totally freak out!"

Annie chuckled. "Let them poop in their trousers . . . if they're wearing any." Everyone hooted at Annie's remark.

An hour later, they had constructed a plan to rescue the women at 19 Yellow Moon Road and contacted Pearl Barnes. Pearl's special skill was relocating people. But it wasn't the same kind of relocation that Simone and Noah would experience. No, Pearl's relocation was far worse. More akin to relocating to hell.

Chapter Thirty-five

Tuesday
Off the Coast of Cuba

Nikki, Kathryn, and Alexis had arrived Monday night on the *La Mancha* and anchored near the *Bella Grande*. In the morning, they joined the others. Everyone was bustling about, discussing the plans and getting their gear together.

Isabelle had been able to cobble together a rough schematic based on the video from the drone. They each had their instructions and were patiently waiting for day's end.

Maggie paced the second deck. "I hate waiting around."

"Yes, dear, we know." Myra smiled at her. "Perhaps you'd like something to eat?"

"Hah. When *don't* I want something to eat?" Maggie grinned. "I miss Charles's cooking. Don't get me wrong. The food has been incredible. But there is something about the food Charles prepares that is, well, just different."

"Perhaps it's because he's preparing it for very special friends." Myra beamed.

Maggie put her arm around Myra and gave her a squeeze. "I can't thank everyone enough for helping me find Gabby."

"And to think, it turned out to be much, much more," Myra said.

"I remember in the beginning you said something about 'woo-woo.' I really believe we were guided to this mission." Maggie spoke with reverence. "Not that we aren't at any other time. But, this. This was simply looking for Gabby and we uncovered so many horrendous things. Things that may have been going on for who knows how long."

Myra put her hand on Maggie's shoulder. "We're always given clues. Signs. It's up to us to pay attention. You could have simply taken Gabby's first call as something odd but not terribly important. But you had a gut feeling."

"Yes, I did." Maggie stared out to the horizon. "And I am so glad you backed me up."

"We wouldn't have had it any other way." Myra gave Maggie a squeeze.

Daniel J. Ruffing greeted his guests in the foyer. Three US senators and the CEO of a large pharmaceutical company. Not counting Ruffing, that would make a two-to-one ratio between the women and the men. It would be an early evening. His biggest concern was if any of these men had a heart condition. If they wanted their ménage-à-trois fantasy, their health was their problem. *I should have had them sign a waiver.* He smirked to himself. The big-pharma guy was slightly younger, but he still looked like he could use a transfusion.

The men were shown to their rooms and given massages before the dinner party was to begin. *That should make the evening even shorter.* While he enjoyed taking their money, he was also very bored with the routine. Everyone pretended to like the others and to be interested in what they had to say. In reality, all they wanted was a fabulous dinner, fine wine and cigars, and a roll in the hay with two beautiful women. It was almost nauseating, but he was used to it.

Each of the men was flanked on either side by a beautiful young woman. Ruffing was quite happy with himself that he was able to accommodate their wish list. The evening progressed as usual, ending with each guest being accompanied by "the hostesses."

Not far from the shoreline, the sisters waited in the dinghies, and Pearl Barnes, who had arrived late that afternoon, was only a few hundred feet offshore in a cigarette boat.

Fergus launched the drone and began to navigate it around the exterior of the premises, using the thermal imaging. As expected, the four guests had shown up earlier and there were now three people per room—four guests and the eight women. There were two more figures moving about from the dining area to the kitchen. One single figure was stationary in the area of Ruffing's suite.

They had cut the engines long before anyone could hear them approach and paddled their way toward the rocks, one on each side of the beachfront.

Yoko slipped out of one dinghy and carefully moved toward the guard. Kathryn had landed on the other side of the small beach area, waiting for Yoko's signal. Like lightning, Yoko took out the first guard, knocking him unconscious. Before anyone could take notice, Kathryn had her target in a choke hold. Each of the guards was given a shot of propofol, the same drug used for short-term anesthesia. It can take effect within fifteen seconds and last for over two hours. Yoko and Kathryn gave each other a thumbs-up and signaled the rest of the sisters, and Isabelle sent a frequency that would disable the security system.

Dressed in their black ninja suits, the sisters and Gabby stealthily climbed over the rocks, Maggie giving Gabby hand signals. Even though Gabby had never been on a mission with them, they needed her to identify Rachel and the other women from The Haven. They certainly weren't leaving without all the women, but the action had to be swift and carried out with as little hysteria as possible.

They split into four teams, with Yoko designated to capture Ruffing. On Annie's signal, the women stormed the mansion. Ruffing barely had time to take a breath before he was out cold. He was dragged to the beach, where Pearl and one of her associates, who had landed, took custody of him while another moved the cigarette boat closer to the shore.

The four teams kicked open the doors of the four rooms, where the men were disrobing. Shrieks and howls filled the air, and the men tried to cover up their flabby white bodies.

Gabby spotted Rachel and pulled down her mask just enough for Rachel to recognize her. Rachel's eyes were as wide as saucers. Gabby whispered quickly, "Let the girls know we're here to rescue them."

Rachel told Diedre, "Go help the others." Everyone was shouting and scrambling. The two staff members fled toward the nearest exits and disappeared into the night.

The women were half-clad, shaking, and crying. Rachel and Diedre assured them they would be okay.

"Come with us! Quickly!" Annie shouted.

Myra wrapped a blanket around one of the women. "Don't be afraid. You're going to be all right." She helped her out to the terrace, where some of the others were waiting, all of them asking questions at the same time.

It was a cacophony of hysteria, but Annie tried to calm them down. "Please, trust us. We're here to help you. But we don't have a lot of time."

Myra checked to see that all eight women were accounted for and at least partially clothed.

Isabelle ran back toward the mansion. Annie shouted, "Where are you going?"

"To get the evidence." Isabelle ran into the house.

"What is she talking about?" Myra tried to grapple with her pearls, but they were tucked tightly under her suit.

"Darned if I know. Come on. We don't have a lot of time." Annie and the others ushered the girls toward the waterline. Fergus and Charles pulled the dinghies as close to the shore as possible.

Myra stood at the top of the terrace, not sure if she should go back for Isabelle, when, much to her relief, she saw Isabelle running toward her, carrying a small black briefcase.

"Hurry!" Myra waved her on and pointed to the briefcase. "What is that?"

"Evidence." Isabelle huffed and puffed.

The two of them ran in the same direction as the others, just as the alarm started blaring, with large spotlights flooding the area. As Myra and Isabelle climbed into one of the boats, they could see the men running around on the terrace, trying to escape from the chaos. It was a sight to behold!

Pearl was way ahead of them, with an unconscious Ruffing lying on the deck of her boat.

As soon as Charles and Fergus had everyone seated safely, they opened up the throttles and hightailed it back to the yachts. It took several minutes for the questions and crying to subside. Myra was on one dinghy and Annie on the other as they explained to the women that they were no longer under the control of Daniel J. Ruffing. They were heading back to the USA.

More questions and more crying as the sisters tried to calm everyone's nerves. Their own included.

When they arrived at the yachts, the eight "hostesses" made their way onto the *La Mancha*. They were shown to staterooms, where they could shower and put on a pair of soft pajamas, each with a sister to assist and comfort her.

An hour later, everyone convened in the main salon, where refreshments and food awaited.

"I am sure you have a lot of questions," Annie began. And they certainly did.

Myra laughed. "Perhaps we should explain. Then you can ask whatever you like."

Annie looked at Maggie. "This is your party, Maggie. You do the honors."

Maggie's eyes welled. She pointed to the women she knew so well. "These are my sisters. We are a team. If someone is in trouble, we try to help." She sniffled and cleared her throat.

"Gabby and I went to journalism school together. She interned at the *Washington Post*, owned by our own Countess Anna Ryland de Silva." She nodded toward Annie. "A little over a week ago, I got a strange message on my voice mail, and being a reporter with a nose for trouble, I had to figure it out." Light giggles filled the salon. "With the help of my sisters, well, here we are."

Some of the women blurted questions while some raised their hands.

Myra stepped in. "There is a lot we cannot divulge, but rest assured you will be okay, and you will never, ever have to deal with Daniel J. Ruffing or his cronies ever again." Applause and tears from the group of rescued women.

Rachel was one of the first to get up and hug Myra. Myra stiffened. "Oh, I am so sorry," Rachel apologized.

"No. No. It's okay." Myra took a deep breath. "Your perfume. Where did you get it?"

Rachel looked slightly embarrassed. "I always carry a small silk pouch that I tie around my waist. I keep a travel-size perfume, lipstick, and mints."

"But the perfume. Miss Dior?" Myra asked, knowing the answer.

"Yes. But how did you know?" Rachel looked surprised.

"It's a favorite of mine." Myra relaxed and gave Rachel a real hug.

"Me too. I got it when Simone took me shopping. There was something special about it. I can't really explain it."

"No need." Charles put his arm around Myra and gave her a squeeze. "Woo-woo, indeed."

Chapter Thirty-six

When the yachts returned to Golden Shores Marina, a swarm of FBI and DEA agents greeted them. Charles and Fergus took the lead.

"I suppose you gentlemen wish to secure these lovely vessels?"

"We do indeed." One of the men was wearing a jacket with FBI emblazoned on it. Another agent wearing a DEA windbreaker approached them.

"Give us a moment to gather our belongings, and they're both yours." Fergus grinned.

"Yes, they are." Both agents answered at once, giving each other a possessive look.

"Good luck to you, mates!" Fergus wheeled one of the dollies carrying the luggage, and Charles wheeled the other.

The government officials wanted to question the women, but Myra and Annie stood between the agents and the women.

"They need to be seen by doctors. They are all in shock. Give them some space, and we'll help arrange for interviews."

The agents began to protest, but Myra and Annie weren't budging. Fergus and Charles shot the agents a look that said, "Don't even think about it." Myra and Annie took the agents' business cards and promised to be in touch as soon as the girls were checked out by physicians.

Two large passenger vans waited at the end of the dock. They divided themselves up and climbed in. The chatter of the women was delightful. It was obvious that they were beginning to accept the fact that they were no longer sex slaves and were back in the US.

Annie arranged for a few extra rooms at the Biltmore until they could find permanent housing for the girls. Jobs, too.

Given the circumstances the women had been forced to live under, they, too, had a bond.

The girls were taken to a highly regarded gynecologist and a trauma counselor. Physically, they were okay. It was the mental stuff that would take a while. The trauma counselor gave each of them her recommendations for therapy, both private and group. They all promised to comply.

Over the next couple of days, the girls spent hours with federal agents, giving them whatever details they could remember, trying hard not to relive them. They were grateful for the therapy sessions.

At the same time, the sisters were helping them decide on living arrangements, such as apartments, or helping them relocate to where they had friends or family members, family members who were upstanding and responsible citizens.

But there was no way Rachel was going back to a crack-den trailer. Diedre had no family with the qualifications, either, so they decided to share an apartment. Jennie had only been at The Haven for a short time and only a few days at 19 Yellow Moon Road. She chose to visit her sister in Boston until she could figure out her next move. Maki, Tanya, Olivia, Collette, and Serena wanted to rent a big house where they could live together. Annie thought a bed-and-breakfast would be a good change of pace and found an ideal location for them in Islamorada. They would live there and run the place.

By the end of the week, everyone had a game plan, including Liam and Gabby. Annie established the Margaret Drew Chair of Psychology at Florida International University for Liam, and Gabby would be his research assistant. Gabby would also do some freelance writing for the *Herald,* for their Arts and Entertainment section. The sisters were curious about whether Liam's relationship with Gabby would evolve. Or not.

Noah was heading to parts unknown, and Simone and her mother were relocated to Barbados. And then there was Ruffing. No, despite all the evidence the feds had gathered, he would not be going to trial and end up in a federal penitentiary. He wouldn't even be indicted the only way he could be, in absentia. Because, strangely enough, despite all the efforts being made, Daniel Josephson Ruffing was nowhere to be found. The FBI and the DEA looked high and low, but their best efforts produced no results.

Courtesy of the Sisterhood, Ruffing was headed for parts unknown. And his domicile would not be nearly as nice as a cell in a federal prison. His encounter with a troop of male baboons being transferred from Africa to the Monkey Jungle in Florida didn't go very well. Ruffing's screams were inaudible amidst the screeching of the most vicious and aggressive of the baboon species. And once the cage arrived in Florida, Pearl made further arrangements for Ruffing to relocate to a place where baboons would be considered tame.

With everything wrapped up, the sisters packed their bags and headed to the executive airport, where Annie's jet awaited.

As they settled into their seats, Maggie made one more remark. "Charles? What's for dinner tonight?"

Everyone broke out in laughter. "Fettuccini carbonara, of course."

Epilogue

One week later
Pinewood

Annie and Myra had just returned from a quick trip to London. They were giggling all the way from the car to the house. Fergus and Charles were waiting in the kitchen. Aromas of Charles's cuisine filled the air.

"How was your visit with Charlotte?" Charles gave her a big hug.

"Wonderful. She and Lincoln are getting along swimmingly."

"So nice to hear." Charles nuzzled her neck. "*Now* will you tell me the real reason for the big rush to get to London?"

"Remember the story about Liam and Noah's mother taking off before their father got arrested?" Annie asked after giving Fergus a peck on the cheek.

"Yes. Rather dodgy of her," Fergus replied.

"Let's save it for when the others arrive," Myra said. "I'm going to change into something more comfortable than this."

Annie chimed in, "I think I'll head back home and unload my stuff. What time is dinner?"

"Seven. The sisters should be here around six thirty," Charles answered.

"Oh good. We'll tell everyone at the same time."

Yelping and yapping from Lady and her pups signaled the arrival of the sisters. Dog treats, hugs, and kisses were shared.

Maggie was the first one to head toward the oven to see what Charles had on the menu.

He swatted her hand as she was about to pull the door open.

"Uh . . . uh . . . uh . . . No fair peeking."

"Do I smell Yorkshire pudding?" Maggie's eyes lit up.

Charles leaned over. "Yes, but don't tell anyone."

In a conspiratorial manner, Maggie whispered back, "Roast?"

Charles winked. "Now fall to it and get that table set!"

As so many times before, the women expeditiously made their way from the china cabinet to the table, placing all the dinnerware and flatware in their place.

Yoko was the last to arrive, carrying an armload of birds of paradise and anthuriums. "Yes, it's a 'theme party.'" Yoko recounted the day at the farmers' market. Everyone cackled with glee.

They made their way to the table, sat in their usual places, took each other's hands, and said grace.

"This smells scrumptious." Maggie handed her plate to Charles. "What's everyone else going to eat?"

Giggles and whooping went around the table.

"All right, old girl. Spill. What were the two of you really doing in London?"

"But first, I want to know what Isabelle found in that black box she took from the estate," Kathryn interjected.

"Oh that?" Isabelle had a devilish grin. "Just lots and lots of video of Ruffing's guests enjoying the pleasure of the girls' company."

"Ew. Ew. Ew," Maggie blurted. "Porn?"

"Yeah. Kinda. But yes," Isabelle said with a sour face.

"What are you going to do with it?" Maggie asked.

"Annie is holding it in a safe place."

"But why?" Kathryn asked.

"You never know when we may need blackmail information." Annie winked. "We think that's how Ruffing was making some of his money. Blackmailing his guests."

"What a swell guy," Maggie blurted. "Enough of that dirtbag. We want to know about your trip!"

"As I mentioned earlier, if you recall, Mrs. Westlake left the country months before her husband was arrested," Myra said.

"Not only did she abandon her children, but she made off with almost a million dollars in cash and jewelry," Annie added.

"Not exactly Mother of the Year, eh?" Fergus replied.

"Exactly. She left two sons entering their last semester in college with nothing. And I do mean nothing. She took whatever she could get her hands on and fled, abandoning her children. We saw what that did to both Noah and Liam. One became a criminal, the other a heartbroken soul."

"At least he tried to make something of his emotional loss," Maggie said sadly.

"Yes, and he did help a lot of people," Myra interjected.

"And I am sure he will help more. He has a very kind heart. And with Gabby with him, who knows what good things will happen."

"Okay, but back to Mommy Dearest." Annie had a gleam in her eye.

"Apparently, Eleanor Adams Westlake has been hobnobbing with some of London's elite. She'd been showing off her jewelry at events."

Nikki looked appalled. "You didn't!"

"Uh, yes, we did," Annie said sheepishly.

"But how?" Alexis asked.

"Do you remember the Julian Marcus jewelry swap? When we switched his wife's real stuff for fakes?" Annie asked.

"Of course!" half the women bellowed.

"But how? I ask again." Alexis was tapping her fork.

"We had a party," Annie said smugly.

"And?" Everyone was almost out of their seats.

"And . . . my dear friend and world-renowned gemologist Lincoln was admiring Eleanor's jewelry," Annie continued. "As he was being so effusive, I was snapping photos."

"Two days later, Lincoln had the replicas ready."

"Then we told her we were having a showing of unique pieces of jewelry and asked if she would be interested in participating," Myra added.

"And?" More urging from the group. Even the dogs were starting to get impatient and began to yowl.

"And, well, we put her jewels on display with some of mine, and a few pieces Lincoln brought in. We made the switch just before the showing, while Eleanor was in the other room having a cocktail," Annie went on. "So Eleanor went home with paste instead of jewels."

"I don't get it," Nikki said with a puzzled look. "How will she find out?"

"This afternoon, Lloyd's of London called her and said they needed a current appraisal for her insurance. That, my dear, would require her to take them to a jeweler," Annie added.

"Imagine her surprise when the appraiser tells her they are worth absolutely nothing!" Myra smiled.

High fives, fist pumps, and screams of laughter filled the dining room.

"What about the real jewelry? What happened to that?" Nikki asked.

"Let's just say there's enough food at the animal shelter to last them a couple of years."